FOOLS ERRANT

MATTHEW HUGHES

FOOLS ERRANT
by
Matthew Hughes

Copyright Matthew Hughes, 1994
Published by Matthew Hughes, 2015
ISBN: 978-1-927880-07-4

Cover illustration by Ben Baldwin
Book design by Bradley W. Schenck

to Jack Vance

CHAPTER ONE

THE LOGODAEDALIAN CLUB was renowned for three things: the zest of its cuisine, the draftiness of its common rooms, and the verbal wit of its leading members. Filidor Vesh could claim no comparable distinctions. His memberships at the Logodaedalian and a number of other select establishments he owed instead to an accident of birth.

He sat in the well-worn ease of the club's salon, sampling tiny, rich pastries and murmuring polite appreciation for the two remaining contenders in a round-table contest of epigrams. The melee of wits had flowed and ebbed around a succession of sumptuous but subtle courses from the club's ancient kitchens. Now, as the stewards deftly whisked dishes from the table, only Fornol Kray and Leetha Hanch remained in verbal arms.

Fornol Kray shifted his ample weight, cracked a walnut between thumb and forefinger, and plucked a word from his opponent's last sally. "It may be, as you say, that 'a life without dreams is no life, yet dreamers live only their dreams.'" Here he paused to admit the meat of the walnut into that process which would transmute it into yet more Fornol Kray. "I will say that life is lived as comedy, though everywhere it is experienced as tragedy."

Leetha Hanch delayed only the moment required to place a tapered finger at her sharp chin before replying, "As with blessings, so with tragedies. If they are everyone's, they are no one's."

The scattering of applause from the assembled members covered Filidor's yawn. A slim young man of refined sensitivities, he lacked both enthusiasm and accomplishment, and was neither deft nor apt in wordplay. He was, however, the nephew and sole heir of Dezendah Vesh, ninety-eighth (or possibly ninety-ninth) Archon of those regions of old Earth still inhabited by human beings. This relationship conferred upon Filidor certain privileges, of which he took full advantage; it also imposed upon him a number of burdens, the full weight of which he would shortly begin to feel.

Filidor's attention drifted. He turned toward the salon's mirrored wall and attempted to admire from the corner of his eye his own delicate profile, then fell to arranging the meticulous folds of his saffron mantle, which overlay an shimmering tunic of spun pearl. His legs, languidly extended, were enclosed in tight-fitting hose of a material that hardened gradually as they descended, to form a half-boot on each pedicured foot.

The contest was dwindling to its end. Fornol Kray had been reduced to the assertion that "insularity is mere map-maker's conceit", against which Leetha Hanch was already forming a complicated trump on the theme of two-dimensionality. While the company awaited the finishing stroke, Filidor gave thought to the possible diversions offered by the rest of the evening. A clutch of young lordlings planned a cruise by barge across Mornedy Sound, a noisy outing which would include potent drink and pliant ladies of the Upper Town. That was tempting.

On the other hand, Lord Afre would soon present a selection of phantasms coaxed through a tiny and transitory breach between this world and an adjacent plane. As Filidor weighed these attractive prospects, a steward appeared at his elbow to inform him that a messenger from the palace waited in the atrium.

Filidor pressed a coin into the man's hand, bade him tell the messenger that no Filidor Vesh was on the premises, and moved swiftly to make the lie a truth. A side door led to a passage connecting the salon to the kitchens. He dodged through the clatter of pots and salvers, and into a storeroom with a small window set in its outer wall. Seconds later, he dropped noiselessly into an alley barely lit by the lantern above the Logodae-dalian's rear door. A few steps away was a public square where he could lose himself among the crowds taking the evening air. From there, it was a short walk to the seclusion of Lord Afre's house in town.

The alley appeared deserted. Filidor padded toward the square, peered around the corner, saw no trace of the distinctive black and green Archonate livery. The square held only the usual stylish after-dinner throng, displaying their finery. He was about to step amongst them when he felt a tug on his mantle.

Turning, Filidor had to look down to see who had laid hold of his garment. He found a very small, very bald man of advanced age and yellowy skin, loosely assembled from knobbed joints and coarse dark cloth. The eyes were black pinpoints in a network of pocks and gulleys, the nose a careless afterthought, and the mouth a thin slice set in an unappetizing grin. The voice issuing from between straggling teeth might have learned speech by copying the creaks and rustles of centuries-old parchment.

"I believe you to be Filidor Vesh," said the dwarf.

"You are entitled to your beliefs, however ill-founded," Filidor replied. "No doubt you will wish to search further for this Vesh, rather than impose your presence upon a man called hence by urgent affairs."

The dwarf transferred his grip from Filidor's mantle to his arm. His gaze swept quickly over the young man's features. "This belief is supported by the evidence, since you answer to a point the description furnished me."

"You are plainly the dupe of some prankster, who abuses the dignity of your years by sending you on a fool's errand," said Filidor. "Were I you, I would seek out the rascal and thrash him."

"I am accustomed to fool's errands," said the little man, "which this may well be. But the Archon orders you forthwith into his presence, and the proof of my assertion is here." He displayed the Archon's personal seal.

The ring seemed out of place among the dwarf's crabbed fingers, but the intaglio of emerald and jet could not be gainsaid. Filidor sighed. A summons from the Archon meant a task to be performed. Invariably, Filidor knew, it would be a service whose significance no rational being could fathom.

He had once been ordered to record the expressions on the faces of spectators at a notorious felon's "restitution", and to write an analysis linking the crowd's eye movements to the prisoner's writhings and spurts of blood. Another time, the Archon had sent him by night to daub illiterate revolutionary slogans on imposing buildings. And, at the premiere of a fashionable author's most wrenching melodrama, he had been required to laugh hysterically until the ushers ejected him into the street. In the gloom of the Archonate library, he had been set the task of counting and itemizing daily reports by officials now centuries dead. The Archon's orders seldom made sense.

Therein lay the crux of Filidor's uncertainty as to his place in the Archonate's affairs. He recognized that, as Dezendah Vesh's sole heir, he must be drawn inevitably into the workings of the Archonate. Remotely, he had even considered that he would some day take for his own the regalia and trappings of his uncle's office. And he hoped that by the time of his investiture he would have learned just what it was that an archon did.

It was universally agreed that the institution of the Archonate was fully right and necessary, and that the Archon wielded ultimate power. But the means of exercising that authority was a mystery to Filidor Vesh, to his friends, and even to their lordly parents.

Presiding at some high banquet or learned seminar, his uncle was the very image of magisterial power. But, equally, he might be come upon in an ill-lit corner of the archives, immersed in mouse-chewed tomes or tinkering with some pointless apparatus left over from a previous millennium. Although he was rarely seen outside the Archonate palace, it was said that the Archon often wandered through the world, guised as anything from an alms-seeking mendicant to a dealer in rare objects. Any stranger might be the Archon, and he might do anything at all to anybody at all; or he might do nothing. These wanderings were also seen as fully right and necessary, and had been referred to since time immemorial as *the progress of esteeming the balance.*

The Archon's summons must be obeyed. Still, Filidor knew from experience that a careful delay in meeting his obligations could take him safely to a point where the order might, from a change of circumstances, lapse. He favored the little man with a disarming smile.

"There is no time for idle conversation. I must hurry to my uncle's chambers, where weighty issues of state may hang in the offing. And so I will bid you the pleasantries of the evening."

Filidor turned to depart, but the grip upon his arm exerted a renewed force, reminiscent of what mountain shrubs apply to vertical cliffs. "Your uncle expressed a concern," the dwarf said, "that this or that matter might prevent your speedy arrival, or indeed that you might lose your way. He instructed me to accompany you, not leaving your side, until you are brought to his familial embrace."

A lift of the dwarf's arm, and an official car thrummed to a halt beside them. In a moment, Filidor was wedged into a rear seat, the dwarf leaping in beside him. The uniformed operator swept them aloft before the door had cycled shut, and Filidor felt his innards briefly rearranging their positions. Then the car levelled off and sped across the city toward the palace of Dezendah Vesh.

The city unrolling beneath them was old, even in a world where little was young. It had worn many names, received the attentions of innumerable builders and conquerors, and prided itself on any number of reasons for being what it was and where it was. It sprawled across the fingertip of the Olkney peninsula, a jeweled nail scratching at the tideless sea. The mansions of the mighty and the hovels of the hopeless straggled up from the shore to the crags of the Devinish Range, where the Palace of the Archonate hung over the city like a black cloud.

The palace was a city within the city, a vast muddle of ramps and towers, keeps and baileys, arches and cupolas added one to another over the millennia of Earth's penultimate age by a succession of archons of all architectural persuasions. In the second level of its seventh terrace, between the minaret known as Holmar's Folly and the half-ruined Connaissarium of Terfel the Third, lay the formal gardens beyond which the Archon maintained his private study. As the last red rays of the ancient sun shifted the green of the grass to black, the car landed and deposited Filidor and the dwarf at the study's outer door. Without knocking, the little man pushed open the portal and pulled Filidor after him.

The room brought back memories of Filidor's childhood, none of them pleasant. It was here that his uncle had made fitful efforts to coax his nephew toward some acquaintance with learning, within walls that stretched high into shadow, each lined from floor to ceiling with books. There were tomes of every age, in every tongue, and in every form devised by humankind or most of the literate galaxy. Many were in languages now scarce remembered; some were merely dust confined between covers; and a few displayed their contents in emanations of light or sound well beyond the human range.

Besides books, the study contained only a chair, a carved and battered table, and a rug with its pattern long since trodden out. On the table lay two volumes, the larger one splayed out as if for autopsy.

"Your uncle does not seem to be here," said the dwarf.

"Let us be bold, and state categorically that my uncle is not here," Filidor snapped, but secretly he took the Archon's absence for a hopeful sign. He might yet escape a wasted night.

The dwarf eyed him coolly. "Impatience," he said. "I remind you that we are here at your uncle's behest. Whatever concerns may delay him are possibly of more moment than a nephew's urge to disport himself among reckless wastrels."

"You misjudge me. I am eager to do my uncle's bidding."

The little man favored the Archon's study with a mild snort, as if about to call upon the crowded ranks of books to confirm his low opinion of Filidor. He crossed to a small door inset among the shelves, and said, "I am sure you can contain your dutiful ardor while I seek out the Archon and report the completion of my charge." Then he left.

Filidor made an impolite gesture to the empty study. He recalled too many hours of imprisonment among its tiers of volumes, warded over by testy tutors. His uncle had urged him, both by instruction and occasionally by resort to punishment, to acquire some smattering of the history of Earth and the dispositions of the people and places of its present latter age. But, since Filidor brought neither willingness nor aptitude to these labors, his uncle in time ceased to press the point, and left the young man to his own devices. The final remission of sentence had been delivered, not without a note of scorn, in this book-filled room. Since then, contact between the Archon and his nephew had been brief, formal, and infrequent.

The dwarf did not soon return. Filidor felt no inclination to browse among the shelves, and after a few minutes he sat down in the room's only chair. Time passed, and no one came. Filidor itemized the things he might have been doing instead of sitting in a hard chair waiting to be sent to do something even less agreeable. In time, it might have occurred to him that his mental list recapitulated the series of empty pleasures, differing more in detail than in substance, which filled his days and caused each to blend indistinguishably into the next. But Filidor seldom followed any train of thought further than its first branching.

He glanced at the two books on the table beside him. The larger of the two lay spread by its own weight. It was an ancient tome, its pages yellowed and cracked at the edges, and covered in a thicket of spiky, black script. The words were archaic, perhaps appetizing to scholars but distasteful to Filidor. He managed to decipher the capitals of the open page's heading, and learned that the rest of the page was filled with the details of the demise of Archon Imreet IV, then he turned his attention to the second volume. This was a slimmer work, bound in blue shamoy figured in gold leaf. Its cover bore the title: *Discourses and Edifications of Liw Osfeo*. No author was noted.

Filidor picked up the book and opened it at random, finding it to be a compilation of tales and homilies in the style of a preceding generation. He riffled the pages, until he was arrested by a singular illustration. A man was being chased by an enraged mob. His eyes slid to the accompanying text, and he began to read.

> *The County of Keraph*, the tale began, *boasted three noble cities, each jealous of its independence and time-honored privileges, yet each cooperating with the others in mutual endeavors.*
>
> *The city of Caer Lyff was largest of the three, and produced the sophisticated baubles upon which, all agreed, civilization depended. The city of Alathe was somewhat smaller; its ateliers and factories manufactured the less intricate but no less necessary goods without which civilization rapidly descends to barbarism. Finally, the city of Dai was smallest of all, but its sturdy citizens raised the crops and kine which fed all Keraph.*
>
> *In the centre of the county, housed in the old ducal grounds, was the Institute. Here scholars and academes rubbed shoulders with chymists and apparaticists, and all combined to provide Keraph with the refinements of modern learning. Besides instructing the worthiest of the county's youth in useful arts and abilities, the Institute undertook research into the creation of yet more subtle devices and systems of great value.*
>
> *It happened that a certain Jever Smee had attained emeritus rank with the Institute, where he conducted private research into the less obvious relationships among time, energy and what the common folk call matter. The fruits of his work were not known until the time of his eventual death,*

*when it was discovered that he had designed and built sev-
enteen intricate mechanisms. The principles by which these
machines operated were beyond the ken of Jever Smee's
colleagues, but their application was soon understood from
notes and jottings left in his workshop. The mechanisms, if
fed with raw materials of the basest sort, transmuted them
into rare and precious substances. Jever Smee's devices
promised immense wealth to the County of Keraph.*

*It further transpired that among his writings was the
last will and testament of Jever Smee. This document ordained that the seventeen mechanisms were to be divided
among the three cities according to a formula arbitrarily
determined by the deceased. Caer Lyff was to receive one
half of the machines; Alathe would receive one third; and
Dai would receive one ninth.*

*The will caused immediate consternation among the
ruling syndics of the three cities, and among the Institute's
Board of Integrators. All saw at once that the lower orders
of mathematics had not been among the disciplines absorbed
by Jever Smee. It was impossible to allocate the seventeen
devices in the proportions stipulated, without reducing some
of them to useless fractions.*

*A long and bitter debate ensued. Some proposed a di-
vision according to the respective populations of each city.
Others insisted on the sanctity of wills, demanding that
Jever Smee's creations be distributed as specified, and any
remaining parts consigned to the scrap heap. A convocation
of fellows of the Institute suggested that the machines be
left where they were, under Institute control, and that their
output of rare substances be shared according to Smee's
formula. Meanwhile, some merchants who imported and
sold such precious wares, in small but profitable amounts,
rioted and had to be put down by the provost.*

*It happened that the Illumino Liw Osfeo was at
that time attached to the Institute as a visiting lecturer in
applied metaphysics. When the imbroglio over the will had*

reached its fiercest pitch, and social war brimmed throughout Keraph, Liw Osfeo put it about that he could adjudicate
the dispute for a handsome fee.

Calling together the Syndics and Integrators, he declared that he was in possession of Jever Smee's prototype.
This had been given him by the late emeritus in recompense
for certain kindnesses, he said, and it had remained unused
in his study. Osfeo volunteered to add the prototype to the
other seventeen, thus making eighteen in all: a number di-
visible by Smee's formula, without the necessity of reducing
any of the mechanisms to fragments.

The Syndics and Integrators readily paid Osfeo's fee,
and the division was immediately made. One half of Jever
Smee's machines – nine of them – went to Caer Lyff; one
third – that is, six – were loaded into wagons and transported to Alathe; and one ninth – or two machines – were
taken to the grange hall in Dai. Osfeo then ruled that the
disaffected merchants be allowed to purchase a monopoly
on the export of the machines' products beyond the county's
bounds, and pronounced the dispute satisfactorily resolved.

The Syndics and Integrators made much of the sage's
wisdom, until it was pointed out by one of his detractors –
for he always had detractors – that the nine, six and two
machines added up to the original seventeen. There remained one unaccounted for.

"Of course," answered the sage. "That is the one in my
quarters, which naturally reverts to me."

It was agreed that Osfeo should retain his property,
since it did not reduce any of the three portions of Jever
Smee's estate. But the enemy was not mollified. While the illumino was being feted by the dignitaries of Keraph, he stole
into Osfeo's rooms and determined that no such mechanism
existed. Returning to where Osfeo sat among the magnates,
his purse weighty with their contributions to his net worth,
the enemy revealed the deception and denounced the sage
for a fraud.

The cream of Keraph were outraged and demanded restitution. Osfeo rose to defend himself. It was true, he said, that the eighteenth mechanism was a mere figment. But what did it matter whether or not a thing existed, so long as it served a useful purpose?

Reason, however, was of no avail. Judging the temper of the crowd correctly, the illumino wisely exited through a nearby window. The magnates pursued him, their retainers and flunkies joining the chase. But the fleet and wily sage soon distanced them, and departed the county by little-used paths.

Filidor turned the page to continue, but was interrupted by the sound of the study door opening. The dwarf had returned, alone.

"We are too late," said the little man. "It seems your uncle has been called urgently away on business."

Filidor rose in both body and spirit. The evening could yet be saved. "How unfortunate," he murmured. "Doubtless he will require me upon his return, but in the meantime..."

The dwarf approached and set his hand in its former grip on Filidor's arm. Two of Filidor's fingers tingled and went numb from the pressure, although the dwarf displayed no sign of exertion. "The Archon requires a service of you, and has charged me to bring you to him without delay. He is presently some distance down the peninsula, in the hamlet of Binch."

"In that case," Filidor grunted as he attempted to free his deadening arm, "I will make haste to arrange transport."

The little man moved easily to retain his balance, and his grip did not slacken. "Your uncle again wondered if circumstances might conspire to detain you, should we somehow become separated. Consequently, I have already laid on a suitable vehicle."

Filidor essayed one last time. "A few necessities for the journey, a brief visit to my chambers," he proposed.

"Such a large palace, so easy to lose one's bearings and miss appointments. Besides, all necessities are in hand."

The dwarf produced from beneath his tatters a small satchel of scuffed leather, and opened it to display its contents. Inside was a selection of ingenious artifacts from the Archon's personal effects. There was the wand of perpetual sufficiency, which could engender nutrition from any organic matter. There was the ward-web, which conferred invisibility and impregnability upon whosoever rested beneath it. And there was the traveler's aide, a small cylinder which telescoped into a staff, and which envigored its wielder on the road or in self defence, besides having several other remarkable properties.

Filidor's eyes narrowed as he surveyed the satchel's contents, which were surely more than would be needed on a short jaunt over well-known roads between the palace and Binch. But the dwarf rebuffed all queries, saying that each item had been specifically requested by the Archon himself.

"There is also this," the little man continued, drawing from a concealed pocket a hand-sized box of tuka wood inlaid with ivory runes. "You are to carry this upon your person at all times, and deliver it into your uncle's hands when he requires it."

Filidor had no time to examine the box. No sooner had he taken it than the dwarf shifted his weight, and Filidor was propelled toward a bookcase which slid silently aside to reveal an unlighted corridor. The little man dragged him through, and the portal closed behind them. They stood in complete darkness, until with a rustle and a series of brief clicks, the dwarf deployed the traveler's aide and raised a light from its upper tip. He then set off down a dust-choked, sloping side corridor and Filidor had to hurry to follow the wavering glow.

Their way took them through level below level of the palace, through suites of apartments and vast echoing halls sealed in decrepitude. Though he had lived within the palace walls more than twenty years, and explored it with all the dedication of boyhood, Filidor had seen none of the myriad rooms and passageways they now passed through. Nor had anyone else in living memory, to judge from the unbroken dust their footsteps disturbed into waist-high billows.

At some point in their passage, Filidor realized that he was still carrying the slim blue volume he had picked up in his uncle's study. His first impulse was to drop it and leave it behind, but that seemed a petty spite. Besides, his uncle might later send him unescorted into this dark warren to retrieve it. He tucked the book away, next to the mysterious box in an inner pocket of his mantle, and pressed on after the dwarf.

The little man offered no conversation, nor did Filidor seek any. Their barely seen surroundings afforded no sights of interest, so for lack of occupation, the young man took to counting his footsteps. Some time after his second thousandth imprint in the dust, Filidor felt the first stirrings of moving air from ahead. A little while later, he followed the dwarf around a moss-shrouded boulder and discovered that he was outside. It was now almost full night, the last ocher gleams fading on the highest reaches of the Devinish Range above them. A few steps from the concealed exit and the dwarf extinguished the glow from the traveler's aide. In the dimness, Filidor could discern the outline of an old surface car.

The vehicle's flared skirts, scarred from encounters with untended pavements, settled almost to the ground as Filidor eased his weight into the passenger seat. The little man scrabbled spryly into the operator's position, and after some initial difficulties encouraged the vehicle's drive system to revive itself. The whine of untuned gravity obvertors set Filidor's teeth to painful vibration.

With a lurch, the car surged toward Binch, thrusting Filidor against the protruding frame of his seat. The wind rushing across the open compartment and the protesting drive made conversation impossible. The little man was in any case intent upon the controls, gnarly hands yanking levers and swinging the steering bar like a war-crazed pilot on a suicide run, whistling tunelessly through the teeth dotting his gums as he rocked the vehicle past imaginary obstacles. Occasionally, he lined up the car's lights on stationary objects beside the road and steered directly for them, emitting noises that imitated some rapid-fire weapon, then swerving away a finger-breadth from fatal impact.

Filidor's sang-froid evaporated in the chill night air. As the dwarf skimmed a derelict retaining wall with barely an eyelash's separation, the young man screamed and wrenched at the controls to bring them back toward mid-road.

"We are going to die!"

"Eventually," agreed the dwarf, shrugging Filidor's grip from the steering bar. He steadied the vehicle's course and grinned at his passenger. "In the meantime, however, why not live life to its fullest?"

The words struck an embarrassing chord within Filidor. Had he not once thrown some such remark at his uncle, rejecting the Archon's urgings toward a sense of duty? He eyed the dwarf's face for some sign of ironic intent, but the little man's features were as inscrutable as an ancient god's.

"Nonetheless," Filidor shouted above the slipstream, "I would prefer to reach my uncle with all my parts in their present arrangement." The dwarf grunted a noncommittal reply, but slowed the car a little, and deleted some of the wider arcs from his course.

Filidor settled back. Irritation at being denied his pleasures was now giving place to stirrings of fear. He knew that he did not like his austere uncle overmuch; it was possible that his sentiments were reciprocated.

The Archonate had no reputation for inflicting harm upon its subjects, but those arbitrarily pressed into its service might not fare so well. Filidor watched the moldering hummocks of the old city's ruins sweep through the car's lights, and began to wish he had paid more attention to his lessons. Whatever the inner workings of the Archonate, he sensed he was about to be drawn more deeply into them than ever before.

THE LIGHTS OF BINCH were dimly clustered on the horizon when the car suddenly coughed and lurched. The dwarf punched at the controls without interrupting his monotonous whistling, and the vehicle roused itself unwillingly to a last effort. But ominous clangs and flutterings were rising from the engine compartment, backed by shudders that rattled Filidor's spine.

"What is amiss? Will we make it?" he demanded.

"As to the first question, I have no idea," the little man replied. "This conveyance was commissioned for the Archon Ondovar IX, now some centuries dead along with those versed in its maintenance. Your second query is best answered by eventualities. All else is futile conjecture."

Filidor looked out into the full black of night. They were well beyond the bounds of the derelict city, passing now through orderly fields worked by the people of Binch. To Filidor, raised within the city's confines all his life, the densely planted crop lands were no less alien than the colony zones where ultra-monds had revised portions of the Earth to resemble the planets of their ancestors.

For him, the dark concealed a jungle thick with vines and tubers. He thought to hear fleshy creepers rustling at him above the wind and the protesting engine. He looked back to the faint glow of the city now far down the Olkney peninsula, and wished himself secure again in its brilliant, hard-edged streets.

Steadily, the few lights ahead grew closer until, shuddering in mechanical despair, the car staggered down Binch's single street and expired in front of the hamlet's business centre. This was a rough-cast country inn hard by an open-air market, whose bare wooden stalls bore a flood of light from the hostelry's garish tavern sign. More light, and a clamor of voices, spilled from the inn's open door, which carried a small placard high on the lintel to advertise the building as a district office of the Archonate.

Seizing satchel and Filidor, the dwarf sprang from the dying vehicle before its final gasp, and hustled the young man through the tavern door. Inside, a fug of smoke, unwashed bodies and yeasty liquors hung from the rafters. The after-market-day crowd ground elbows the full length of the bar, and filled the close-packed tables. Intent upon their drink and shouted conversations, the men of Binch paid scant heed to the little man who nudged his way through their mass, nor to the dandy he dragged behind him. To Filidor, the composite odor of sweat, soil, and undefined agricultural material was over-powering. His passage through the densely packed crowd left him feeling as if he had been processed through some fleshy machine.

The little man ducked beneath a raised glass and scrambled atop the bar to speak to the publican. Filidor could hear nothing above the din. He attempted to bore closer, only to be stopped by a picket of elbows and fustian clad shoulders. The barman, a large Bincher with a porous nose and migrating eyebrows, was nodding in agreement at something the dwarf had asked, and raising a stumpy finger toward the tavern's ceiling. They exchanged a few more words, then the dwarf clambered back over the front rank of drinkers, bringing with him a pot of dark ale, which he pressed into Filidor's hand. Some of the jar's contents slopped onto the young man's pearly chemise.

Filidor had to stoop to hear what the little man was saying. "Wait here. I must see if your uncle is upstairs."

"Here? You expect to find the Archon amidst this ill-smelling country rabble?" cried Filidor. One of the rabble, over-hearing, fixed the young man with a measuring stare. Filidor attempted to return the look in kind, but the effect was diminished by the kinked posture necessary for hearing the dwarf's next words.

"The Archon is found where he chooses to be found. Now remain here, endeavoring to give no further offense to persons both larger and more numerous than yourself." The little man then squeezed into the crowd like a bird diving through water, and was lost to sight. The small space he had occupied was instantly filled by a towering, leather-clad farmer, Filidor was jostled, and more ale was added to the spreading stain on his front.

The young man elected not to protest. Adopting an air of noblesse oblige, he resolved to appear as if he frequently enjoyed a rustic celebration. He tasted the drink in his hand, to learn whether it eased thirst as effectively as it discolored apparel; but the ale was warm and bitter, and foreign to a refined palate. With a grimace, Filidor sought to return the pot to the bar. Finding his best efforts easily blocked, he at last poured the liquid onto the tavern floor, where it quickly bleached the strewn rushes a pristine white. Filidor did not care to consider what it would have done to his stomach.

The noise and press of bodies was becoming more than he could bear. Filidor began to insinuate his way toward a staircase that departed the room from its far corner. He was making laborious progress through the crowd, when suddenly the crush parted before him and the barman blocked his way. A beefy hand flattened against Filidor's chest, and the publican said, "You owe for the ale."

Filidor fumbled for his belt clutch, but found it missing. As he felt with growing alarm through the folds of his mantle, he saw the barman's eyebrows migrating southwards into foul weather range. The tavern fell silent, then was swept by a murmur of low growls.

"My money is gone," Filidor said, casting a look about the cluttered floor. "Has anyone here..."

He had intended only to ask if anyone had seen his lost purse, but the Binchers took his words for the beginning of an unjust accusation. He was shouted down amid several threatening gestures. The publican exchanged his arresting palm for a handful of Filidor's chemise, and the young man's heels left the floor.

"Now, now, gentlemen," said the innkeeper, "I'm sure this is nobbut an honest misunderstanding." But he pulled Filidor into the shadow of his nose and said, "Yet you must pay."

"I have rings," offered Filidor, displaying a jeweled hand.

"Not like to fit," said the barman, showing a hand larger than Filidor's face.

"My companion will pay."

"He's not here."

"He just went upstairs."

"I did not see him go. Did anyone see this one's companion?" the barman asked the room. The response was a ripple of snorts and "nay's".

Filidor regathered a portion of his dignity, despite the lack of floor beneath his feet. "I am the Archon's nephew, and you are obstructing the discharge of my duties."

The Binchers laughed. A number claimed they too were various relations of Dezendah Vesh, one old gaffer attesting to be the Archon's saintly grandmama. The innkeeper quieted them after a moment. "All right, then," he said. "Where's your sigil, where's your plaque? Identify yourself."

"My companion can verify all. Allow me to seek him upstairs, and I will..."

"Seek out an open window, more like," cackled the Archon's granny. The barman's face closed, and he shook Filidor slightly.

"We rustics have simple ways, easily grasped by our betters. The rule here is: those who can't pay in coin pay in kind. You may wash pots, serve at table, or entertain the paying clientele. Choose."

There was neither escape nor succor reflected in the faces of the Binchers. "It has been said that I own a fair voice for a ballad," Filidor said.

The barman lowered him at last to the floor. "The lad will sing," he informed the crowd. "Clear him a table." A clatter of pots told Filidor that a space was being made behind him, then he was hoisted by several hands onto a shaky platform of rough boards.

"Now, sing," said the taverner.

The room's hubbub subsided somewhat as the Binchers settled themselves to listen. Filidor smoothed his garments and contemplated for a moment, while the rustics sniggered and nudged each other. Then the young man raised his voice in a thin but serviceable tenor.

Thou orb which doth the welkin limn
With ocherous ichor aflame
Ywis the verdant mount may rim
And bid the night to claim
Her stygian realm...

So far did Filidor succeed in introducing into Binch the works of one of his city's lately popular composers, before someone put lips and tongue together to emit a sound more commonly associated with a lower orifice. Loud laughter followed, and several hands rocked the boards on which he stood. "If you can't sing, how about a dance?" a burly farmer shouted, as Filidor struggled to keep his footing. The crowd roared anew as he lost his balance and fell backwards into their waiting arms. Filidor was tossed from hand to hand until one receiver missed his catch, leaving the young man to sprawl face down in the foul rushes.

The taverner appeared and hauled Filidor almost to his feet by seizing the back of his collar. In a stumbling run, he was brought to the door and propelled from the inn by the force of the barman's boot, not coming to rest until his forehead struck the side of the collapsed surface car. Behind him, the laughter abruptly muted as the tavern door slammed shut.

He slumped motionless for a long moment, then painfully righted himself, to see the little man perched lightly on one of the car's air vanes, regarding him with interest.

"Your uncle is not here," he said. "He has gone on."

Relief seeped through Filidor's aches and bruises. "Then we return to the city," he said.

"Alas, not," the other replied. "Here we remain until we receive further instructions. In any case," he gestured at the car, "this vehicle has achieved a state of permanent inanimation."

"Can we not require the Archonate's office to send another?"

"I have been given no leave to do so. Besides, the office is now closed for the night."

"I find this intolerable!" cried Filidor.

"Perhaps you should seek to extend the limits of your tolerance," said the dwarf. "Unless you would prefer to retrace our route back to the city on foot, against your uncle's wishes, and alone in darkness which may hide who knows what feral beasts?"

"I will not pass the night in that deplorable inn!"

"It is doubtful you would be welcome," said the dwarf. "In fact, I would think it better to be well clear of this place before its patrons are set loose, lest some of them remain so affronted by your person as to offer you further remonstration."

Filidor considered the little man's words and limped away. The rest of Binch, however, offered no apparent hospitality, even were he to forego his usual standards of accommodation.

"Where shall we sleep?"

"Wherever the ground is flat, dry and relatively soft," replied the dwarf, jumping down from the car and walking toward the darkness. Filidor followed, shivering as a sudden cold breeze crept between him and his mantle.

"Are we to pass the night exposed to the elements?" he asked.

"No need. The ward-web will shelter us from any inclemencies, as well as from insects, night haunters and any other perils you may imagine."

"I am far from content," said the young man, but he followed the dwarf to a nearby copse of mournful wystol trees. The ward-web was deployed and found to be functioning on all points, except for an irritating ultra-sonic keen from one of its components. This, along with the irregularities of the ground and the snores of the little man, kept Filidor long parted from sleep. He tossed and turned in search of comfort. Something sharp lodged beneath his ribs. Reaching to remove it, his hand closed upon the small box of tuka wood which it was his mission to carry to his uncle. He drew out the box, fingering it in the darkness and wondering what it might contain. Then he found the traveler's aide and fiddled with it until he coaxed a light from its tip.

Turning the box over in his hands, he traced the unreadable runes inset on all sides. He shook it, hearing something heavy rattle inside. Then he examined it minutely for a catch or stud which would open it to reveal its contents. If any such device existed, it eluded his efforts, and finally Filidor tucked the box back into his mantle. In doing so, his fingers touched the book of Liw Osfeo. With sleep only a remote possibility, he drew forth the slim blue volume and began to read.

> *Osfeo was in the marketplace at Elizen-Gat when he saw a crowd of people wildly cheering a trio of men, hung about with ropes and grapples. Inquiring of a seller of baked buns for the cause of the agitation, he learned that the three had just returned from a mountaineering expedition to remotest Hakwert, where they had conquered that region's highest peak.*
>
> *Eager to hear more, Osfeo pushed through the crowd. "Is it true," he asked the leader of the team, "that you have conquered the mountain?"*
>
> *"Yes," was the proud reply.*
>
> *"And have you brought back any tribute?" asked Osfeo.*
>
> *"Of course not," scoffed the mountaineer.*

"What about prisoners of war?" was the next question.

"Ridiculous!"

"Well, did you at least get signed articles of surrender, and a promise of lasting peace?"

"Who is this fool?" shouted the mountaineer. *"Are you trying to imply that we did not in fact conquer the mountain?"*

"Certainly not," replied Osfeo. *"I was just wondering how you can be so sure the mountain has admitted defeat."*

It seemed to Filidor that something was amiss in the logic of the anecdote, but being disinclined by nature to follow abstruse chains of thought, he let the question drop. Instead he riffled through the pages in search of another short excerpt.

Osfeo, he read, *for a time set up as a diviner in the village of Jaem, near Esrick. This allowed him an income and the leisure to sit in the village's piazza drinking hot spicy klat. To amuse himself, he often played practical jokes on the villagers.*

After some weeks, his neighbors became annoyed at his constant pranks, and formed a delegation to demand that the disruptions cease.

"Has it not occurred to you," replied Osfeo, *"that there might be a deeper meaning to my antics?"*

"We require a demonstration," said the neighbors.

Osfeo then directed their attention to a house across the square, where a large can of water balanced precariously upon the partially open front door. As they watched, a young boy came out, pushed aside the door, and was drenched.

"Now," said Osfeo, *"pay heed. That youth carries in his pocket a box of lumets, with which he intended to play near the village's communal barn. The lumets now being soaked to uselessness, the danger is averted."*

The villagers rushed across the piazza and examined the boy, finding all to be as Osfeo had said. After summarily whipping and warning the young miscreant, they returned to the diviner and praised his prescience.

"Regard," said Osfeo, and directed their attention to a potter now entering the square from an alleyway, carrying a large ornate amphora on his shoulders. Osfeo pulled taut a string which he had stretched across the mouth of the lane, and the potter tripped, dashing the valuable vessel to the cobbles.

"Attend," said Osfeo. "That man was recently told in a dream that some catastrophe would soon befall him. Ever since, he has been near incapacitated by dread, fearing the disaster he knew to be looming over him. Now he will assume that the breaking of a costly pot must be the calamity he feared, and will be able to face the future with an optimistic mien."

The villagers questioned the potter, who confirmed Osfeo's analysis, and joined in extolling his far-reaching wisdom. Then all settled down to await the sage's next prodigy.

Soon after, they espied a wealthy merchant, well known for his grasping ways, crossing the piazza in his richest robes. As he passed the group around Osfeo, disdaining so much as to notice their presence, the diviner peeled a karba fruit and deftly tossed the slippery skin beneath the merchant's heel. The plutocrat skidded and rose into the air before crashing down on his well-padded fundament.

The villagers laughed and hooted at the merchant's misfortune until the man had limped out of sight. Then they turned to Osfeo for the hidden meaning behind his prank.

"Has it never occurred to you," he answered, "that I might be doing these things merely from malicious merriment?"

There was more to the tale, and Filidor would have read on. But at that point, a yellowy crabbed hand reached across and extinguished the light.

"Sleep," rasped the dwarf, and Filidor was left staring into the overhanging black of the ward–web's energy matrix.

BY THE TIME the innkeeper had laid before him what the Binch hostelry's fly-specked menu described as a hearty country breakfast, Filidor had identified no more than three parts of his body that did not pain him. A fitful sleep on hard ground after a manhandling by the tavern crowd had left him newly conscious of the locations of his muscles and joints. His arm ached where yesterday the dwarf had seized him, as he lifted a battered spoon to poke at the mess filling the bowl.

The spoon broke the film of grease overlaying a clump of half-cooked dumplings flecked with scraps of grayish meat. The smell of the stuff pushed its way into his nostrils, and Filidor felt a wet bubble of nausea rising in his gullet. He laid the spoon in the bowl and pushed both to arm's length across the table. The chill light of dawn, which he had never seen at the beginning of a day, made little progress through the tavern's single smeared window. Filidor doubted that the full rays of noon would do much to lighten the place's gloom.

With the food banished from his immediate surrounds, his stomach settled, and he wished half-heartedly for the wand of perpetual sufficiency, which could have turned the inn's slop – or even the boards of the table – into something more suited to his palate. But the wand was in the satchel, the satchel was with the dwarf, and the dwarf was in the Archonate office up-stairs, awaiting instruction from Filidor's uncle.

Filidor hoped the Archon was nearby, within quick reach of the vehicle that would surely be sent. He could then deliver the small box that had left an impression in his ribs, be relieved of his duty, and go home to a soothing, scented bath.

His reverie broke under the sounds of the little man clumping down the stairs. The ever-present grin a further affront to Filidor's pains, the dwarf mounted the bench on the other side of the table, from which vantage he clawed Filidor's untouched breakfast toward him, dug fingers into the soggy mass, and shoveled some into his mouth. Filidor was surprised that such loud smacks could come from such thin lips. His stomach expressed a different reaction, and he turned away.

"Is there word from my uncle?" he asked the tavern wall.

The dwarf worried a slab of meat clenched in his fingers. "He has sent a missive to you, through me, by the usual means." A flake of meat jiggled on his lower lip as he spoke.

"Let me see it," said Filidor, turning and finding his gaze reluctantly drawn to the bobbling scrap. The dwarf's pointed tongue swept his lips and the ort disappeared.

"Since it came by the usual means," answered the little man, "there is nothing to see. You are of course familiar with the usual means."

"Apparently not."

"It is of no moment. You will just have to trust me." The dwarf scooped up another handful of dumpling and chewed it with gusto.

"Trust you! I don't even know you. I don't even know your name!"

The little man considered this a moment. "Quite right. A name is called for. I have had several I can remember, and doubtless many more I have forgotten." He tapped his root-like fingers on the table. "I have it: you may call me Gaskarth – a name for which I have always had a peculiar fondness." The dwarf expressed his pleasure at this name-taking by seizing Filidor's spoon and rapidly stripping the young man's bowl of its remaining provender.

"That is not your real name," said Filidor.

"Remind me to ask you some day just what it is you mean by a *real* name," answered the little man. "As it is, we must now be off."

The day was scarcely begun as Filidor followed Gaskarth from the inn. The aged sun spread its weary light over the fields of Binch, the energy seeming to arrive almost spent from its journey, as if it would soon cease to make the effort to come at all.

Between the dusty fields stretching away at either hand, the road led west down the peninsula to the city and east into the interior. Gaskarth shouldered his satchel and set off inland at a fast rate despite his half-length legs. Filidor straggled along behind, unable to close the distance without resorting to the painful indignity of running. A few hundred paces along the road, however, the dwarf stopped and waited. Wordlessly, he drew the traveler's aide from his baggage and handed it to Filidor, then walked on.

After a few false starts, the young man managed to fumble the traveler's aide into a staff as long as he was tall. The ancient device's inner workings ground into operation, sending subtle emanations into Filidor's muscles, allowing him to match Gaskarth's crab-legged speed. The aches and stiffness of the night began to ease, and walking in the open air settled the young man's stomach. This organ, relieved of distress, realized that it was without useful work, and sent this information on to those other parts of the body responsible for providing it. "I'm hungry," said Filidor.

Without breaking stride, the dwarf drew out the wand of perpetual sufficiency, activated its mechanism, and touched it to a wayside bush. The branch at once changed color and texture and broke off of its own weight. Gaskarth deftly caught the transmuted material, tore off a portion, and popped it into his mouth. The remainder he handed to Filidor, who nibbled gingerly on the spongy mass, then took a delightful bite.

"Why, it tastes exactly like mazhouki," he exclaimed, identifying a rich confection that is part of every child's best memories of growing up in Olkney.

"That does seem to be the setting on this indicator," confirmed Gaskarth, examining the wand's inset controls.

"What other flavors will it produce?"

"Regrettably, none," said the dwarf. "It is a very old artifact, quite unrepairable in these later days, whose workings are frozen with disuse. I fear that the necessary parts would be well beyond availability."

"Then we must eat mazhouki or nothing?" cried Filidor.

"There is always grass and a wide selection of slow-moving insects," Gaskarth replied.

The cake's thick taste had already begun to cloy Filidor's palate. He threw down the uneaten portion. "Nothing but mazhouki until we reach... hoy, stop a minute! You have not yet revealed my uncle's message. Where are we bound?"

"I had thought you uninterested in all but your present discomforts and appetites," said the little man. "But, since you now inquire, I rejoice to enlighten you: we make for Ektop. No doubt you are well aware of its location and the intervening distance."

Filidor was now beyond vain pretense. "I cannot mask my ignorance. My command of geography is feeble. I have ever been unable to compass places I have not been."

"Unable, or merely unwilling?" asked the other.

"Are they not the same?"

"You are learning," said the dwarf.

Ektop, Gaskarth informed Filidor, was a land some two days by foot from Binch. Its borders, like most boundaries of the aging earth, were subject to alteration at the whims of its inhabitants. It was generally thought to commence somewhere on the thither side of a crumple of hills which slipped away from the main Devinish Range. The land extended to the lip of the Amavic desert in one direction, and bordered the Republic of Zeel in all others. Ektop's peculiarity, in a world and time devoted to peculiarities, was that its founders had conceived of their land as a bastion of "the natural life", and their descendants strictly observed the founders' will.

"The Ektopians," Gaskarth continued, "strive to live in perfect harmony with their environs, refusing to inflict the least scratch upon nature's innocence. They pursue this ideal so assiduously that their strictures apply equally to even those few outsiders who enter their realm. In Ektop, a stranger treads well who treads exceeding soft, as the saying goes."

"They sound a strange folk," said Filidor.

"No stranger than you to them," he was answered. "In this penultimate age, the world is speckled with nations pursuing odd aims with intense determination. It is the character of our times. Coming whence you do, you doubtless assume that the mores and customs of your own land arise from the workings of simple human nature. But human nature is far from simple, and what appears natural in your own milieu may seem chillingly alien when transported into some foreign sphere."

"Surely, though, men and women are much the same wherever one goes."

"Only in that they are born and eventually die, and that in-between they eat, sleep and futter each other in divers ways. All else is open to the spirit of inventiveness." The dwarf paused in thought a moment, then went on. "Consider the common Olkney practice of exchanging children among one's neighbors and friends during the annual Fete of Melpoi."

"A very sensible custom, of benefit to all," pronounced Filidor.

"Yet," said Gaskarth, "there are cultures wherein such behavior would be universally deplored, and even subject to legal sanctions."

"Amazing," said Filidor. "Next you will tell me that, should I venture into the adjacent country and blow my nose, I will be set upon by outraged natives."

"Not in the next country, although public evacuation of the nases is a misdemeanor in the Dominion of Hom, across the Behannon Gulf. Curiously, however, one is expected to spit frequently."

Immersed in this educative discourse, Filidor's mood lightened, and he passed a not wholly disagreeable day. Gaskarth, now that he was no longer engaged in dragging the young man forcibly toward their mutual goal, emerged as a diverting travelling companion. Filidor began to sense that his life to this point, confined almost entirely to the palace and its surrounds, had been attended by a constant but unnoticed ennui. Now, freed from his mundane routines of pallid pleasure-seeking, he felt an indefinable change settling upon him. Perhaps, he mused, when this errand ended in Ektop and he had flown back to the palace, he would consider further travels.

The little man had obviously sojourned throughout the world, acquiring a familiarity with all its unknown complexities. As he listened to Gaskarth's reminiscences, Filidor was gradually brought to realize that the intricate sophistication of his own culture was but one small thread in the weft of the world's weaving. Sensing that there was a wider pattern to be seen, he began to desire to see it.

Day's end found them among the slopes of hills beyond which lay Ektop. Sustained by the subtle energies of the traveler's aide, Filidor was only mildly fatigued by a day of almost unbroken march. He warmed himself by a small fire while they dined on more mazhouki, augmented by certain berries and succulents Gaskarth had gathered along the way. The little man then deployed the ward-web and was soon wrapped in his noisy slumber. Filidor was wakeful, and sat awhile feeding the flames.

He watched the slow wheeling of the stars, with the counterpoint of more quickly passing motes of light, which he knew to be objects thrown into nearer space for some forgotten reason in a bygone era. He was a little disappointed that the sky above these hills was no different from that viewed from his chamber windows. An outlandish sky would have better suited his sense of being launched upon an adventure.

The fire cast enough light for reading, and Filidor took out his book of Osfeo, thumbing through its pages until his attention was caught by an illustration. It showed the sage bound and kneeling at the feet of a fearsome barbarian lord. Filidor turned to the text.

Osfeo, seeking a shorter route between Uz Narim and Yahk, chanced his luck in crossing the Vaandaye panhandle. The ever-vigilant Vaandayo border guards noted his passage, however, and he was straightaway seized, beaten and hauled in chains before their paramount. The Vaandayos being notorious cannibals, Osfeo listened in trepidation to the guards' argument over how his carcass should be divided among their larders, once the formalities of sentence were carried out.

But as the order for his execution was about to be delivered, the illumino cried out to the barbarian chief, "Wait! Spare my life and I will perform a great service for you!"

Surveying his prisoner's rags and spindly frame, the paramount sneered, "What possible service could be expected of so hapless a wretch?"

Osfeo, who knew of no real service he could render, but who did not want to end his days in a Vaandayo cooking pot, blurted out the first thing that entered his mind. "I can train dung beetles to gather gold dust instead of dung!"

Now, the Vaandayo value only one thing more than the taste of human flesh in their mouths: the feel of gold in their fingers. The chief's court put down their knucklebones in mid-game to listen.

"Is this true?" they asked the sage.

"Indeed! Indeed!" he swore. "In fact, I braved the journey into Vaandaye only because in this land alone are found the least obtuse dung beetles suitable for training."

"Very well," decreed the paramount, "sentence is stayed pending a demonstration of your skills as a trainer. How long will it take?"

"About ten years," said Osfeo.

"Ten years?" cried the Vaandayos.

"Even the least obtuse dung beetle is a slow learner," he replied.

Amid some grumbling, the Vaandayos agreed to the illumino's terms, and made room in the palace compound for a laboratory and living quarters where he could work under guard. Men were sent to gather dung beetles and bring them in for training. A small store of gold dust was weighed out and provided. Osfeo set to work.

The chief's clown, a shrewd fellow for an anthropophage, had witnessed Osfeo's performance in the court. He came to congratulate the sage on his wiles, and found Osfeo diligently shaping gold dust into dung-shaped portions and prodding beetles toward them.

"Truly, you are a fellow of surpassing guile," said the clown. "For you have translated instant death into ten years of comfortable living at the imperator's expense."

"Hmphf," said Osfeo. He did not look up.

"And, in that time," the cannibal continued, "much may happen. My master may die. You yourself may die of natural causes. You may even be entirely forgotten and thus able to flee. Or, at the end of ten years, you may contrive to gain an extension. I applaud your wit."

But Osfeo remained intent upon his beetles, and the fool went away. "If I can just make this work," the sage muttered to himself. "Wealth beyond counting!"

The firelight was still bright, the dwarf still snoring, and Filidor remained far from sleep. He passed on to another tale.

In those days, he read, *Osfeo decided to try his hand as a fisherman, believing that a simple life among those who toil might enrich his enlightenment. But he found the fisherfolk of northern Baersund a silent and surly lot. His efforts at friendship sullenly rebuffed, Osfeo lived apart from them, in a salt-stained hut beyond the village precincts.*

Baersund was a stony place washed by a cold sea. Year by year, the fishermen's catch had dwindled, so that they labored hard for a scant reward. Osfeo did not sail with them as they traversed their fishing grounds each day. Instead, he rowed a small boat, which he put together from scraps of wrecks, to places where everyone knew there were no fish to be had. His gear was a worn and raveled net rescued from the village midden, yet each evening he brought back his little craft almost sinking under a weight of fish.

The Baersund men, coming ashore with barely a basket or two to show for an entire day at sea, were first amazed, then outraged at Osfeo's success.

"How is it," they snarled, "that we who battle tides and tempests, struggling to wrest a living from the inhospitable sea, can gain so little; while you, who do the least work of all, should receive so much?"

"Perhaps," replied the sage, "you have never offered the fish an opportunity to cooperate."

And with that, Osfeo left them the boatload of fish and went up to the land of Menai. The Baersundians mocked him in his absence, and continued to wage unequal war upon the elements.

Filidor slept, and his dreams were easy. With morning, he awoke only slightly stiff, and soon he and Gaskarth were afoot again for Ektop. Before twilight of that day, which passed enjoyably for Filidor, they had topped the backbone of the hills and were descending with the sun toward their destination. Filidor now detected a change in the character of the countryside through which they walked. Accustomed to view nature as a generally unobtrusive background to civilized pursuits, he sensed that here the usual distinction had been overthrown. In Ektop, flora and fauna held centre stage, and humankind edged gingerly around them.

His tranquil mood began to fray as they came down from the hills into heavily wooded slopes, where gnarled trees and thick ropy vines obstructed their passage. There was almost a detectable contempt in the way birds and small creatures regarded them from the forest's edge, and Filidor was once forced to give way to a disreputable little furred something which refused to yield him the path.

"We are now within the Ektopian marches," Gaskarth advised, as Filidor skirted the chittering creature. "You will do well to offer no offense to being, beast, or vegetation. Remain upon the surface of the roadway, which is both ancient and impervious to harm – much to the despair of the Ektopians, who account it an affront to the ecology. Unhappily for them, they lack the resources with which to remove it; but, happily, the road's presence spares them from having to walk on the grass, which hereabouts can be a capital crime."

Picking their way with care through deepening twilight, they came in a short time to an Ektopian border post. This was a tumble of rocks forming a rough shelter from the elements. A scattering of bones before the natural dolmen showed that it had seen long service as the den of some carnivore. Being presently uninhabited by anything feral, the shelter was now occupied by two naked and unprepossessing Ektopian border guards. These emerged from beneath the overhang, bearing fist-sized pebbles, which they presented in a threatening manner as they demanded the purpose and destination of the travelers.

Displaying the seal of the Archonate, Gaskarth demurred when the guards raised the question of a body search and the confiscation of contraband materials. Under Ektopian law, which was fortunately superseded by the authority of the Archonate, this would have required the seizure of the outlanders' clothing, it being made of forbidden organic stuff. Ektopians were restricted to wearing inorganic materials, of which they had none: no factories existed in the land, nor had they any goods to barter in exchange for imports. Consequently, Ektopians went naked in all seasons.

For implements and utensils, they employed what durables had been handed down across the generations, or made do with stones or bones abandoned by animals. Some found shelter in the few ancient structures their forebears had been unable to dismantle, but most housed themselves in caves and hollow trees untenanted by beasts – as had the border guards – or simply lay down in the open air. This latter course was not recommended, since the many carnivores at large in Ektop were accustomed to regard humans as easy game.

All this Gaskarth explained as they left the customs post and descended into Ektop. "Surely they must starve," wondered Filidor. "Wherefrom do they derive sustenance, if even the picking of roadside fruit will earn the most severe punishment of the law?"

"Not if the fruit has already been worried at by birds and left for whosoever chooses to finish it," answered the dwarf. "As well, the carcasses of dead animals or fish washed ashore may be licitly consumed, if no scavenger arrives to claim the carrion before it begins to rot. And seeds which fall upon stony ground may be gathered and eaten without penalty."

Despite Gaskarth's explanation, it still seemed to Filidor that the Ektopians sacrificed much for principle, gaining little in return. The border guards had not looked the image of natural health; if anything, they were perched on the brink of extinction. Mulling such thoughts, he arrived with the little man at the capital of Ektop, a town of those ancient but indestructible buildings that were long ago scattered at random through the world by a capricious and unremembered international regime. These towns, each as like to one another as the techniques of mass production could achieve, would remain as they were until the old sun simmered down to a final cinder, or until the slow passage of geological time buried them beneath aeons of sedimentary rock. The buildings were an offense against the sensibilities of the Ektopians, but Filidor noted that the locals had conquered their repugnance enough to be living in them.

The travelers found their way to the town's square, collecting along the way an entourage of sullen inhabitants. Little of the square's impermeable paving could be seen, since generations of Ektopians had used it for a refuse heap. Filidor and Gaskarth waded through a sea of debris, which in some places rose to such a height against a building that the doorway was partially buried, leaving only a crawl-hole beneath the lintel. The Ektopians, it seemed, refused to impose their detritus on the environment, and therefore kept it to themselves. The resulting smell was the nasal equivalent of deafening.

The two outlanders plowed toward a building that bore a plaque identifying it as a regional office of the Archonate. The doorway had been swept clear, and a few flagstones showed between the portal and the accumulated garbage. Here the dwarf instructed Filidor to remain, while he sought within for the Archon or news of his whereabouts.

The young man, left standing amid the foulness of generations, could not conceive of his austere and magisterial uncle being found within nose-reach of the place. His musings were cut short, however, when he realized that he had become an object of scrutiny for a motley crowd of naked Ektopians, who viewed him with marked disfavor.

Filidor returned their sentiments. The locals were of divers ages, sexes and sizes, but all bore the common brand of scrawny ugliness. Even the young seemed decrepit. As a lifelong resident of Olkney and a frequenter of the resorts of the elite, Filidor was well used to seeing the human form unadorned by raiment. But the forms to which he was accustomed would be clad in healthy, rosaceous flesh, not these grey-skinned starvelings ringing him amidst their ancestral rubble.

The crowd milled about with open hostility, growing more numerous as more distant Ektopians hurried through the filth to be affronted by his presence. Some hissed, others muttered, and one raw-boned youth pursed cracked lips to send a glob of yellow spittle in the direction of Filidor's boot.

Filidor backed a step, and then another. The flags were slimy underfoot, but he slid backwards until he felt the wall of the Archonate's building against his shoulders. The mob closed in. Growls and muttered threats arose on all sides, and one voice from the back of the pack urged threats that were all the more worrisome for being too indistinct for Filidor to understand. The young man raised his staff, worked a dry throat through the mechanics of swallowing, and addressed the Ektopians. "Desist and withdraw, or I shall come amongst you!" His quavering tone lacked conviction, and the mob jeered; but something in his voice penetrated to the semi-sentient innards of the traveler's aide. It began to emit a foreboding blue radiance, then a series of hard *clicks* as a number of lethal devices sprang into prominence at both tips. The staff began to rotate in complex yet crisp maneuvers, its motions drawing Filidor's hands into a succession of martial positions.

A few passes of the staff's infinitely honed hooks and blades beneath their noses prompted the nearest Ektopians to turn and squeeze between those immediately behind them. The new front ranks of the mob, now seeing the potential dismemberment being offered by the criminal outlander, made rapid shift to follow their compatriots from the area. Filidor was soon left in welcome solitude. The traveler's aide sheathed its claws and became once more an unobtrusive walking stick.

Despite its successful conclusion, Filidor's first encounter with the Ektopians had dulled his developing taste for foreign travel. He ardently hoped that he would soon be through with his mission and could return home by the fastest available transport. Thus he turned with sharp anticipation a few moments later as Gaskarth emerged from the office.

"I trust you were not bored in my absence," said the little man, and continued before Filidor could relate the events that still left him atremble. "Alas, we have failed once more to catch up with your revered uncle. Duty has called him on to parts as yet unknown, and we must remain here to await further word."

Filidor was reluctant to endure the niggardly hospitality of Ektop, and protested bitterly. "I cannot believe that my uncle would abandon me to the scorn and contempt of unwashed ruffians. I advise the summoning of an air car, followed by an immediate return to the palace, where we can doubtless effect point-to-point communication with the Archon, arranging to meet him at some designated place."

The dwarf shrugged. "Your advice is duly noted. Its merits are admitted. Unfortunately, it conflicts directly with your uncle's specific orders. We are required to attend upon his next missive, taking pains not to mislay or in any way part with the box which you are conveying to him."

Filidor felt in his mantle, found the small oblong of tuka wood, and said, "I have it still."

"Good," answered the little man. "Oh, and by the way, your uncle reminds us that it is mandatory for all officials of the Archonate, while traveling, to be of service to those amongst whom they journey. He therefore enjoins you to find some way to be useful to the Ektopians while we are within their borders."

"Useful to them?" exclaimed Filidor. "I can scarce imagine any possible service I could render such dregs, short of providing my own flesh for the filling of their bellies – an outrage with which I am sure they are familiar. Furthermore, the Ektopians and I share a deep, mutual abhorrence, and I can imagine no point at which our interests might cooperatively meet."

"Nonetheless," answered Gaskarth, "it is in the nature of the Archonate to be useful to the citizens under its purview. And since you are now in the service of the Archonate, a fragment of that constant duty falls to you. However, this is a debate for another time. The Archonate's office is now closed for the night, and the approaching darkness will lure beasts into the town; we had best seek a place of rest. Perhaps the morning will bring some opportunity of service."

"Is there a decent hostelry?" Filidor asked.

"Unfortunately not. I suggest we leave the town and sleep out of doors under the security of the ward-web. The ground will be hard, but at least the air will be breathable."

With that, the little man clutched his satchel to his chest and kicked his way through the refuse-laden square. A few catcalls and obscure obscenities followed Filidor as he plowed his way after, but most of the Ektopians were intent on barricading their houses against the perils of the night. A few minutes walk through the gathering dark took them out of town, to where the forest spread pools of shadow beneath its looming boughs.

"Shall we gather grass and leaves for sleeping couches?" asked Filidor.

"Certainly not," said the dwarf. "It would only exacerbate the raw spots we have already rubbed into the Ektopian hide by our foreign presence. Not even our official status could prevent their taking strong action. No, let us travel to some point where the road widens, and make our camp upon its adamantine surface. Disturb no blade of grass, else we will suffer."

They pressed on through deepening darkness, lighting their way by the traveler's aide, until they rounded a bend in the road only to see the pavement disappear before them into a vast expanse of water. A lake stretched like a sheet of opalescent glass across the right of way, its surface reflecting the first stars of evening, broken only by the upraised trunks of a few trees now become green islands.

"This was not here when last I passed this way," said Gaskarth. "I would judge it the work of castorels." At Filidor's blank look, the dwarf explained that castorels were a species of large, semi-aquatic rodent, about twice Filidor's weight. Their giant incisors made short work of any tree, and they used the trunks to construct vast dams across free-running streams, creating private meres for their own purposes.

"They are also fearsome predators, deadly in their natural element and not inconsiderable on land. Obviously, they have chosen to block some stream which formerly flowed through a conduit beneath the road, thus forming this lake. Equally obvious is it that we can proceed no further, so here we will camp."

Filidor looked out over the smooth surface, thinking to detect the ripples of large subaquatic beasts possessed of an appetite for his person. "Perhaps we should withdraw to the relative safety of the town."

Before the dwarf could reply, both heard the hunting

cough of some large flesh eater back along the road. "Better to remain here," advised Gaskarth. "Calm your fears. The ward-web is an ample safeguard."

So saying, he activated the field above them. Together, they lay upon the ancient but unmarked pavement, the little man soon falling to the yowlps and snorts which accompanied his sleep. There were long moments, however, when Gaskarth appeared to stop breathing. In these silences, Filidor heard the snufflings of animals outside the ward-web. And, once, the still lake surface carried to his ears the sound of an immense flat tail slapping the water with a force like the crack of artillery. Despite all these alarums and discomforts, Filidor eventually slept, awakening to find the dwarf preparing a breakfast of mazhouki derived from discarded scraps of bark.

When they had eaten, the little man said that he would go back to town to seek further word of the Archon's where-abouts and to learn if any instructions had been transmitted. If no message had arrived, he would wait until word came.

"In my absence," he finished, "you might bend your thoughts to some way in which we may offer service to the Ektopians, as ordered. But I warn you: give no offense to any living entity, no matter the provocation, and even though you think yourself unobserved."

Filidor did not, in any case, remain long unobserved at the castorels' lake. Soon after the dwarf's departure, a crowd of Ektopians came grumbling up the road and gathered a small distance away, where they huffed and turned baleful glares upon the outlander. Some carried rocks and bone clubs, and Filidor regretted that Gaskarth had taken the ward-web. But the young man retained the traveler's aide, and the emaciated natives had to content themselves with rude signals and mut-tered remarks that Filidor could scarcely hear.

For his part, the young man regarded his detractors with equal distaste, speculating that the most useful service he could proffer would be to douse and scrub a few of them in the lake. If they came up lacking some of the filth and scurf that discolored their skins, they would have profited. And if they did not come up at all, he thought, then the world would be that much better off.

After a while, Filidor put aside such thoughts and endeavored to think of some practical benefit which he could bestow on the Ektopians, in fulfillment of his uncle's wish. But he arrived at nothing that would not be immediately rejected as a violation of their deepest convictions.

While he thought, the morning wore on. The mob eventually settled on the road, keeping watch over Filidor in an attitude of morose malice. He, in turn, grew tired of the sight of them, and gave up his mental search for a way to do his duty. He would ask Gaskarth when the little man returned. The heat of the morning, coupled with his lack of sleep, made him drowsy. To remain awake, he opened the book of Osfeo.

Osfeo, he read, *became a hermit near the great city of Melchipor. The people of the city soon heard that the eminent sage had made his abode in the region, and agreed that his presence conferred a certain added dignity upon their otherwise mundane existence.*

They then reasoned that, if having Osfeo live nearby was a benefit, having him installed within the city proper would constitute an even greater distinction. A delegation of the ruling Melchiporian ealdormen therefore came out to Osfeo's bare cave and invited him to relocate to the city.

Osfeo declined, saying that he had chosen solitude and poverty on purpose, since he meant to concentrate on finding the meaning of the universe.

"But surely, illumino," said one ealdorman – a merchant of favors and insubstantial wares – who saw a potential increase in sales to pilgrims drawn to the sage's wisdom, "surely you would be able to concentrate even more deeply without the distractions of a stony bed and the whistling of the wind about the cave mouth at all hours."

"I had not given it any thought," said the sage, "but

you may be right."

After considerable encouragement, the ealdormen secured Osfeo's agreement to take up residence in Melchipor. They furnished him with a mansion in a select district, with servants to attend to his provisioning and unlimited funds to purchase what he desired. He was thus able to devote his full attention to his researches. In return for their subsidy, he announced that the people of Melchipor would be the first recipients of his findings.

A few years passed, and the people of the city were well pleased with his residency amongst them. Osfeo was in those days a popular sage whose thoughts were extolled and retold in divers lands. A steady stream of seekers and mystic pilgrims came through Melchipor, enriching the merchants who sold to them and to the tourists who flocked to see the metaphysical circus.

But, as in all human endeavors, there are fashions in illumination. Osfeo was eventually decreed to be no longer au courant; the stream of visitors slowed, then dwindled, then stopped.

Still, Osfeo pursued his researches amid the luxury provided him by the merchants of Melchipor. When several years had passed without result from his labors, some of the city's magnates came to grumble at the expense. They resolved to address the sage, demanding to know what progress he had made in determining the meaning of the universe.

A delegation appeared at Osfeo's mansion, finding him reclined on a divan while servants rushed to anticipate his every need. The ealdormen were angered at witnessing the luxury they had themselves imposed on Osfeo. The most offended of them cried, "Tell us, illumino, what you have learned at our expense about the meaning of the universe!"

Osfeo pondered a moment and said, "I have determined that the universe is immensely large."

"Is that all?" demanded the ealdormen.

*"First things first," replied Osfeo. "I have also deter-
mined that the universe is immensely complex."*

"And?" they cried.

*"And I have lately decided that fine foods are more
easily digestible than uncooked grains," said the sage.*

*"Sheer banality!" shouted the merchants. "We already
knew that!"*

*"Then you will be pleased," answered Osfeo, "to have
your views confirmed by one as erudite and respected as I."*

While Filidor read, the Ektopians had fallen still. The
lakeshore was silent save for the constant buzz of gnats and
midges expressing their simple pleasure at the quantities of
blood to be found in Filidor's vessels. Mindful of the dwarf's
warning, he raised not a finger in defence, but endured, grimly
motionless. He willed himself not to notice the swarms of
insects, and thus did not mark the v-shaped wake far out in the
lake, which now turned to point like a watery arrow at the spot
where Filidor sat.

He turned the pages of the book and passed on to another
story.

A TRAVELLER CROSSING the wastes of Goroth came upon Osfeo piling stones one atop another. Thinking the sage deranged by his advanced years or the fierce heat of the sun, the man asked, "Tell me, old one, what inspires you to undertake such grueling toil?"

"I am creating a structure which, by the properties of its design, will focus certain arcane energies in this region. These energies will prevent floods," said Osfeo.

Knowing him now for a madman, the traveller scoffed, "Then your construction must focus these energies in both directions of time, since this land has been desert for thousands of years."

"You are unusually perceptive," replied the sage. "If you would care to assist me in moving this boulder, I would be pleased to enroll you as a disciple."

But the traveller declined with laughter, and continued his journey across the sun-baked bed of an ancient sea.

The attentions of clouds of midges could be borne, but a bronze-bellied hornet was something else entirely. As the thumb-sized creature made its first pass in front of his eyes, Filidor flinched and waved the book to ward it away.

There was an immediate hubbub among the Ektopians. Several leapt to their feet, exhorting their fellows to take note of the outlander's offense against innocent nature. Filidor, intent on his swooping, humming attacker, paid them no heed. The hornet homed in again, and the young man aimed Osfeo in a slap against it. The book flew from his hand, and the insect sideslipped and went off in search of less militant prey, but the Ektopians were now on the march.

A jagged rock whirred past Filidor's head, and he turned to find the mob stalking toward him. Another missile followed, as he raised his staff. The traveler's aide shivered, then emitted a burst of energy that left the flying rock an expanding puff of dust that stung his cheeks. But other rocks now came thick and fast, and more Ektopians were pressing up the road, drawn by the enraged cries of their compatriots. A stone rebounded from the ground in front of Filidor and struck his shin. Another grazed his shoulder. He was driven back to the water's edge, and farther.

The silt sucked at his boots as he splashed about in the shallows, dodging and defending himself as best he could with the staff, which prevented any of the larger missiles from crushing his bones. He stumbled and quickly got back up, coughing water from his nose, to be met by a new hail of bric-a-brac.

Warily, Filidor backed farther into the gradually deepening lake, until the water was waist deep and he was beyond the Ektopians' effective range. Curiously, his attackers did not venture beyond the shoreline, although the water was shallow and they could easily have reached him with a concerted rush and a fresh volley of rocks. Perhaps, he thought, they were loath to risk crushing some subaqueous plant or vermin, for they seemed content to stand at the water's edge, regarding Filidor with grins of complacent triumph as he stood with the lake lapping his belly. Some took up sticks of driftwood and thrashed the shallows to foam, pausing from time to time to beam with happy anticipation at their outlander victim. Indeed, it seemed to Filidor that they were now not watching him at all, but directing their gaze behind him.

He turned to look, but at that moment he felt a pressure wave through the water against his legs. Ripples boiled around him, as two hand-like paws gripped his ankles and yanked him from his footing. He heard the Ektopians raising a derisory cheer, and then sound was cut off as the castorel dragged him under and out toward deep water.

He had a glimpse of a broad furred back and a leathery dark-skinned tail, then he was moving at speed through darkening water. Filidor was hauled feet first down and along the bottom of the lake, its submerged brush snatching at his skin and clothing. Light dimmed, then faded to blackness, and his lungs began to burn.

He still clutched the traveler's aide, but the slipstreaming pressure of the water prevented him from bringing it to bear upon the beast. Then shoulders and head thumped against the lake bottom, and consciousness had begun to ebb when he felt himself being dragged through a narrow underwater tunnel lined with sticks and debris, and thrust into stale air upon a pile of cracked bones. Darkness was absolute, and around him he heard the noises of hungry beasts.

It was a continuous chittering, interrupted by occasional low growls, and it came from too close a distance to be comfortable in the fetid blackness of the castorel's lair. Filidor felt about him: he was on a narrow ledge above the water-filled entrance to the animal's den. The ledge was built up from matted sticks and logs, and gave beneath him as he shifted his weight. He edged away from the water, until his back was against a wall of meshed branches curving inwards to meet somewhere not far above his head. That much he determined by feeling with one hand while the other sought to activate the traveler's aide.

His fingers poked at studs and buttons with frantic hope but no discernible results. Perhaps the ancient instrument had been damaged by its immersion in water. Desperate, he punched at it, while vibrations of the ledge and rustles in the darkness told him that something stealthily approached. Then the warmth of foul carnivore breath washed over him; with a wordless shout, Filidor swung the useless staff like a club, striking fur-sheathed bone scant inches from his face. There was an angry yelp, and the sounds of a heavy body scrabbling back.

Whether it was from the jarring effect of the blow or because his panicked exclamation had registered in some still functioning part of the mechanism, Filidor would never know. But now the traveler's aide produced a wavering glow sufficient to reveal the full peril of his predicament.

He was in a domed chamber perhaps half again his height and about twice that distance in width. The walls were a matting of logs and branches, some as thick as Filidor's body. He crouched on a ledge which extended in a demi-lune around half the den's perimeter, above a pool of black water from which emerged the head and forequarters of the beast that had captured him. Directly opposite Filidor, at the other end of the ledge, the beast's mate rubbed the sore spot on her nose where his staff had made contact. Around her, three castorel pups the size of brag-hounds blinked their rattish eyes and gnashed finger-length teeth in anticipation of the coming feed.

The male eyed Filidor with disinterest, then hauled his huge body out of the water to join his mate. They both exchanged ill-tempered grunts before the male, his role as provider complete, pushed aside the pups and lay down to sleep. Then the female, urged on by the hungry chitters of her brood, shook her head, bared yellow incisors as long as Filidor's hand, and heaved her bulk toward him.

Filidor thrust out the staff, and was relieved to see it emit a crackle of energy which struck the castorel dam square upon her wet black nose. She leapt back with a snarl and sneezed. Then after eying Filidor a moment, on she came once more, making conciliatory clucks low in her throat, while driblets of drool spattered from her chops. A second bolt of energy sent her yipping and reeling back again. She cocked her head and gave Filidor a look of puzzled disappointment, then turned and waddled back to her end of the ledge, swatted the pups into silence, and settled down to wait.

Filidor considered his situation, and found it far from ideal. He recalled Gaskarth saying that castorels sited their lairs deep within the massive dams across the waterways they blocked. Hence he must be somewhere beneath an enormous construct of meshed timbers and debris. The sole exit would be the underwater tunnel through which he had been dragged, and it offered no hope of escape.

If he dove now into the black water, he would be pursued, savaged and drowned long before he could reach its deep water exit. Even if some miracle let him escape the castorels, he could probably not hold his breath long enough to find his way down to the exit and up again to the surface. He was not a strong swimmer.

He examined the traveler's aide. He knew it to be solely a weapon of defence, designed to aid long-ago pilgrims whose ethical tenets did not permit them to indulge in assault except in reply to real and present dangers, and then by only the minimum degree of force. It would discourage the castorels, but its energy discharge could not be scaled up to incinerate them completely. Besides, Filidor realized, immolating the castorels would leave him the choice of being cooked in a blazing hive of wood, or drowned in the tunnel.

However, a rescue from outside was unlikely. The Ektopians had cheered the prospect of his dismemberment and consumption by the forces of nature. The dwarf would not know his whereabouts; even if he did, what could Gaskarth do against the unanimous opposition of the locals?

The heroes of romance and fable, Filidor knew, often encountered and bested much more dread perils than his. He had whiled away many an afternoon amid the exploits of such legendary paladins, who inevitably conquered all before them. Usually, though, these invincibles had the help of a particularly devastating weapon, or at least some magical talisman which, when rubbed or entreated, could summon a convenient elemental spirit to their cause. Filidor had only an ancient and unreliable device, which at any moment might exhaust its energies, or find some other excuse to malfunction.

Cast upon his own slim resources, Filidor examined his

surroundings. The den was a bubble in the mass of flotsam and timber from which the castorels had built their dam. It must be above the level of the lake's surface, else there would be no air. Somewhere above the castorels' domed ceiling lay the outside world, Filidor reasoned, but he doubted if the beasts would allow him to climb their walls and begin to pull apart the roof.

The wall at his back was matted branches, seemingly loosely meshed. He pulled at one, to see if he could insinuate himself through the tangle and crawl laterally away from the castorels' stinking lair. But, though the wall was just tangled brush, that tangle rested beneath many tons of wood, and the branches could not be widened by more than a finger's width.

Very well, thought Filidor, my only course is to cut through. He took another look at his staff's controls. Yesterday, it had spontaneously produced a number of points and edges suitable for cutting Ektopians. If he could contrive to produce one now, it would serve to cut wood.

The she–castorel, taking his concentration for sleep, made another rush down the ledge. The staff shot a bolt in her direction, and she squawked and hunkered back. But it seemed to Filidor that the energy discharge was less than last time, as if the staff's reserves were dwindling.

He pressed a stud at random, hoping to see something sharp snick into place from the tip. Instead, he was rewarded with a tinny voice singing a roundelay called "The Feckless Wanderer", a tune Filidor assumed to have been favored by some erstwhile owner of the staff. The song did nothing to soothe the savage breasts of the castorels, and their intended dinner frantically punched the controls until the ballad and their growls subsided.

His next attempt to find a cutting tool produced a recorded critique of inns and hostelries to be found along the Bay of Shipslitch, and the next after that created a cloud of acrid green vapor even less pleasant to the sense than the odor of castorel. When all the studs had been pressed to no avail, he began to try them in various combinations. After some time, during which the staff offered him a range of wares from foot powder to tonsorial implements – interrupted by yet another sortie from the she-castorel – the staff finally responded to his need.

From one end sprang a crescent of thick metal something like a pruning hook, with a curved inner edge keen enough to separate individual molecules from their closest neighbors. Driving back a castorel cub which was investigating the taste of his boot, Filidor turned and began attacking the matted wood.

The first few branches came away without incident, and a shallow indent appeared in the wall. Filidor edged closer and cut deeper into the tangle, pulling out sections of wood as thick as his arm. The hole was now deep and wide enough to admit his head and shoulders. He reached in with the staff and cut more wood. As he pulled it into the castorels' den, he heard a series of snaps and pops deeper within the wall. The sides of the den shuddered, and the female and her cubs let loose shrieks that set Filidor's teeth to tingling.

Their noise awoke the male. The giant rodent peered at Filidor with a dislike so intense as to be almost human. The young man redoubled his efforts, chunks of debris tumbled from the hole, and the wall surrounding it perceptibly sagged inwards. The male castorel growled with a sound like tearing flesh, and launched itself down the ledge at Filidor in a bone-scattering rush.

The staff fired a weak bolt, which barely slowed the beast. Filidor quickly reversed his grip and swiped at the animal with the hooked end, shearing off a portion of the castorel's stubby ear and gashing its neck. The big male shook itself, splattering a halo of blood, and glared. The muscles in its shoulders and forearms knotted as the beast prepared to spring. Filidor braced the staff against the floor and hoped it would serve to keep the castorel's shovel-like teeth from his throat.

Suddenly, a crack like a rifle shot sounded from within the wall at Filidor's back, followed by snaps and pops from all sides. The roof of the den directly above the male castorel bulged downward, the ends of broken branches poking through.

The animal looked up, as if estimating whether there was still time to rend Filidor before they were all crushed beneath the sagging mass of timber. Then it shook itself, turned and dived into the water of the exit tunnel. The female hissed once more at Filidor, before she batted her pups off the ledge and plunged after them and her mate.

Filidor turned at once to the hole he had cut in the wall, chopping with the hooked staff as hard and fast as panic would allow. He sliced and pulled, hacked and drew back, sweat trickling into his eyes while sharp twigs scraped at his shoulders and belly. He hauled himself head first into the tunnel, lying on his back and cutting above and ahead as far as his aching arms could reach.

He was soon deep into the tangled mass of the castorels' dam, entombed in a sloping tunnel that angled up and away from the animals' den. The more he cut, the louder and closer came the sounds of shifting, snapping supports, as he chopped a weakness through the vast network of wood. Now his tunnel shook as parts of the woven structure came under stresses the castorels had not intended them to bear. A thick branch crashed through the tunnel, just missing Filidor's nose, and he carefully sliced it away before resuming his slow upward progress.

Sharp pains now shot from his wrists to his shoulders, the ache building until his muscles burned from strain. He paused to rest and wipe the stinging sweat from his eyes. The staff's light was beginning to fail, leaving him in dim-shadowed darkness. He covered its waning glow with his hand and turned to peer forward, hoping for a glimmer of day through the meshed branches. But no sliver of light was there to encourage him. He looked back along his own length, and saw far down the sloping tunnel a glint of reflection from the staff's illumination.

For a heart-stopping moment, he thought the shimmer came from the eyes of one of the beasts, returned and now creeping up after him, to catch him supine and defenseless in a space no wider than himself. Then a demure gurgling sound informed him that what pursued him up the tunnel was not the castorels, but their lake. The structural inefficiencies he had created in the dam were causing it to subside, and the water was rising to catch him.

His aches disappeared as Filidor threw himself at the wall of wood between him and daylight. He hacked and scrabbled at branches, worming his way over and under whole logs he dared not sever, lest the dam give way completely before he was free of it. The staff's light dimmed further, then faded to black, but he did not need its beams to tell him that cold water now lapped his feet.

He swore and cut harder, tearing at the wood with bleeding hands, hauling himself higher – and was rewarded with a faint chink of honest sunlight, and a whisper of cool air in the stifling dark. But the strength was leaving his arms as the staff's energies were no longer available to fortify him. Desperate, he cut at the branches beyond his head, and pushed with soaked knees against the walls of the tunnel.

The dam quivered like a racing beast at the starting gate, and made a sound like a great wooden sigh. The water that had been lapping Filidor's knees suddenly surged over his belly and chest and kept rising until it covered his head. Panicked, he flailed upwards, chopping with the staff and pushing his way through the wooden bars of his prison, getting above the rising water. He slithered around onto his belly and butted his way up through branches that no longer resisted as staunchly as those deeper within the pile. He yanked a severed log from his way, and suddenly his head was out.

Filidor looked down and saw that he was high up the downstream side of the sagging gigantic structure. He scraped and tore a space wide enough to free his shoulders, just as the water caught up with him. The lake was now bulling through the tunnel with conviction, forcing him out as if it were giving him a hasty rebirth into the sunlit world, and he had to cling to the side of the dam or be propelled into empty air and a long fall.

The traveler's aide dropped from his fingers as he clung

to the matted wood. It fell into the thick torrent that was now arcing out from Filidor's exit hole and roiling the streamlet below the barrier. He let it go. Exhausted but jubilant, he scrambled up the slightly sloping wall of wood and hauled himself onto its top. He had won free of violent Ektopians, ravenous castorels, and cold black water. He stood up on the shaky mass of timbers, raised his arms and opened his mouth for a joyous victory shout. At that moment, the dam collapsed under him.

The lake smashed through the breach with the zest of long-frustrated gravity. Filidor plunged feet first into the widening flume, to be hurled through a narrow ravine now greedily filling itself with emancipated lake waters intent on resuming the seaward journey interrupted by the castorels.

Currents sucked the young man beneath the surface, drubbed him against rocks and debris, then flung him briefly back to air and light. Chunks of wood torn from the dam or sucked up from the lake bottom battered him as he was sped along. A log grated over his shoulder, and he clasped it to keep afloat, fending off other trunks that sought to crush him in the narrow ravine. Together, they swirled into an eddy where the ravine widened into the old stream bed, and Filidor was briefly circling below the overhanging boughs of a tree growing on the bank.

He had no means to reach the dangling branches before the current would sweep him out of the eddy and back into the rushing torrent. Dazed, spent from the effort of his escape, he had not even the strength to release the log and swim ashore. He had gone as far as he could, and probably further. He laid his head against the log and closed his eyes. The prospect of imminent death no longer seemed worth struggling against; at least it would be peace and quiet.

His resignation was broken by a steam-whistlish toot hard by his ear. The traveler's aide, equipped with a homing device keyed to its last user, as well as several means of propulsion when necessary, had plowed through the detritus to float beside him. Its batteries partially recharged by exposure to sunlight, it awaited his need. Filidor seized the staff and extended it hope-fully toward the tree above him; the traveler's aide fired a small grapple from its tip and gently winched him ashore.

He crawled out of the flood and lay shivering on the grass, beyond caring how many of the Ektopians' prized stems and blades might be crushed beneath him. For quite some time, he gave himself over to the simple pleasure of continued breath-ing. Then, as the sun's heat drove some of the chill from his muscles, he raised himself up and examined limbs and torso for damage. His fingers found bruises and scrapes, and a sting-ing lump on the side of his neck, but no fractures or wounds.

He surveyed with satisfaction the wreck he had made of the castorels' dam, entertaining the hope that whole crowds of Ektopians had been downstream when the mass of debris had smashed along the course of the old stream bed. He was savor-ing this prospect when a tap upon his shoulder brought him around to face the grinning dwarf.

"I congratulate you," said Gaskarth. "You have survived a stoning, a capture by ferocious beasts, and the collapse of a weighty structure. None could deny that these are enviable abilities, well worthy of note."

"I am not given to vanity," replied Filidor, with controlled rancor, "but I will point out that your absence required me to endure and prevail by my own merits."

"Solitary accomplishment is said to bring the greater sat-isfaction," observed the little man. "But I regret that we have no leisure to exchange philosophical trifles. While you were engaged with the castorels, I received word from your uncle. We are commanded to attend him forthwith. If you are recovered from your exertions, therefore, we must depart in haste for the adjacent territory of Zeel."

Filidor rose slowly, leaning on the traveler's aide, and paused to wring water from the hem of his mantle. The dwarf made as if to depart, then stopped and riffled through the con-tents of his satchel. "I found this near the site of your capture," he said, producing the slim volume of Osfeo. Filidor tucked the book into his sodden clothes and set off after the departing dwarf.

"I am glad of one thing," he said.

"And what might that be?"

"The urgency of my uncle's instruction relieves me of any requirement to linger and perform some unappreciated service for his nation of despicable scatherlings!"

Gaskarth turned to allow Filidor to catch up. "I can understand whence such sentiments arise," he said. "But a wider acquaintance of the world in this penultimate age will reveal to you that the Ektopians are no worse than many another community, and overall less dangerous than most. In any event," he said as they walked on, "you have in fact conferred a number of boons upon them."

Filidor snorted. "All unknowingly, I can assure you."

"Knowledge can be a hindrance to right action," answered the little man. "There are those who hold that, if we but knew the full ramifications of even our least deeds, the ensuing concatenations of cause and effect would paralyze us with indecision."

"I will not argue the proposition," said Filidor, "but I confess to curiosity as to how my near consumption by castorels benefited the Ektopians."

"Doubtless you were too occupied to notice," said the dwarf, "but your experience redounded to their aid on several points. The castorels, which had devoured several Ektopians, are dead, since you arranged to have them battered and drowned by the flood. Large quantities of seasoned wood are now available to the Ektopians for fuel and building materials, as are a great number of edible animals and fish cast ashore by the receding deluge. You have protected, fed, warmed, and housed a multitude."

Filidor could not frame a reply. "Perhaps more important," Gaskarth went on, "is the contribution to their emotional well-being. As you might imagine, the strictures of Ektopian law create considerable social and personal tension, which they find difficult to discharge. Your presence amongst them afforded an opportunity to vent their repressed choler upon your person.

"All taken in all," the dwarf concluded, "I am confident that your uncle will say that your performance outran his expectations. He will surely honor you with distinction when he at last clasps you to him."

As the dwarf spoke, Filidor's exhilaration over his triumph faded. Pride in accomplishment gave way to resentment at being used. He was not given to contemplation of life's mazes and contradictions, yet it seemed there should be some axiom to be taken from his late experiences. A man sits placidly by a lake, seeking no involvement, and is then attacked by mob and beast, put in peril of his very existence, and delivered only by his own desperate exertions; all of this serving to benefit his persecutors. Something must be out of balance.

Gathering himself together, he asked the dwarf, "Was all this in some way planned and predetermined?"

Gaskarth turned upon the young man a thoughtful gaze. "There are those who say that all is planned, to the placement of the last mote and mite. There are others who say that nothing is purposed, and that the galaxies themselves swing where they will. And then there are some, like me, who prefer to walk on, saying as little as possible."

"I am confused," said Filidor.

"That, too, is frequently said," answered the dwarf, and then said no more, because they must now begin to force their way into the untamed forest of Ektop. Within minutes of leaving the stream, they were deep within wilderness, seeking a path through tangled underbrush. Thorns and hooked leaves snagged at hair and clothing. Unseen things clumped away in the middle distance, or hissed at them from nearby thickets. At the dwarf's urging, Filidor took the lead, flailing at brush and nettles with his staff. In time, they broke onto a dung-littered game trail that snaked away among the trees. Gaskarth sniffed the air a moment, then pointed left. Filidor set off in the direction indicated.

The forest of Ektop was a dank place, and much less hospitable than the familiar terraced park lands descending from the Archonate palace. Filidor noticed a tendency to hunch his shoulders together, as if to reduce the landing space offered some fanged attacker. He looked often behind, but saw only Gaskarth marching stolidly in his train. To the fore, the trail stretched never more than a few paces before turning out of sight behind some tree or moss-hung bush. Constant rustlings and squawks attended their passage, and several times Filidor heard large beasts breaking through the brush on either side.

In his former life – and it was as if that were already years instead of days behind him – he had given over the occasional evening to read some picaresque tale of brave deeds and hairsbreadth escapes. Such accounts often put their protagonists to journeys such as this, through dark woods where danger might lurk beyond each bend in the path. Yet the heroes who disported through those romances had only to keep their eyes steadily fixed on the quest before them. Their antagonists were always large but ever vincible. No roots lay in wait for their unwary toes. No cobwebs drooped invisible until they suddenly draped the face from chin to brow. No swarming ticks cast themselves from hanging branches, burrowing snouts at the ready, onto blood-rich hero skin. No stink of moldy rot wafted among the trees, thick as mist.

"I am mired in despond," said Filidor. The dwarf did not answer, and the young man trudged on, wondering where the thrill of adventure might have gone. He had known it as he had chopped through the last sticks and hauled himself up the side of the dam, but all before and since had been sustained fear broken by moments of intense discomfort. It might have cheered him to know that his staff, responding to its holder's emanations of fright, was now emitting certain infrasonic tones to prompt predators to depart their places of ambush and take their appetites elsewhere. Unaware of its assistance, Filidor swung the instrument at a particularly ugly fungus, and noted that it had begun to rain.

"Where did you say we were going?" he asked over his shoulder.

"The land of Zeel," was the answer.

"How far?"

"We should reach the River Sampo by mid-day tomorrow. Across it and we are in Zeel."

"What manner of people will we find there?"

The dwarf did not answer. Filidor glanced back. Gaskarth's face bore a bleak, far-away look. He walked in light-footed silence, but he seemed to have shrunk even smaller. Perhaps it was only the gloom of the forest and the effects of cold drizzle, but the ragged little man appeared burdened by more than the old satchel slung from one shoulder. He did not look up as he asked Filidor, "Have you still the box for your uncle?"

Filidor felt in the tucks of his mantle and nodded. "Will we see my uncle in Zeel?" he asked.

"Perhaps," said the dwarf, in a voice from far away.

"Is something amiss?"

"I am not sure. Perhaps I'll find out in Zeel," said Gaskarth, but he spoke as if to himself, and waved away further colloquy.

The tree-shaded darkness of the forest gradually deepened into night. They camped where a giant conifer had crashed to earth through overhead canopy, letting the faded stars drop dim light on its dead limbs. Filidor broke off some kindling and made a fire. The small blaze sputtered irritably in the rain, sending small tendrils of smoke up through the rent in the forest roof, where they were easily flicked away by movements in the upper air. The travelers ate mazhouki, and some mushrooms the little man pointed out to Filidor. The brief meal finished, Gaskarth sat beside the fire, his black eyes following the ins and outs of the flames.

"I sense that something is wrong," Filidor finally edged into the other's silence.

"Something may be," said the yellow man. "Or nothing. I cannot tell for the moment. In any case, it does not touch upon you. At least, not yet." He looked across the fire into the dripping darkness, and Filidor's further inquiries brought only a shake of the hairless head. Soon after, Gaskarth spread the ward-web beneath an arch of the fallen tree, and lay down to sleep.

Filidor was exhausted and stiff from his exertions, but sleep seemed merely an idea too difficult to grasp. He threw more wood on the fire, raising a glow of light in the stygian woods, and took out the book of Osfeo. He opened it at random, as if playing the child's game of auspices, half-heartedly seeking enlightenment.

In the Muzeywan jungle, Osfeo came upon a young bull garoon pinned beneath a trapper's deadfall. Moved by pity, the illumino braved the predator's venomed spines to lever up the log that held it fast. The garoon shook its triangular head, regarded Osfeo from its great round eyes, and with a soft exhalation of "hoo, hoo," the beast withdrew into the undergrowth.

Years later, in passing through Urzendhi, the sage transgressed one of the Ten Thousand Canons, and was taken up by the city's harmonizers. They instantly adjudicated the case and sent the illumino to purge his guilt through combat in the municipal amphitheater.

Osfeo was handed an antique bombarde, a cumbersome weapon capable of one discharge at short range, then he was pushed into a large enclosure whose sandy floor reeked of old blood. Across from him, a door opened and into the arena slid a mature bull garoon.

The creature shook its frills, spraying spectators in the lower stands with toxic drops, and undulated across the sand toward the sage. Then, at lunge's length, the animal abruptly stopped and twisted its sinewy neck to inspect

Osfeo from several angles.

The illumino fired his weapon, and the garoon's head was instantly obliterated. The harmonizers promptly set him free, and Osfeo left Urzendhi the same afternoon.

Years later, he related the tale to his disciples, one of whom asked why he had not accepted the beast's friendship. "You assume," said the sage, "that this was the same monster I had freed, that it would remember my kindness, and that remembering would prompt it to mercy. These are the elements of a good morality tale, but they are tenuous assumptions on which to hazard one's life. Whereas a headless garoon is almost certainly harmless."

Filidor recalled that, as a child, he had never enjoyed much success with auspices. If there was any connection between the Osfeo tale and his predicament, it eluded his understanding. He slid his fingers between the book's pages at hazard, and opened it to another place. There was a picture of Osfeo seated beside a great river.

Osfeo studied as a young man with the revered sage Nassal im-Fatarj. One day, Master Nassal observed that the man who sits patiently at the river's edge will in time see the corpse of his enemy float by. The master's words struck a chord in Osfeo's youthful mind, since he was at that time engaged in ritual enmity with the sire and sons of a certain powerful family. Buoyed by his teacher's lesson, he took staff and bowl and ensconced himself beside the nearest river.

Days piled into weeks and became months as Osfeo waited patiently at the water's edge, eking a meager living from whatever passersby would cast into his bowl. Through his constant perspective of the water rushing past his feet, he learned much about rivers that was not apparent to the cursory glance. By noting what floated past, he deduced happenings many leagues upstream. As well, he made progress in a number of solitary disciplines requiring ample leisure and few distractions. But the corpses of his enemies did not fall under his gaze.

After more than a year, Osfeo began to wonder whether he had fully apprehended Master Nassal's teaching. A few months later, still without a sign of his enemies, he reluctantly concluded that he had erred in interpreting the lesson. Dispirited, he left the river and returned to the town where the master kept his school.

Stopping at the town gates, Osfeo went to the imprintor's booth to hear what news had transpired during his lengthy absence. The official put aside his stamps and inks, and regaled the young man with all the noteworthy tidings since Osfeo's departure. Osfeo was interested to find that the man's report confirmed many of the deductions he had reached from his study of the river.

But when he asked after news of his ritual enemies, the imprintor informed him that the family had some time ago fared west on a commercial expedition. Crossing a distant river – not that which Osfeo had sat beside – their craft had capsized and all were lost.

Hearing this, Osfeo hurried back to Master Nassal. "Master," he cried, "I am delighted to be able to confirm your wisdom from my own experience!"

The master nodded his acceptance.

"But if only I had stayed longer in school," Osfeo continued, "I would have learned how one goes about choosing exactly the right river."

This time, as he considered the picture of Osfeo seated beside the water and the tale's reference to drowning, Filidor felt sure there was some correspondence to his own experiences of the day. But if so, the relevance escaped him. He banked the fire and crawled beneath the ward-web to sleep.

THE MORNING CAME WET, and the little man went about his ablutions with an air of despondency. Filidor, however, awoke refreshed; youth and a night's rest had somehow combined to put behind him the rigors of the preceding day. It was good to taste fresh air, to hear the sounds of the forest, to feel the springiness of leaves beneath his feet – and even the cold drizzle filtering through the trees did not repress his spirits.

Filidor sensed change in his being, as if he were shedding a disused skin, emerging fresh but vulnerable into a world made different because he was different. He wanted to communicate these novel sentiments to Gaskarth, but the dwarf had begun to perform the complex Lho-tso exercises by which an adept can concentrate life-force and redirect it to those parts of the self that require energizing.

When he had completed the final graceful motion, the little man drew a slow, measured breath, and at once launched himself into preparations for the day's march. Their scant gear was soon assembled, and the dwarf tossed Filidor a handful of fungi to eat along the way, to be followed by the inevitable mazhouki. Then he led the way back into the trees.

They moved at a brisk pace, saying nothing, Gaskarth's mind seemingly immersed in whatever a dwarf might think about in a forest. Filidor was content to travel in the other's wake, exercising the newly developing strength in his legs, and taking unaccustomed pleasure in the sights and sounds the woods offered him.

As the morning wore on, his pleasure dwindled. The farther they progressed toward Zeel, the less wholesome became the forest. At first it was too small a change to notice, but each turn in the trail presented Filidor with a stretch of woods a little less green, a little less alive. The undergrowth thinned imperceptibly, until only a few oily-leaved bushes hugged the ground between the boles of the trees. The trees themselves began to lose their grandeur: lofty devadars gave way to unpretentious rowan, which in turn yielded to gnarly clumps of conifers. The few birds Filidor saw seemed ill at ease, and the forest was now silent save for their footsteps on the grey, brittle grass. An acrid odor of burning hung over the land.

By noon, the drizzle gave up, and a brassy sky showed through the thin cover overhead. The stink of combustion strengthened and was reinforced by wafts of more biting vapors. Filidor coughed as the sharp-edged fumes rasped the back of his throat. The dwarf looked back at him and commented, "It is truly said that no one comes upon Zeel unawares."

"Never mind that," choked Filidor. "What is that stench?"

For answer, the dwarf turned off the trail and skittered down a brief slope. Filidor followed and shortly found himself on the graveled shore of a milk-white river. The dwarf pointed across the foul-smelling flow. "This is the Sampo, and that is Zeel," he said, "and the effluvium offending your nostrils is what the Zeelotes call the odor of progress."

The landscape across the river was obscured by hanging smoke pouring from what seemed to be whole ranks of manufacturies. A low rumble of incessant clanking sounded from over the stream, and the horizon was shot with arcs and splashes of light.

"I cannot imagine how the Ektopians can endure to share a border with such a polluted realm," said Filidor. "Surely a state of permanent war must obtain against the Zeelotes."

"Indeed," confirmed Gaskarth, "and it would be cause for alarm were the Ektopians not completely unarmed, and the Zeelotes not fully occupied with more immediate concerns. Come, there is a bridge."

It was a structure of gleaming chrome that swept across

the Sampo in one unbroken arch, ending at the Ektop shore where neither road nor trail came out to meet it. The span, though empty of traffic, was wide enough for several omnibuses to have engaged in competitive races along its length. As the travelers advanced onto the sliding pedestrian mover that ran along one side of the crossing, they observed that work crews were just completing the last stages of the bridge's construction. The Zeelotes, clad in brightly colored coveralls cinched by tool-bedecked harnesses, were in feverish haste to rivet a row of decorative plates across the superstructure.

As the mover carried them up the arch, Filidor could see farther upstream another bridge being dismantled with equal energy by other Zeelotes dressed in drab garb. The second span seemed in no way derelict, and appeared to differ from the new crossing only in details of design and embellishment. Reaching the mid-point of the bridge, Filidor saw other gangs of laborers on the Zeelote shore, diverting a road that had run to the old bridge, so that it could now extend to the new. The workers' every motion seemed powered by a frantic desire for speed, such that it made Filidor tired even to watch them.

At the Zeel end of the bridge, the travelers encountered a customs post on which the paint had yet to dry. Within was an officious personage in a crisp black and orange uniform whose identity plate proclaimed him to be Discriminator (Third Class) Hostain Klorvy of the Excise Corps.

"Next!" shouted Klorvy, as Filidor and Gaskarth entered the otherwise empty booth. The official then produced a palm-sized card from which he read a stream of regulations and instructions too rapid for intelligibility. The recitation over, the Zeelote stepped smartly forward and said, "Welcome to Zeel. Please deposit all your possessions into this device."

Filidor clutched the traveler's aide against Klorvy's attempts to seize it. "I protest!" he cried. "I expected no confiscation!"

"No confiscation is intended," answered the Zeelote, taking a step back as the staff sent a warning jolt up his arm, "but inspection of all manufactured goods is mandatory. Your possessions will be returned to you, doubtless before you have secured lodgings."

Filidor looked to Gaskarth, who motioned him to unconcern. With a shrug, he surrendered the staff and such oddments as he carried about his person. As he made to withdraw the box of tuka wood from his mantle, however, the dwarf subtly inclined his head, and Filidor returned the thing to its hiding place. Meanwhile, the Discriminator had quickly sorted through Filidor's offerings, choosing out those of manufactured origin while disdaining the book of Osfeo and the small vial of Filidor's infant teeth which – like all his people – he carried for reasons ill-defined but ancient. Klorvy emptied his selections into the inspection machine's hopper, save for the staff, which he examined with great interest, pressing several studs and murmuring at the results.

"This is quite new, most excellently new indeed," he exclaimed. "Clearly a breakthrough in both design and multiplicity of function."

"To the contrary," countered the dwarf, "you hold in your hand a veritable relic, a curio deriving from the Episcopal Dynasty of Nur h'Din, making it in fact more ancient than most of the geological features of this region of the globe."

A terrible change flooded the Zeelote's face, and he let drop the staff as though it were a small animal that had just deposited a natural but unwholesome substance in his lap. He snatched a napkin of disposable fiber from its wall dispenser and wiped his hands thoroughly, then took another to remove the sheen of sweat that had sprung from his brow and upper lip. He wadded the rags with white-knuckled fingers and stuffed them into a disposal vent, then turned upon the travelers an expression of icy disgust.

"How long do you propose to inflict your presence upon my country?" he inquired.

"A matter of hours only, perhaps a day or two at most," replied Gaskarth.

"And what employment will you undertake during this sojourn?"

Filidor was taken aback. "My companion has just informed you of the brevity of our stay. What useful employment could we conceivably seek in so short a time?"

Klorvy's face paled further, then flushed in anger. He stepped back and drew himself to attention.

"Entry denied!" he snapped. "This is outrage! Sheer insouciance! You attempt to import into Zeel an object which is – and you will excuse my language, but there is no other word for it – old, and then glibly announce an intention to gad about without conscience or gainful occupation! It strains all tolerance. It is provocation beyond demurral, even for foreigners. I order you to remove yourself forthwith, or I shall summon proctors!"

Gaskarth approached the Discriminator with placative gestures. "It seems that misapprehensions becloud us. My young colleague spoke from ignorance of the revered and ever-improving laws of Zeel. We are, in truth, full-time employees of the Archonate, whose seal you see I bear, and therefore far too occupied to seek other employment.

"As for the staff," he continued, "its origins may not be new, but the technology of the Episcopal Dynasty of Nur h'Din was so thoroughly expunged by the succeeding regime – a revolutionary cabal who called themselves the Phalanx of Rigorous Piacularity – that it is now unkenned by Zeel or any other land. In this sense, which you will agree is an important one, this instrument's workings and principles are fully innovative. As indeed you perceived them to be on first appraisal."

A creature of doubt left its tracks across Klorvy's face. He regarded the two travelers and their staff a moment, then he shook his head and let some of the rigidity out of his stance.

"As a simple Discriminator (Third Class)," he said, "I am ill-matched against outlander sophistry. I will defer the point to the deliberations of my superiors. In any event, I must yield to the superordinate authority of the Archonate, and grant you entry to Zeel. But I warn you to bend no canon or prohibition, and to give no offense to right-thinking Zeelotes, else you are liable to be drafted into a dismantler squad."

"What of our possessions?" asked Filidor.

"They will be returned to you in good order at the office of the Archonate, which until tomorrow" – he consulted an informatrix on his wrist – "is located in the Avenue of Relentless Endeavor. Good day."

Filidor had no opportunity to voice any of the several questions about Zeel that had already come to mind, because the little man prodded him from the customs post without further delay. They stepped back onto the pedestrian mover and sped away; but not before Filidor glanced back to see that Klorvy had retrieved the staff and was examining the device with an expression that mingled distaste and speculation.

The mover carried them a short way from the bridge to a nexus, where Gaskarth chose another sliding belt that took them toward the nearby city of Zeel. Even before they reached the outskirts of the city proper their route was flanked by continuous signs of activity. At one site, a complex of new buildings was under accelerated construction, even as an equal number of quite serviceable warehouses and transport termini were disappearing into the maw of a herculean destructor. Construction and demolition crews, sharply distinguishable by the bright garb of the former and the drab grays of the latter, built and dismantled at break-neck speed.

Filidor was agape at the frenetic pace of the Zeelotes. Gaskarth noted this, and commented, "Here innovation and a brisk approach to the world are the prevailing virtues."

Filidor shook his head. "I wonder that any of them can survive the day."

"I have heard that mortality rates have risen," replied the dwarf, "although the statistics are skewed by the recent institution of capital punishment for aggravated unpunctuality."

There was no leisure for further conversation, because they had now travelled deeper into the city, and the pedestrian

ways had filled up with bustling Zeelotes. Filidor was frequently jostled by those who sprinted along the already moving belt.
On the streets, velocitators and jitneys sped by, their operators
intent on pursuits that demanded strict adherence to ambitious
schedules. At no time did Filidor witness a Zeelote in an attitude of repose. They did not stop even long enough to remon-
strate with each other about the frequent collisions which were
a natural result of their constant haste: instead, they exchanged
imprecations on the fly. Filidor himself was addressed as a
"piece of history" by one surly Zeelote whose too rapid passage
along the pedestrian mover spun the young man almost from
his feet. There was no doubt the epithet was meant as an insult.

At above the crowded streets, the city was further enlivened
by swarms of air cars and free-floating advertisements which
exhorted all but the deaf and blind to consume a bewildering
array of goods and services. On many buildings – even those
yet uncompleted – huge banners urged one and all to: *Compete!
Gain!* and *Surpass!*

At a building whose entire facade bore such garish en-
couragements, Gaskarth pulled Filidor from the pedestrian way
and through the portico. They struggled into the lobby against
a crowd of porters who were hoisting cartons through the
front door from a pantechnicon which waited with its engine
running at the curb, where another gang of workers were refit-
ting the mechanism of its off-loading ramps.

Tugged in the little man's wake, Filidor squeezed across
the packed lobby and down a side corridor equally crowded.
They arrived at a door which bore the Archonate's crest in
shiny gold leaf. Here the dwarf left him, and slipped through
the portal.

Filidor tried to gain entry himself, but the door's sensors
would not admit him. Cast again onto his own resources, he
pressed himself as deeply into the shallow doorwell as he
could, to avoid being jostled by the stream of Zeelotes hustling
in both directions. He soon noticed that there were two distinct flows: one composed of brightly dressed porters carry-

ing sealed cartons of new goods into the building through the
front door; the other comprising grey-clad individuals lugging
unboxed equipment out through a rear service exit. The in-
coming Zeelotes went about their labors with zest and determination, while the drably appareled showed distaste for their
work, or at best a patient resignation to their lot.

Not so patient were they with Filidor, whose stationary
presence in the corridor – though no barrier to their scurryings
– clearly posed an affront to their sense of propriety. He dis-
tinctly heard himself referred to as a "paralytic codger", but the
speaker was out of earshot before Filidor could compose and
launch a suitable rejoinder. He was subjected to other indignities, and his temper had begun to fray by the time Gaskarth at
last emerged from the Archonate office and quickly led him
back out into the stampeding mobs on the street.

Only the dregs of tolerance remained in Filidor's cup.
As the dwarf sought to lead him into the thick of the throng,
the young man set his heels and resisted with all his strength.
Zeelotes bumped and cursed him as he impeded their hurtling flow, but Filidor stood his ground and drew the little man
toward him.

"I will not be chivvied along at this unseemly pace. Whatever else I must be in this life, I remain a gentleman, and gentlemen are not to be hurried. I demand to know: first, the whereabouts of my uncle; second, how soon I may be discharged
of my errand; and, third, where in this land of supercharged
bedlam a person of refinement may find rest and repast. I am
hungry."

Before Gaskarth could answer, a sleek vehicle whined to a
halt beside them and disgorged a Zeelote dressed in a uniform
similar to that worn by Discriminator Klorvy. He thrust into
their hands the possessions which had been taken for inspection, proffered a receipt book for the dwarf's signature, and
was speeding away from them before the car's entry hatch was
levered down. The little man quickly ascertained that the contents of his satchel were as they should be, and made as if to

depart. Filidor had loosed his grip on his companion to receive back his traveler's aide and pocket items; but now he reestablished his hold upon Gaskarth's collar and hoisted the dwarf, feet dangling free, to eye level.

"I have asked you a question," he said. "In fact, three questions, all of which require answers before we take another step."

The little man eyed Filidor speculatively a moment, then nodded. "Fair enough," he said. "I offer apologies and an explanation: in my travels, I have acquired the facility of taking on the characteristics of whatever folk I find myself among. A matter of protective coloration. Thus, in Zeel I am Zeelotic, inhaling bustle and haste as if from the air. If you would be so good as to lower me, we will seek a place of refreshment, and I will answer your first and second queries."

Feeling like a caught-out bully, Filidor reset the little man upon his feet. "I, too, apologize," he said. "Hunger and the shock of being thrust into this ant hill of a city..." he grunted as yet another Zeelote trod upon his foot, "have disturbed my equilibrium. Please lead on."

Gaskarth pointed their way back onto a pedestrian mover, and steered them through a confusion of transfers and interchanges, until they arrived at a low building crowned by a gigantic luminous sign. A complicated array of colored lights and baffles at least two storeys high, this advertisement delivered to the world the single commandment *EAT!* at sufficient candlepower to be visible, Filidor was sure, from the moon that some said had orbited Earth long ago in the planet's youth. They stepped from the pedestrian way and entered.

It would have been too much to hope, the young man knew, that Zeelotic eateries would be arranged so as to encourage diners to linger over their food. Nonetheless, he had been expecting chairs. Instead, he stepped onto a moving belt which immediately erected a cubicle about him no wider than himself. Cocooned in its embrace, he was fed past a battery of devices which analyzed his wants and met them with a succession of foodstuffs delivered directly into his mouth. An extender reached from the wall into his pockets, extracted coinage and made adjustments for non-Zeelotic currency, and withdrew as Filidor was expelled to make room for the restaurant's next patron. The expulsion was in keeping with the place's abruptness: Filidor yelped as the floor dropped from beneath him, and he slid through a glistening tube back onto the street. As a courtesy, during his brief passage to the outside, his garments were efficiently cleaned by electrostatic charges.

No sooner had he gained his feet than the dwarf popped into place beside him from an adjacent tube. Gaskarth arrived in mid-grumble, wiping traces of soup from the crown of his head while commenting darkly on the limitations of machinery designed for standard-sized persons.

Filidor's patience was far from replenished by his experience with Zeel's cuisine. His stomach now growled from outrage, and it matched his temper. He wanted answers and clarifications, and would not draw the line at shaking a response from his companion. But the scruff of neck he reached for was already receding in the direction of a crowded omnibus hurtling past the curb.

The vehicle scarcely slowed to board and disembark passengers, and Filidor was forced to leap the pedestrian belt and grasp a stanchion barely before the omnibus's doors wheezed shut behind him. Gaskarth was too short to be seen, but the dwarf's passage toward the back of the conveyance could be tracked by its effects on the other passengers jammed into the central passageway. Filidor thrust himself into the press of standing Zeelotes, nudging a few with his staff, until he at last accosted the dwarf near the rear exit.

"Now..." he began, but at that moment the omnibus took a tight corner at speed, and all were thrown to one side. Filidor found himself inclined upon a stout Zeelotic woman of disapproving mien. Muttering an apology, the young man levered himself back upright as the vehicle resumed a level course.

The Zeelote eyed him with distaste. "Outlander?" she inquired.

"Out of Olkney," Filidor replied.

"Backwards place, I hear," pronounced his interrogator, to the approving grunts and nods of her compatriots.

Remembering how he had fared at the hands of strangers in Binch and Ektop, Filidor forbore to answer in kind. "Perhaps," he admitted, "but if you will excuse me, I have some matters to take up with my travelling companion here."

He turned to address Gaskarth, but the large Zeelote was not yet through exerting her cultural superiority over strangers. "What's this, some piece of outlander junk?" she sneered, poking her fingers into the controls of the traveler's aide. By chance, her proddings engaged the inventory command, causing the staff to display in sequence all its capabilities. The results were astonishing, even to Filidor, who learned that he had not yet witnessed a tenth of what the device could do. When the staff ended its performance by raising a brightly colored parasol from its tip, there was a moment of suspended breath followed by a wave of outright applause from the Zeelotes.

"I've never witnessed the like," said the stout woman. "I must have one."

A chorus of similar sentiments erupted among the other passengers, though they were all thrown forward as the omnibus decelerated to a near stop. Filidor allowed a smug smile to take charge of his face, in anticipation of acquainting the Zeelotes with the staff's complete singularity. But Gaskarth denied him that pleasure, seizing the young man's arm and dragging him through the exit. The vehicle sped away, Zeelotes still demanding information on the traveler's aide from the open windows.

"We are here," said the dwarf.

"More to the point," said Filidor, eying the imposing building before which they now stood, "is the question of whether my uncle is here, leaving aside the matters of what place this is, and why we have come to it."

"Regrettably, your uncle is not yet able to receive you into his embrace," replied Gaskarth. "I am informed that he wishes us now to depart Zeel for the Free Dominion of Jamp; hence we are here at this almost-completed aerodrome, where one may purchase an outbound passage."

"And after one has reached this next realm – having sought in vain through Binch, Ektop and Zeel – might then one encounter one's uncle, deliver one's mysterious box, and go home?"

The dwarf raised his eyebrows. "It is possible."

"But not certain."

"Certainty," mused Gaskarth, "can be an inhibiting prospect." The comment seemed more addressed to himself than to his companion.

Filidor sighed. "Tell me but one thing," he said, gesturing to indicate the scurrying Zeelotes flowing into and out of the aerodrome, "This land of Jamp: do its citizens rush hither and yon in mad pursuit of gain and novelty?"

"No more than the norm," answered the little man. "In fact, most Jampeians devote themselves to the attainment of excellence in pastimes of leisure."

That seemed to Filidor a brighter prospect. "Then I will be content," he said, and followed the dwarf into the teeming maelstrom of the Zeel aerodrome.

The travelers worked their way through a tide of buffeting shoulders and viciously wielded elbows that ebbed and flowed through the terminal. The congestion was worsened by the work crews who swarmed up and down skeletal scaffolding to put the finishing touches on the building.

By paying careful attention to floating ribs and other sensitive parts of their anatomy, Gaskarth opened a way through the crowd of Zeelotes surrounding the ticket dispenser. By the time Filidor had made shift to follow, the dwarf was back with two travel vouchers. Together they joined the mob flowing toward a ramp that led out and down to the airfield.

The ramp led them past a row of shops and stalls purveying goods of use or interest to outbound travelers. Zeelotes eddied their way into and out of these establishments, clutching haversacks and pouches stuffed with their purchases. Passing one such emporium, which advertised its wares by means of a rotating collage of utensils above the open door, Filidor was jostled by an exiting customer, and was amazed to be thrust aside by a travelling staff identical to his own. Behind the Zeelote came another, also bearing a close copy of the staff. As the crowd's surge bore him away, he craned his head and saw a stream of Zeelotes leaving the booth, clutching staffs. His attention now drawn to it, he observed that almost all the people around him now carried traveler's aides differing from his own by nary a jot nor a tittle.

At this point, Filidor was propelled slantwise across the flow of Zeelotes moving down the ramp, as Gaskarth used him for a shield to thrust their way into an inconspicuous entry just before the sloping corridor met the airfield. A placard on the wall of the small side passage identified it as leading to the embarkation area for passengers leaving Zeel. No Zeelotes followed, foreign travel tending to corrupt, or at the best to offer continual affronts to the Zeelotic moral standards. Filidor and the dwarf proceeded at a moderate pace to the passageway's end, where they presented their vouchers to a screening panel set in a portal, which then opened to admit them to the in-transit lounge.

They entered a large room, indifferently furnished, and sparsely peopled by outlanders awaiting flights from Zeel. A family of Niffelinders – recognizable by their brocaded headgear and slashed buckskins – dozed among their baggage at one end of the lounge. A trio of ultramonds clad only in their own intricately woven plumage exchanged mournful whistles as they sought to arrange their multiple limbs on chairs that would have denied comfort even to the humans who made them. A lean and wiry Schtort paced a tight circle near the passenger loading tube, the plaited tassels at shoulder and hip swinging in time to a droning chant, to the annoyance of a garishly uniformed Ta'am mercenary sitting just outside the limit of the tassels' arc. But the Ta'am kept his hands well clear of the panoply of weapons in his harness; a Schtort's implanted neural and muscular enhancements could prompt him, if violently provoked, to irreparable excesses.

Filidor and Gaskarth crossed to a crescent of empty seats and composed themselves to wait. After consulting an illuminated marquee above the lounge's main window, the little man announced that their airship would arrive soon, and would board passengers after taking on cargo.

Filidor released a long breath of satisfaction. "I am relieved to be freed of any long stay among these teeming Zeelotes." He gestured at the window, through which they could see various craft being stuffed or unstuffed with goods. Zeelotes fled to and from the airships like ants butchering a grasshopper. "All is graceless haste."

The dwarf reclined in his seat and observed the activity outside. "It brooks no denial that Zeelotic zest and briskness exact a rigorous seasoning of the newcomer. Malchance, it is equally true that many visitors may expire of the strain before they can make the requisite adjustments."

"I would not doubt it," said Filidor. "For myself, I rejoice that no further adjustments need be made."

"Really?" inquired the other. "I had thought you were coming along nicely. This is, after all, the first foreign land you have visited in which the citizenry did not form enraged mobs and attack you."

"Jest if it suits you," answered Filidor. "I will not rise to the bait. I am content to be leaving, and to have been spared the burden of providing some service to these hurtling myrmidons."

Gaskarth pursed his thin lips. "I regret to diminish your contentment by the recitation of mere fact; but a service was indeed levied upon you, and you have discharged it admirably. The Zeelotes are already reaping benefits from your presence amongst them."

"I cannot conceive how, unless they have taken me as an example of refinement and tranquility they would do well to emulate."

"Then I shall elucidate," said the dwarf. "It is an abiding tenet of the Archonate's deft governance that people should be endowed with what they need, whether or not they will willingly accept it.

"In the case of Zeel, it will not have escaped your notice that here is a land wedded, if not flatly addicted, to innovation. Zeelotes must always have the new, yet this overweening desire inevitably leads to dissatisfaction, for novelty is a transient quality. The Zeelotes have exhausted their own inventiveness; but, disdaining most outland manufactures as retrograde, they are reduced to designing and producing goods which differ from their previous editions only in details of style. The Zeelotes being uncomfortably aware of the lack of true freshness, the absence of verifiably new and improved products imposes upon them considerable social and personal strain."

"This is admirable logic," answered Filidor, "yet I fail to discern my contribution to resolving the conundrum."

"You contributed by presenting for inspection your travelling staff, which employs principles of energy flux and the organization of its parts that are wholly unknown even to Zeel's most knowledgeable savants."

"Which they have slavishly copied," said Filidor.

"I am pleased that you noticed. Foreign travel seems to be broadening your perceptions beyond the bounds of personal comfort."

"In any case," Filidor retorted, "you advised them plainly that the device is impossibly archaic."

"Just so," agreed the dwarf, "but so archaic as to be entirely novel to Zeel. And they have responded well. Before we had traversed the distance between the customs post and the Archonate bureau, Zeelote technicons had disassembled the staff and analyzed its principles of operation, finding them – in this place and age – wholly new. By the time we had dined and made our way to this aerodrome, the device was already being manufactured. We arrived here just as the first retaileries began vending staffs to the populace."

"Surely, however, one exemplar of forgotten science offers no panacea to a widespread cultural dilemma," argued Filidor.

"Your perspective requires expansion," countered Gaskarth. "The exemplar was not in the thing itself but in the surrounding concept: that unrecalled technologies might be mined as if they were new-found discoveries. Into the Zeelotic ethos, we have injected the philosophical axiom – well known to the field of fashion – that the outmoded only remains so until it becomes unremembered, after which it may justly return as the avant-garde."

Filidor did not care to hear more. "Now you will doubtless inform me that I have imparted fresh vigor to the Zeelotic polity, and that my uncle will reflect upon my actions with favor."

"Rely upon it," said the dwarf.

Disinclined to further conversation, Filidor announced that he would occupy himself until their ship arrived by perusing the thoughts of Liw Osfeo.

"Wisdom is welcome, whatever the source," quoted Gaskarth, and composed himself for a brief nap.

LIW OSFEO HAD been living off a small inheritance in the town of Arvile, but eventually his funds dwindled. Rebuffed by the townspeople when he sought employment, and fearing that the oncoming winter would add hunger to his penury, he marked off a plot of land in his yard and spent a coin for a sack of seed.

Laboriously, he prepared a garden, scratching at the earth with clumsy tools he made from refuse. But the soil was poor, weeds infested his rows as fast as he could clear them, and the weather did not cooperate.

Osfeo's neighbor watched from the window of his well-stocked, warm house as the sage swinked among his sparse crop, but offered no help save the occasional proverb on the dignity of toil and the virtues of self-sufficiency.

In time, as his last few coins were running low, Osfeo managed to harvest a few bushels of thin legumes and fibrous roots. These he cleaned and stored against the winter.

But then, just as the first sleet-edged winds came rolling down from the icy heights of Ban Teyve, Osfeo met with good fortune. He was summoned to exorcise several frits from the draft animals of a caravan whose owner had crossed the Sinchen Waste without due regard for the rituals of passage. For his fee, the illumino received wealth enough to keep him through the winter and into the spring.

The next day, Osfeo's neighbor called to congratulate the sage on his luck, and perhaps to join in whatever celebration seemed appropriate. To his surprise, the man found

Osfeo gnawing on the gritty roots and stringy pods of his hard-won crop.

"Osfeo," he cried, "why do you force this barely digestible provender upon your innards, when you might dine on more toothsome fare?"

The sage chewed and swallowed with difficulty. "Tomorrow I shall eat my good fortune," he replied. "Today I am eating my sweat."

"Surely, this is folly," said the neighbor.

"True," answered Osfeo, "but you must agree it has a certain charm."

There was a long footnote appended to the story – something about the validity of Osfeo's actions under the doctrine of declarative causality, a philosophical system of which Filidor had never heard. He thought the commentary detracted more from the story than added to it, and was leafing through the book for another episode when a brusque voice from the air around him announced the imminent arrival and departure of their flight. He woke the dwarf, and together they gathered their possessions and entered the passenger tube.

Some property of the tube relieved them of weight and inertia, and wafted them up several storeys to the landing deck of the airship. Here, on a thinly railed platform ringing the crew and passenger quarters of the vessel, their tickets were taken by a surly fellow clad in brightly checked – though coarsely woven – breeks and tunic, topped by an unlikely brimless hat. This, Gaskarth observed as they made their way to a spacious cabin, was the uniform of an airman-ordinary in the Krzyztadl state fleet, elements of which continually criss-crossed the world, carrying goods and persons from anywhere to anywhere else, to the benefit of Krzyztadl's national treasury.

Having found their cabin and briefly refreshed themselves, the two travelers returned to the landing deck to inspect the airship – the first of its kind Filidor had seen – and to watch as the Krzyztadlis loaded cargo. The surface on which they and their cabins stood was the middle level of an oblong of wood and metal suspended by filaments from an array of spheres charged with buoyant gas. The deck below contained cargo holds and whatever engines moved the craft at the will of the captain and officers on the bridge above Filidor's head. The entire ship, when underway, was surrounded by a translucent shield which obviated wind, weather and whatever airborne objects might hinder its passage. The field was now dormant so that crates and bundles might be shunted up a loading belt into the holds.

The men and women of the ship's crew attended to the loading without benefit of assistance from the Zeelotes or from their own officers, one of whom perched languidly on a container at the base of the ramp and directed his subordinates' efforts. Filidor remarked on the contrast between the officer's ease and the others' exertions, between his beribboned attire and their rough garb, and on the absence of any machinery with which to lift the heavier crates onto the loading belt.

Gaskarth explained that in Krzyztadl rigorous class distinctions pertained, with rulers and the ruled strictly segregated as to duties and privileges. Social divisions ran deeper than in most lands, and the lot of those low on the scale was not to be envied. On an official vessel such as this, the separation between officers and other ranks was greater than that between the magnates and the meanest of Olkney.

"I wonder that the underclass does not rebel," said Filidor.

"But they do," replied the dwarf. "At least once in every generation."

Filidor shuddered. "I presume they are put down with ruthless slaughter."

"Rarely," said the dwarf. "More usually, rebellion succeeds into revolution, and the uprisers assume the places of the erstwhile aristocracy. I believe the last unsuccessful rebellion – ignited by one Radik the Inept – occurred some three hundred years past, and upwards of a score of lives were lost. Naturally, numbered among them was the memorable Radik."

"I am mystified," said Filidor.

"You would be less so had you paid attention to your youthful studies, but I will instruct you briefly. Krzyztadli politics pursues a changeless cycle of abuse, guilt and expiation, punctuated by short and remarkably civilized revolts. Today's aristocrats are yesterday's helots, inflicting revenge on their underlings, who were in turn once their dominators.

"In time, the sweetness of revenge will cloy, and tinges of remorse will begin to haunt the ruling class. As this process accelerates, the lowest classes – that is, the former oppressors – will sense that they have expunged their own guilt from their last term in power, and will agitate for the removal of the boot heel pressing hard into their necks. At a certain critical point, these two trends will intersect. Then a few petards will be tossed, a wholesome riot or two will enliven the streets, and with an appropriate flourish of arms, the transfer of authority will take place."

"Surely this must wreak havoc among the everyday affairs of commerce and the lives of the populace," wondered Filidor.

"Not so," said Gaskarth. "The broad spectrum of Krzyztadli society remains uninvolved in what is essentially a dispute between the lowest and highest of the realm. Indeed, most look forward to the revolts as a welcome distraction from the mundanities of getting and spending which occupy their daily existence."

Filidor digested the dwarf's remarks in silence. Then a shade of apprehension clouded his visage. "I trust that we, as aliens cast by circumstance into the Krzyztadli social dynamic, enjoy the same unembroiled status as the Krzyztadli middle classes? That is to say: the Archon does not require us to adjust the political balance by our direct and possibly perilous participation?"

"I have no such instructions," Gaskarth assured him. "We are to move with all speed to the Dominion of Jamp, and this Krzyztadli craft was the earliest available transport."

"Then I shall endeavor to enjoy the voyage, in the hope of finding my uncle awaiting as we alight at the Jamp terminus."

"Better to travel in hope than to arrive in trepidation," the dwarf quoted obscurely. "And now, since I see that the vessel's hold is fully laden, let us seek the common room and discover what other hardy souls share our travels."

The common room was a well-windowed chamber which occupied most of the ship's stern, affording a panoramic view of the haze generated by the manufactories of Zeel. A table for the officers' mess and another for the passengers had been placed at left and right, with the intervening space reserved for a blue Irax carpet of delicate weave and soothing pattern. A scattering of comfortable upholstered chairs were arranged beneath the windows, and here the travelers encountered the ship's other passengers.

As they were shown to their seats by a sullen Krzyztadli steward, they were greeted by a large man of middle years, his bulk swathed in robes of taupe and vermilion.

"Well met and welcome," boomed this energetic individual, spreading bejeweled hands to beckon Filidor and Gaskarth forward. "Join a merry coterie of voyagers and be all at your ease. I am Nofreg, an aficionado of the sport of pelaste, en route to Magne Stade for the celebrated tournament. Doubtless my ebullient and expansive nature has already discovered me to you as a native of Aralothe."

Filidor's obvious unfamiliarity with the nature of Aralothians made no impression on Nofreg, who proceeded to introduce the three other people seated around them. These were: Mezra of the Isle of Cyc, whose long-bladed epiniard in a lacquered scabbard identified her as an accomplished swordster; Chasmar of Ord-Issel, a handsome woman of an indeterminate age who wore slightly indelicate garments, and whom Nofreg described as "now at her leisure after a career in mercantile pursuits"; and a long-nosed, thin-headed man in a cowled grey habit, introduced as Jenbo Lal, of the Order of Pelerins.

Mezra planned to retire from competition and to accept a teaching post at a training school in Jamp. Chasmar was enjoying a retirement of travel after amassing a respectable fortune in the commodities trade. Jenbo Lal's aims and destination went unstated, save that he was bound for regions north of the Ahman nation.

Filidor made those gestures which formality requires. "I am Filidor, and my companion is Gaskarth, both out of Olkney."

A twitch of Jenbo Lal's sleeve betrayed a sudden interest in the two travelers. Long fingers eased his cowl lightly forward so that his lean features disappeared into shadow, and Filidor noted a curious design etched into the nail of one index finger. The Pelerin's voice was oily enough to have left a smear on his thin lips, had he not licked them so often. "Olkney, is it? I had thought the folk of the Peninsular more apt to embrace the comforts of the near and known than to put themselves about in this unsettled world."

Filidor, who had formed no opinions about Pelerins, found that he did not like this one. His answer was cool. "Yet some may rise above provincialism. For myself, I am engaged on a mission of –"

"A mission of edification," interrupted Gaskarth. "My young companion has elected to transcend the parochialism of his country in the sincere belief that, as the maxim states, travel enlarges the outlook."

Irritated, Filidor took a seat next to Chasmar, and was momentarily fazed by the volume of scent she exuded. "Just so," he continued, "but we are also charged by my uncle –"

"To return with whatever outlandish bric-a-brac as may enrich the family's connaissarium," the dwarf finished, shooting the young man a hard look and sinking with a small shake of his head into the chair beside Nofreg.

"Travel is indeed enriching," opined Chasmar, shifting her ample flesh toward Filidor and engulfing him in another wave of perfume. "Since the passing of my husband and partner

Yrle" – she patted an absent tear – "I have found my wanderings through foreign lands to be an unfailing source of compensatory experiences." She placed a warm, damp palm over Filidor's hand.

"I am not one to deny the broadening effects of distant lands," offered Nofreg, "yet I have often said that the chief benefit of travel is to allow the returned sojourner a renewed appreciation of his native milieu. I am always glad to re-enter the towering gates of Aralothe; all other places seem puny by comparison."

"We are well aware of the Aralothian preoccupation with size as an ultimate criterion," put in Mezra.

"There is much to be said for size," Chasmar mused, "although I would accord equal value to vigorous enthusiasm." Her hand now idly traced Filidor's arm and disappeared into the folds of his outer garment.

Her remark seemingly addressed to no one in particular, Nofreg ignored it and replied to the swordster. "Mark you not, my friend, how stature and weight carry the initiative in the world? Does not the largest buck enjoy the most numerous herd of cows? Does not the tallest tree in the forest spread its needled limbs above the crowns of lesser growths? Does not the largest vein make the most prosperous mine?"

"By restricting your argument solely to the animal, vegetable and mineral, you choose safer ground," answered Mezra. "Yet I have often faced your armored Aralothian hoplites in the arena. And while they swipe and swing their great falches, grunting and sweating with effort, I parry and pink and prick them with my little epiniard, until they faint from blood-loss and exhaustion."

"Agility is nice, too," said Chasmar, "although distracting if taken to excess." She now employed both hands to investigate Filidor's person, as if she were one of the eyeless seers of Fihkskan scrying the future from his lineaments. It was becoming clear to Filidor what immediate future Chasmar intended for him. Unused to the forthrightness of the mature females of Ord-Issel, and embarrassed by her direct attentiveness, he blushed and made to rise from his chair. "Madam," he whispered, "I am not accustomed to such familiarities on first acquaintance!"

"Oh tush, sweetling," Chasmar breathed, rising with him and insinuating her hands beneath his mantle to join them at his lower back. "We of Ord-Issel know what young bravos crave, and we are forthcoming about it."

Filidor cast a helpless look toward Gaskarth, but the little man's attention had not wavered from Jenbo Lal. Flustered, the young man twisted out of Chasmar's embrace, but as he stumbled away, her hands seized his clothes and the contents of some of his pockets fell to the Irax carpet, among them the box of tuka wood.

Jenbo Lal leaned forward at this, and Gaskarth noted a gleam in the man's shrouded eyes. The rune-covered fingernail stroked the bony chin, and a half-smile moved upon the Pelerin's lips. Filidor stooped to retrieve the objects, repocketed them and tugged his clothing back into order. The amorous Chasmar had subsided with a girlish toss of her coiffure, but Filidor reseated himself next to the dwarf, at a safe distance from her inquisitive fingers.

Mezra and Nofreg continued their debate as if nothing had happened; clearly, this was no recently begun argument. Nofreg called more examples to defend the Aralothian doctrine of worth through magnitude. Mezra countered with texts from the Cyc philosophy of minimality, which declares that tiny but well-aimed causes may result in mighty effects; she cited the legend of the pebble and the avalanche which buried Hemistor's Grand Militia. Chasmar contented herself with the occasional smoldering glance in Filidor's direction, while he and the dwarf gave whatever nods and assents seemed appropriate when called upon by one party or another in the continuing clash of ethoses. Jenbo Lal had lapsed into pensive meditation.

As the debate wound down to mutual snorts and implied aspersions on national characters, Gaskarth rose and announced that he and Filidor would repair to their cabins, there to rest until the evening meal. Sliding out from under Chasmar's parting leer, Filidor let go a long sigh of relief once they were out of the common room and into the corridor to their quarters. But, as Filidor sought to unlock his door, Gaskarth drew him instead into his own adjacent compartment. The dwarf sealed the door and carefully inspected the small chamber before seating himself on the bunk.

"I detect more than your usual air of incomprehensible mystery," said Filidor.

"As well you might," said the little man. "Then let me dispel it." He went again to the door and listened. Satisfied that no ears but Filidor's would hear him, he drew close to the young man and whispered, "A potential for danger looms."

Filidor snickered. "The woman of Ord-Issel is formidable, but I do not fear that she will be one too many for me." He indicated the sealed door and quoted: "Locks laugh at the lovesick."

Gaskarth passed a crabbed hand over his hairless crown and sought guidance from the ceiling. "You mistake the peril. Chasmar is as she is, and posits no harm to a well-knit youth possessed of any penchant for new and untried experiences. The threat is in the shape of Jenbo Lal. He is no true Pelerin. From his interest in us, our origins, and most particularly the box you carry, I suspect we have encountered a thaumaturge. And perchance a nasty one at that."

"A thaumaturge?" Filidor scoffed. "You mean a magician with spells and cantrips and a cauldron fashioned from a nygrave's skull? Am I a child to be fretted by dark lurkers under the nursery bed?"

Gaskarth sighed. "Had you spent less time investigating the contents of bottles and young women's undergarments, and more days in the Archonate library, you would laugh less. Let me stop up yet another chink in your understanding, wide though it gapes.

"You should know that there is a slow cyclical flux, an ebb

and flow, in the way the world journeys across the Great Wheel. The immutable laws which govern cause and effect are in fact quite changeable, mere happenstance of time and place. In this age, for example, what you would call rationality is again in the ascendant; the arcana of magic is reduced to a secondary role. Imperceptibly, however, as age transmutes into age, the balance shifts. Laws of mechanics and entropy grow less dependable, and the logic of magic regains its force, to hold sway until the cycle revolves once more.

"For the most part, and for the mass of this world's dwellers, the cycle makes no difference. What does it matter that this craft is lifted by buoyant gases rather than levitating sprites, or that it is powered by energies generated by a machine rather than a wizard's will? It lifts and moves; the effects are identical, though the causes differ."

"I defer to your erudition," Filidor said, "but manifestly we inhabit a world in an age of triumphant science. What powers may a thaumaturge command, for good or ill, if magic must limp along like the younger brother in the *Tale of the Two Orlicants?*"

"Little," agreed the dwarf, "but little is often enough. In either phase of the cycle, the lesser order always retains some vigor. In the previous age of magic, a spark would still light a fire, and water would extinguish the flame. In this age of science, a spell will not blast a realm to rubble, yet if properly cast it may induce a person's atoms to take leave of one another. The detonation is less spectacular, but quite sufficient for the individual most directly concerned.

"Besides," the little man concluded, "we are but a century or so from the cusp of transition. Devices now gradually lose their reliability, while the power of a word or gesture assumes a growing potency. But in either age, that box you carry could have terrible significance in the wrong hands. The magician must not get his hands on it."

Filidor's interest was engaged, but Gaskarth said he wished to consider certain matters in silence, although he wanted his young charge to remain in the security of the room. So, while the little man took thought in a chair, Filidor stretched his length upon the bunk, and slept. When he awoke, it was to the sound of a small drill being applied by the dwarf to the bulkhead separating their cabins.

Gaskarth extracted the drill, then did something that caused the tool to fold in upon itself and become the size of a thumb. He stowed the drill in his satchel and took out an obscure device consisting of a cluster of opticon tubes. This he fitted to the pin-prick hole in the bulkhead, made some small adjustments, and then activated its mechanism. At once, a three-dimensional simulacrum of Filidor's vacant cabin appeared in the air before them. Although Filidor knew that no lights lit the empty space next door, and that his cabin was filled with the dark of early evening, the simulacrum rendered all within as if lit by full day.

"Do you thus intend a remote chaperonage, or is there some more pointed reason for arranging this surveillance?" Filidor asked.

"Observe and deduce," was the dwarf's noncommittal reply. "For now, I wish you to compose a brief note to the insistent Chasmar. Take pen and pay heed."

Filidor wrote as Gaskarth dictated, though he avowed no intent to fulfill even a tenth of what the missive promised. When the note was done and signed with a manly flourish, Gaskarth bade him fold the paper and give it to a steward, with instructions to pass it to the woman along with the key to Filidor's cabin. But first they dissolved the simulacrum and placed a high-backed chair so as to hide its mechanism from casual view. Then they went next door, where they disabled all the lighting elements in Filidor's quarters, and moved his goods into Gaskarth's cabin.

As they exited the darkened chamber, a steward passed down the corridor, gaily proclaiming that a fine repast would soon be served in the common room. Filidor noted the jaunty gait of the ill-clad Krzyztadli, commenting that he was the first member of the crew who seemed content with his lot.

"More than content," said the dwarf. "The man almost glows with delighted anticipation."

Below the common room windows, starlight fell on the tors and tarns of Dimpfen Moor, a wild and barren place of bogs and boulders where no traveller tarried long. Nothing could penetrate the airship's protective field to shriek in the rigging, but somehow the sense of constant chill winds infiltrated the awareness of anyone disposed to contemplate Dimpfen's tussocks passing silently below. Accordingly, none of the people in the common room felt so disposed.

At the passengers' table, Chasmar, Mezra, Nofreg and Jenbo Lal greeted Gaskarth as their diverse natures prompted. Filidor paused at the entrance to the room to place note, key and a coin in the hands of another cheerful steward, who heard the young man's whispered instructions and signified carefree complicity. Filidor chose a seat well down the table from the woman of Ord-Issel, while the dwarf slipped into the chair she had been keeping vacant beside her. Conversation had apparently lapsed before their arrival, but Gaskarth immediately struck up a low-voiced colloquy with Chasmar, accompanied by nods and motions of the head in Filidor's direction. In the same direction, from the other side of the table, was aimed the scrutiny of Jenbo Lal.

After an exchange of courtesies, while smiling stewards served a course of piquant appetizers and Phalum wine, the cowled magician essayed a few remarks that demonstrated a familiarity with the Olkney peninsula.

"You have visited there?" Filidor inquired.

"On occasion," said Jenbo Lal, "in the conduct of my researches."

"I was not aware that the Pelerins interested themselves in academe, being more a contemplative order than scholarly," put in Mezra at Filidor's right.

The magician returned the Cyc a cool glance. "Just so. However, we are allowed our avocations. Mine happens to be the collection and categorization of small caskets and the like, of ancient origin."

"Extraordinary," said Nofreg, seated at Jenbo Lal's elbow. "It happens that I have in my baggage a relic box which once held the eyebrow pluckings of the Blessed Etheln, who – as I am sure you will have heard – was reputed to be the most immense demi-god in the entire Glavinian pantheon. Picked it up in the bazaar at Tormstale the other day. Fellow swore it was pre-sixteenth aeon without doubt."

"Fascinating," hissed Jenbo Lal. "Please do not fail to let me see it." He turned back to Filidor. "And you, young man; might you have acquired any such items in your travels? I would be willing to purchase."

"Regrets," said Filidor. "I own nothing to pique your interest."

"Indeed? I had thought to see you let fall just such an object during our earlier conversation."

"A trick of the light, perhaps," answered Filidor.

The magician's eyes narrowed. "I am well versed in tricks of light, or of darkness, and prone to trust my senses. I therefore assert that I saw a small box, somewhat carved and figured, of tuka wood or mayhap seastro."

"Oh, that. A mere bagatelle. A container for small personal necessities, fashioned ineptly by myself in an idle hour. Still, if you would care to examine it..." Filidor felt among his garments, pressing the box firmly down into its pocket. "No, I seem to have left it in my cabin. Though I hesitate to submit the product of my limited skills to the judgment of a connoisseur, perhaps in the morning you would favor it with an evaluation."

"Perhaps in the morning," Jenbo Lal echoed.

"And I would like you to look over my reliquary," boomed Nofreg.

The thaumaturge's eyes narrowed to slits, but he put down the impulse to do an injury to the Aralothian. "Certainly," he said.

At that moment, the passengers' attention was called to

the other side of the room by the arrival of the airship's complement of officers. These Krzyztadli aristocrats who trooped into the common room and assumed seats at the second table might have been the dejected remnant of a defeated army. A pall of profound gloom hung over each, as if they contemplated an inevitable and imminent doom. Even the ribbons of rank tied at the shoulders of their splendid doublets drooped mournfully. By contrast, the ordinary matlos serving their superiors fairly cavorted about the table, dispensing tankards and platters with reckless abandon and expansive flourishes.

Thankful for the distraction from Jenbo Lal's insistent queries, Filidor commented to Mezra, "The deportment of the officers and crew seems to have altered since we boarded."

The swordster nodded. "It may be that the Krzyztadli social dynamic has entered upon a climactic stage. I trust this will not alter our travel arrangements."

Nofreg turned to view the spectacle. "I have heard of the phenomenon, but never thought to witness an entire social class bought low by guilt and remorse." He took a draft of the excellent Paeshan vintage which had accompanied the prepared greyfish course, and continued. "Of course for true atonement there is no greater example than the history of the Unequaled Escreot – an Aralothian, it must be said – and his remorse over the unjust execution of his third wife and her entire clan. After the sixth wife had been exposed as the true author of the usurper's plot, and punitive measures had been taken, Escreot personally gathered the gnawed bones of the innocent executees, buried them with his own hands – in separate graves, mark you – and carved a stone for each. After which he named the first day of each month as an occasion of national grief, and would appear ash-bedaubed in the market for all to witness his repentance."

"Or unbridled exhibitionism," said Mezra, at which the swordster and the pelaste enthusiast fell to their customary wrangle. Filidor fixed his gaze upon his plate, ignoring or turning through inconsequential remarks the further probings of Jenbo Lal, until the meal was consumed. The Krzyztadli officers did not stay at table, but departed the common room without a word, their chins grazing their chests. The gleeful stewards then served a round of stimulating beverages and digestive pastilles, which the passengers carried to the chairs ranged before the great windows. Chasmar, however, declined the proffered drink, and left the common room with hurried farewells and a meaningful look for Filidor. The young man went to sit with the dwarf.

"What that woman contemplates is more than human capabilities will allow," he said.

"I concur," said Gaskarth, watching the swing of strongly constructed hips as they disappeared into the corridor. "And to ensure that she is not disappointed, I have furnished her with an atomizer that disperses an odorless mist: its ingredients, when inhaled, so act upon the faculties of the male as to render him helpless with lust while possessed of boundless potency. I urged her to use the stuff in minimal measure, but I judge her nature to be such that she will now be filling the air in your darkened cabin to overbrimming with aphrodisiac miasma. The effect in such a confined space must be devastating."

"I do not wish to be thus devastated."

"You will not be," said the dwarf.

"Then will she not eventually emerge in a rage of dissatisfaction, when none appears to inhale the mist and consummate her expectations?"

"If I am not mistaken, someone else will shortly take your place. See Jenbo Lal."

The thaumaturge had risen and was bidding the others a good night. Filidor and Gaskarth watched as the cowled figure swept from the room in the pungent woman's wake. "You told him at table that the box remained in your cabin," said the little man. "He goes now to test the truth of that intelligence, as I thought he would. Let us give him a moment and then see what he has found instead."

The corridor was empty as they let themselves into the

dwarf's cabin, but a series of muffled thumps and odd noises came from the next compartment. Gaskarth removed the chair he had placed against the spy-hole and activated the simulacrum. A vivid tableau of the scene in Filidor's lightless cabin appeared before them.

Jenbo Lal stood pressed immobile against the opposite wall, fingers clasping his long nose to prevent an indrawn breath. His free hand traced intricate patterns in the darkness, as he attempted to dispel by magic the aphrodisiac cloud. A visible disturbance in the folds at the front of his habit revealed, however, that the mist had already achieved some partial effect upon the lower regions of the thaumaturge's brain. Meanwhile, Chasmar had freed herself of all restraint and apparel, and was groping her way through the dark between Jenbo Lal and the door, making small sounds as if summoning a reluctant pet to accept a caress.

"A quandary," observed the dwarf. "Few spells are efficacious without the utterance of a word or two. Yet, should he part his lips to speak, the mist will enter and he will be lost. And now Chasmar closes the gap between them." The little man grinned. "I believe Jenbo Lal's current stasis is about to dissolve into reckless dynamism."

As he spoke, Chasmar's questing hand groped through the dark and found that part of Jenbo Lal which was most prominent. With a cry of triumphant discovery, she seized him through the cloth and squeezed. The magician gasped as she swung him around and propelled him backwards onto the bunk. Then the aphrodisiac took full charge of Jenbo Lal's senses, Chasmar threw herself upon his body, and in a moment he was engulfed. Filidor and Gaskarth paused a moment to witness the spectacle, then the dwarf extinguished the simulacrum. Small sounds could still be heard through the bulkhead.

The little man withdrew a timetable from his satchel and consulted a page. "We are scheduled for a brief stop in Thurloyn Vale shortly after sunrise," he said. "Since Jenbo Lal will likely be indisposed at that hour, if not still actively engaged, I suggest a surreptitious disembarking. We can find some alternative means of continuing on to Jamp after some safe distance has been put between us and the magician."

"Will not Chasmar be angered when she discovers the substitution?" asked Filidor.

"Possibly," conceded the dwarf. "On the other hand, she may well be satisfied with a novel experience. In either case, she is unlikely to have much energy for remonstration after our lean friend has exhausted all his reserves in her service."

It was agreed that they would take turns keeping watch until dawn, with Gaskarth standing the first stint. Filidor curled up on the bunk. He thought that the thin wails now coming through the bulkhead would keep him from slumber. But this had been one of the longest days of his young life – from Ektop to Jamp and into a matching of wits with a thaumaturge – and it seemed only a moment later that he was being awakened to exchange his bed for a seat by the door, while the little man sought some rest. The dwarf's snores soon filled the compartment, overpowering the intermittent noises emanating from next door.

Filidor considered reading from Osfeo, but his eyelids drooped from fatigue, and he gave himself instead to retrospection. His days of leisure and diversion in Olkney now seemed impossibly distant, though it was scarcely four nights since the dwarf had accosted him in the alley behind the Logodaedalian Club and set him upon this desultory pursuit of his uncle. The morrow or the day after might well see him brought into his uncle's presence, the mysterious delivery made, and a return home arranged by the shortest route.

Yet Filidor was mildly surprised to discover in himself a disinclination to resume his old ways of life. He could not say that he had enjoyed individually every part of his recent adventures. He had been subjected to sustained exertion, poor victuals, cultural dislocations, the abuse of strangers and moments of sheer physical terror. Seen in hindsight, however, the events of the preceding few days now took on the glow of pleasant accomplishments recalled at leisure.

He drew from his mantle the object of his mission, the box which had engaged Jenbo Lal's avarice and led the magician unexpectedly to his present occupation. Filidor traced the ornate designs graved into its surfaces, and wondered idly whether they were mere ornament or some archaic script. Again, he felt the edges and sides for some spring or catch to render it open and display its contents. But the thing resisted all probings, so he returned it to his pocket and fell again to musing.

Shortly before dawn, Filidor's sleepy ruminations were disrupted by a heavy concussion in the airship's frame, somewhere forward of the passenger quarters. A second detonation followed close upon the vibrations of the first, causing the vessel to shudder and yaw. Before the second explosion racked the ship, Gaskarth was awake and on his feet, gathering their possessions and throwing open the door. With the single injunction: "Come!", he was out and down the corridor, Filidor following, to the open deck.

The airship was at a dead stop, hovering at what would have been tree-top height, had Dimpfen Moor boasted any growth higher than a shrub. Most of the crew were gathered in an area where the open deck held wide covered hatches above the cargo holds. The matlos seemed afire with enthusiasm, as several of them used a length of pipe torn from the superstructure to batter at a door which barred them from the companionway leading to the bridge. Above them, the ship's officers disconsolately watched their progress from the command deck windows. Another group was energetically tearing off a hatch cover to expose the cargo. The airmen exhibited a carnival spirit, laughing and encouraging each other with shouts, as the cover was lifted and dashed to the deck. Two of them immediately clambered onto ladders and disappeared below.

Nudging Filidor to follow, Gaskarth approached the group standing about the open hatch. The dwarf tapped the arm of a Krzyztadli who wore the sash of a subadar, and politely inquired as to the source of the recent explosions and the crew's present exuberance. The subadar, a stocky individual possessed of a wandering nose, close-set eyes and a bifurcated chin beard, turned and clapped the little man on the shoulder. "By Hannie's single teat, 'tis the glorious revolution at last!"

In the next few moments, in-between directing his crew to swing the lifting tackle of a gantry over the open hold and raise up the crates below, the subadar related in a sequence of asides the progress of events. Gaskarth and Filidor learned that a certain cryptic message had that evening been received over the ship's communications gear, signaling that all Krzyztadl was in the throes of revolt. Pursuant to their long-standing plans, the crew had forthwith mutinied. A demolition commando had blown the door off the small-arms locker, while another had attended to the largely symbolic bombing of the captain's cabin. The captain had been at the time on the bridge, engaged in tearful self-recrimination with most of her officers. The remaining command staff had been hustled from their quarters and chased to join their fellows, so that the mutineers could seal the door before bringing up the traditional battering ram.

At this point, the subadar asked one of the grinning airmen to take Gaskarth and Filidor aside while the heavy crates were brought on deck. The two returned to the exit leading from the passenger accommodations, where they found their fellow travelers gathered in a sleepy-eyed huddle, guarded by two of the matlos. Mezra wore her epiniard and kept one hand to its hilt, while Nofreg gazed about with a tourist's fascination for the picturesque. Chasmar leaned against a bulkhead, loosely draped in a blanket, with an air of spent serenity. She regarded Filidor with mild consternation when he entered her field of vision.

"Your powers of recovery are astounding," she said. "Even more astonishing is it that you should arrive on deck before me, when I had left you but a moment since, lying breathless and scarce able to raise a digit."

Filidor did not know how to reply, but was saved from

embarrassment by the dwarf. Gaskarth engaged Chasmar's attention and began to weave a plausible tale, in which it transpired that Jenbo Lal had innocently entered the wrong cabin and become enmeshed in her amorous stratagem before the little man could act to prevent the error. "And once the inevitable had ensued," finished the dwarf, "it seemed inappropriate to enter and attempt to set matters straight."

The woman of Ord-Issel considered Gaskarth's explanation for a drowsy moment, then shrugged, causing the blanket to slip alarmingly from her shoulders. Filidor looked away as she followed the shrug with a yawn which opened even more disconcerting vistas to his gaze. "Well," she said, "the evening was not entirely wasted."

The Krzyztadli mutineers had by now hauled the last of the crates on deck and finished battering in the door to the bridge. The officers, ribbons and plumes adroop, descended the companionway and were immediately put to work dismantling the crates, to the jeers of the revolutionists. The subadar watched long enough to see the work underway, then strode over to the passengers.

"Honest gentlefolk," he began, "the new Provisional Government of Krzyztadl sincerely regrets your present inconvenience, and ...hold on, one of you's missing! Where's the tall one, the Pelerin?" But the two guards swore they had searched all the cabins and brought the entire passenger complement on deck. The subadar snorted and called over a number of the other mutineers, instructing them to employ the surveillance instruments on the command bridge to locate the missing Jenbo Lal. The Krzyztadlis ran to do his bidding, while he continued his address to the passengers.

"Pursuant to Plan Seven, this vessel is now commissioned a warship of the Provisional Government and will return at once to Krzyztadl, there to assist in the overthrow of the despised tyranny. As a ship of the line, it offers no accommodation for superfluous personnel – that being yourselves – and we regret the necessity of asking you to disembark with your hand luggage. Your larger equipage may be reclaimed from the Navy upon presentation of appropriate documentation after the revolution."

It took a moment for the import of the subadar's words to penetrate the passengers' understanding, then there erupted a babble of protest from all save the dwarf, who went to the rail and looked out across the barren moor. He scanned the barren heath for movement, then turned his eyes to the dawning sky. There was something that might have been a great bird, but it was lost in the dimness.

Meanwhile, Chasmar harangued the Krzyztadlis, promising a lawsuit, and Nofreg threatened an avenging phalanx of Aralothian might. Filidor invoked the Archon, while Mezra swore once and half drew her epiniard. But the subadar and the guards backed smoothly away, leaving a clear field of fire for the ison cannons that had been removed from their crates. One of the weapons was now deployed in the direction of the passengers. Mezra sheathed her blade, and the clamor quickly died.

"Sincere regrets, unavoidable circumstance," murmured the cheery mutineers, as the passengers' gear was brought on deck and a boarding net lowered to the peaty surface of Dimpfen Moor. Those sent to use the command deck's surveillance equipment returned to report that no trace of Jenbo Lal could be found, and the baggage handlers said that the Pelerin's belongings were gone from his quarters.

The subadar removed his brimless hat and disordered his hair, but had neither time nor disposition to pursue the mystery. Instead he had the ison cannons sweep the area immediately below and around the airship – "to discourage night predators," he said – and then put the passengers over the side. The Krzyztadlis swiftly pulled up the boarding net, bid the stranded travelers good fortune, and turned the ship for home.

CHAPTER SEVEN

IN THE CREPUSCULAR DIMNESS of Dimpfen Moor, the five marooned travelers stepped from tussock to tussock and sloshed through black pools toward the only landmark in view: a twisted spire of agglomerated rock which loomed over a mound of hardpacked bare earth a short distance from their landing place. Gaskarth had spied the tower from the airship's rail before they had been put overboard, and now led the way. They walked through ozone-smelling mists still crackling with residual energies of the ison blasts, but thanks to the efficacy of the Krzyztadli barrage they reached the earth mound unmolested.

The mound was not much higher than Filidor, the spire stretching above it about as far as he could have thrown a stone, had he experienced such a futile inclination. The place was no less desolate than the rest of Dimpfen Moor, but it was dry. Here the travelers stopped and individually considered their predicaments. The air was cold, and mist dampened their garments. Chasmar, shivering in the blanket that was her sole covering, pressed against Filidor for warmth. He wrapped a fold of his mantle about her, then gently disengaged the hand with which she automatically began to investigate his person. Mezra and Nofreg squatted in glumness, while the dwarf took counsel with himself.

They sat in a lengthening silence, until Chasmar shook beads of moisture from her hair, swathed the blanket about herself and rose, declaring, "Well, what do we do now?" A vigorous discussion followed. Mezra was for staying put until another craft should pass their way and offer a rescue. Nofreg favored an immediate march in the direction of the nearest town, which Filidor recalled to be Thurloyn Vale: less than an hour by air, but probably more than a day's trek across the sodden moor, he thought.

"Much more than a day," put in Mezra, "since we will doubtless be lost beyond hope in this wild and trackless waste before we have walked an hour. Least done, least risked. I say we stay."

Nofreg rose and exhorted them to follow, saying, "It is not my nature to endure in passive hope. Action creates possibility: therefore let us have action, preferably at once and on a grand scale! I say we march!"

The Cyc swordster sneered. "March if you will. Wander at large, and feral beasts will contend for your bones. I will remain in this position of relative safety and await the next airship."

The two philosophical adversaries fell to their old wrangle, while Chasmar appealed mutely to the skies for deliverance. Filidor sought to put in a word, but there was no point at which the others would allow an entry into their long-standing wrangling. He turned to the dwarf, and asked, "What shall we do?"

Gaskarth eyed the two disputants, then shrugged. "I have been giving it some thought," he said, "and cannot decide whether it is better to go or to stay." At this, Mezra and Nofreg flung their respective views at him, each vying to out-voice the other, and continued until the little man sprang to his feet and with surprising volume roared them into silence.

"Now," he said, when they had subsided, "we have the option of remaining where we are, in hope of rescue – which is unlikely, since there are no fixed airlanes across the moor, and the odds of another airship passing soon within hailing range of this spot are not promising. Or we strike out for Thurloyn Vale on the equally unpromising chance that we can find our way across unfeatured terrain which must contain any number of ferocious predators. Neither choice is attractive. I therefore propose a vote."

"Go," said Nofreg.

"Stay," said Mezra.

"Stay," said Chasmar, eyeing the pools of cold water that stretched from the base of the mound to the mist-shrouded horizon. She took Filidor's arm.

"Go," said Filidor, eyeing Chasmar.

"Then it falls to me," Gaskarth sighed. "Are we to go or stay?"

"Of course, you will stay," said a raspy voice from the base of the mound.

The travelers pulled together at once, and Mezra drew her blade. Five pairs of eyes searched the earth where mound met moor, but there was no sign of the speaker. Then what had appeared to be a dark spot on the lower edge of the hummock began to widen, and resolved itself into a hole, from which emerged the head of a neropt.

It was a roughly triangular head, the size of a cooking pot, with two protruding eyes, a pair of segmented antennae, and a mouth that was a collection of smaller working parts nestled between two curved mandibles. Except for the eyes, which were red, the head was bone white, as were the thorax, abdomen and six jointed limbs which followed it out of its tunnel. The creature scrambled up the mound and paused before the travelers, its antennae waving.

Chasmar trembled. "What is it? What does it want?"

"A neropt," answered Gaskarth. "A species of social insect. And I believe it wants us."

"Come, come," said the insect, in a voice like that of an asthmatic bird. "This is the busy season. There is much to do." Then it scuttled forward and seized Chasmar's blanket in its mandibles, and began pulling her toward the hole from which it had emerged. The woman screamed, Mezra flicked the wrist of her sword hand, and the neropt's head trailed a colorless ichor as it bounced down the slope.

"Hurry, hurry," said an identical voice behind the travelers. They spun around to find three more neropts climbing toward them. "This way," said the one in the lead, reaching to grasp Nofreg's robe. "There is fungus to be tended, and..." The insect's voice ended as the Cyc decapitated it, but the next one following finished the sentence without missing a beat. "... tunnels twelve through thirty-six must be resurfaced."

Mezra repositioned herself to kill the neropt, but the dwarf pushed down her sword arm. "As well to try slaying a man cell by cell," said Gaskarth. "These are mere workers, and easily killed, but the odor of their spilled blood can bring soldiers, which are twice the size, thickly armored and terribly single-minded." The swordster took but a moment's thought before she sheathed her blade and rapidly kicked earth over the stuff that leaked from the dead neropts.

A score of tunnel mouths had now appeared at the base of the mound, and from each emerged a file of insects. Most swarmed out onto the moor, gathering lichens and bracken which they rolled into moist bundles and brought back to their subterranean hive. A dozen climbed the mound toward the travelers, tugging at their garments and impelling them toward one of the tunnels.

Filidor struggled against them, the memory of his capture by castorels still fresh. "Must we submit?" he cried to the dwarf. "Can we not flee?"

The little man shook his head as he was drawn toward the tunnel mouth, and pointed downslope in another direction. A soldier had shouldered its way into the open air, its antennae questing for the source of the neropt blood it smelled. Filidor took one look at the beast's barbed mandibles and began to tug his captors all the faster toward the base of the mound.

The tunnel mouth was a narrow fit for Filidor, and had to be widened to allow Nofreg to enter. Chivvied by the workers, the travelers crawled on hands and knees the length of several paces, until the ceiling suddenly rose and they found themselves in a room-sized chamber dimly lit by a nacreous glow from luminescent fungi spattered about the walls. Although the floor of the chamber was beneath the sodden moor's ground level, its surface was a dry concrete which, Filidor later learned, was secreted as excrement by worker neropts.

The floor was broken in several places by holes twice the width of Filidor's shoulders. Out of some of these, a myriad of workers were swarming toward the outside world, shepherded by occasional soldiers. Into others, returning workers were hurling their bundles of vegetation. And toward one of these latter holes, one at a time, the travelers were dragged, lifted up and dropped.

Filidor was first to go, and scarcely had time to cry out before his captors' grip left his clothing and he plunged straight down into darkness. The walls of the shaft were smooth, but they burned his palms as he reached out and tried to slow his fall. A second later, however, he felt friction against his back, as the shaft bent to become a curving slide, which corkscrewed downward, slowing his descent by degrees, until he shot from its nether end onto a heap of damp vegetation which filled a large subterranean chamber lit by more of the glowing fungi. He had time to note that several narrow tunnel mouths broke the smooth walls of the chamber before a whoosh of air and a terrified moan preceded the arrival of Chasmar.

She shot from the shaft, blanket flapping about her head, to plant her feet square in Filidor's belly. Gasping, he dragged her out of the way just before the arrival of Nofreg, Mezra and Gaskarth, who came almost one on top of the other. These last three had not waited to be thrown into the shaft, but had jumped quickly when a soldier neropt, scenting worker blood in the vicinity, had taken an interest in them. As soon as they had disentangled themselves from each other, Mezra drew her epiniard and meticulously cleaned its blade and her hose with handfuls of marsh grass scooped from the chamber floor, then buried the smeared clumps deep within the pile.

The dwarf, meanwhile, had begun to investigate the chamber. It was roughly circular, about thrice the height of a person and perhaps twice its height in diameter. Several unlit tunnels led out of the place. Some reached upwards to the antechamber at the surface, to judge by the bundles of vegetation which tumbled out of them. Others presumably led into the neropts' hive. From three of these latter tunnels came wafts of musty air. From one came the acrid reek of formic acid. Gaskarth sniffed and peeked into each in turn; then, his investigation complete, he rejoined the others at the centre of the chamber.

"Hypothesis:" he announced, "we are in a collection and storage area for harvested vegetation. That tunnel leads into the hive proper. Those three tunnels opposite lead to the neropts' gardens. We will be put to work tending those gardens."

"Are we not to be devoured?" Chasmar asked.

"Not directly," returned the dwarf, but before he could let the crypticism out of his answer, a squad of workers plopped from the delivery chutes and hustled the captives into a tunnel. Again they must crawl on hands and knees, butted and dragged by neropts, through a dark, narrow passage. The air was thick with an odor of rotting vegetation, and the walls of the tunnel were streaked with fine dust which, dislodged by their passage, burned their eyes and made them sneeze. Thus, in tears and racked by sternutatious spasms, they were prodded and pulled into another chamber.

Here the air was slightly clearer, and gradually the five humans recovered their equilibrium. When he had wiped the streams from his eyes, Filidor saw that this place was many times larger than the storage area where they had first arrived. It was a vast, circular room, lined in neropt concrete, and lit by the luminescent fungi. From the floor of the chamber, a series of rocky terraces swept up almost to ceiling height. And each terrace was thick with globular black fungi, some beds filled with specimens as small as peas, others ripe for harvest with fungi twice the size of Filidor's head. The dust clouding the air was a mixture of dessicated soil and myriads of spores expelled in small explosions by the mature crop.

But Filidor had little time to examine his surroundings. "Work," said the nearest neropt, and dragged him toward a terrace. The others, too, were seized and pushed toward the banks of fungi. The neropt workers then left, but a soldier replaced them in the mouth of the entry tunnel. The big mandibles clacked once as their guard's antennae caught a faint whiff of neropt blood, but the trace being too faint to be actionable, the insect lapsed into a posture of frozen vigilance. A fine powdering of dust began to settle on the soldier's chitinous mantle, dulling its sheen.

The captives soon deduced the nature of the work expected of them. More worker neropts arrived, packing loads of vegetation from the storage chamber, then turning back for more. One part of the humans' task was to spread the wet plant matter on the terraces as compost bedding for a new crop; the other was to deposit mature fungi into a smallish hole in the floor at one side of the vast chamber. Gaskarth opined that the shaft beneath the hole led to a distribution nexus which would serve the neropt nest. The dwarf then divided their party into two groups: himself and Chasmar to harvest; Filidor, Mezra and Nofreg to lay compost.

The Aralothian balked at drudging for insects, arguing that their energies would be more usefully applied to seeking a means of escape. Gaskarth indicated the soldier neropt, and suggested that Nofreg advance his arguments in that direction. Nofreg declined, and grumbling bent to lift an armload of marsh grass.

The air in the underground chamber was cool, but the labour soon had Filidor bedewed with sweat. And each footstep planted on the mushy earth of the terraces raised wisps of the same fine dust that coated the entrance tunnel. By the time he had stopped counting the bundles of soggy grass he had lifted and carried up into the terraces, Filidor's hands and face were sticky with accumulated dust, and his back ached less from its burdens than from the steady succession of sneezes which interrupted the monotony of his efforts.

As the chamber gradually filled with puffs and eddies of dust, the travelers tore strips from the clothing to cover their mouths and noses, gaining some relief. Their guardian soldier had no such protection, and eventually became agitated as the dust clogged the breathing spiracles along its flanks. The humans watched with interest as the neropt's rudimentary lungs essayed the insect equivalent of a sneeze, then were gladdened to see the soldier shake the dust from its mantle and withdraw through the entry tunnel.

"Good," said the dwarf. "Now, while we have time, let us examine this chamber for possible exits."

Mezra peered down the entry. "I presume that our guardian has taken up a new station at the other end of this tunnel," she said.

Nofreg examined the hole down which ripe fungi were thrown. "Obviously, too small," he concluded. "Could we enlarge it?"

"If we could, it would likely only lead us yet deeper into the nest," said Chasmar.

"We are trapped," said Filidor.

"Perhaps," replied Gaskarth. "But I have read that neropts are prone to rearrange their architecture from time to time. This chamber may once have had another function, and these smooth hard walls may therefore conceal the mouth of a disused tunnel. Let us see." With that, he began a slow circuit of the walls, tapping and listening, tapping and listening. The others hurried to follow his example.

A neropt worker entered through the tunnel, dropped its load of marsh grass and regarded the humans with what must have been puzzlement. At length it said, "Work."

"We are working," answered the dwarf.

The insect considered this reply for a moment. "You are not working effectively," it said.

"Fungus spores have disrupted our neurological processes," said the little man, continuing to tap.

"Is this disruption permanent?"

"Purely temporary."

The insect rotated its head to regard, each in turn, the five humans assiduously tapping the walls of the chamber. Filidor

kept his face averted, but a shiver walked up his spine; somewhere, deep in the nest, a larger intelligence looked out at him
through the worker's unlidded eyes, and weighed his useful-
ness to its purposes. He tapped faster, ignoring bruised knuckles.

"Recover soon," said the neropt, and left the alternative
hanging.

The travelers fell to tapping with a renewed will, and it was
only a few moments later that Chasmar cried out in triumph.
The others ceased their efforts and listened, as the woman of
Ord–Issel thumped her hand at a spot on the wall at the end of
a high terrace. "It's hollow," Nofreg bellowed.

"Shhh!" cautioned Mezra.

"Back to work," ordered the dwarf. "Filidor, the traveler's
aide." The little man took the proffered staff and leapt nimbly
up the terraces to Chasmar's discovery. Moments later, one of
the instrument's drill–bits was keening as it bored a finger-
breadth hole through the neropt concrete. Gaskarth applied his
nose to the hole and sniffed. "Up and out," he concluded.

"Then let us go," shouted Nofreg, throwing down his
burden of marsh grass and chunting his bulk through the
banks of fungi. The others followed in his wake.

"Stop!" cried the dwarf. "We cannot leave yet."

"Surely," said Filidor, "we are not required to render a
service to our captors. If so, I say we have done enough already."

Gaskarth made dismissive motions. "In the first place,
the noise we would make opening the tunnel would attract attention and soldiers. And even if we could hold them off long
enough to enter the tunnel, and even if the passage leads unim-
peded to the surface, they would catch us outside. No, we have
discovered an opportunity; now we must plan how best to use
it. Should the first attempt fail, it is unlikely the neropts will
afford us a second."

They went back to work, sticky and sneezing in the swirling spores. The next neropt to deliver a load of grass watched
them briefly; then, apparently satisfied, it went off for another

load.

Filidor hauled armloads of grass to an upper terrace and spread the vegetation across a bed from which mature fungi had already been removed. The humus he was covering was dank and ill-smelling, threaded throughout by hairlike mycelii, the roots of harvested fungi. Even as Filidor trod the new grass into the soil, fresh spores were settling from the air to begin the next crop.

The work was monotonous and unrewarding, Filidor noted, yet it tended to occupy the mind with the immediate demands of coordinating motion, balance and direction. The bedding could be laid in a variety of patterns; different routes of ascent and descent could be chosen between a terrace and the growing pile of grass. He speculated on how a lifetime given to dull, repetitive labour might condition the laborer to habits of discipline which might be praised as virtuous. Perhaps, when he was restored to his proper station in life, he would undertake a period of voluntary effort – at least several days – to determine whether his character would be enlarged by the experience.

Abruptly, his train of thought was interrupted by a sharp pain lancing through his sole as he trod a wad of grass into the humus. Filidor rubbed the offended part, then bent to investigate. His probing fingers encountered something hard and pointed, meshed about with the fibrous roots of the fungi. He slipped his fingers around the hardness, gripped, pulled, then pulled harder, and sat down abruptly as the thing came loose from the soil.

Filidor found he held by one mandible the eyeless head of a worker neropt. At first, it seemed curiously light, until his examination revealed that all flesh had been stripped from its surrounding chitin by the web of mycelii that covered the head and penetrated every orifice. As he turned the relic, the fungi's fine roots brushed across his wrist like drifting cobwebs, and Filidor shuddered and threw the insect's head far down the terraces, where it bounced and rolled to a stop at Mezra's feet.

Wiping the mycelii from his fingers in disgust, Filidor turned
to see Gaskarth regarding him from nearby.

"We have found the legendary neropts' graveyard," the
young man said, but the tremor in his voice revealed the in-
stinctive revulsion he felt at the touch of the fungi's devouring
filaments.

Mezra drew her epiniard and speared the neropt's head
on its point. She raised the object, inspected it briefly, then cast
it aside.

"I have only one question," she said, turning to Gaskarth.
"Are we to assume that this creature became infested with
fungus after its demise, or before?"

A worker brought more grass and departed. Gaskarth
waited until it had left before replying. "The latter, I surmise,"
he said.

"Then I have at least ten questions," boomed Nofreg, "all
of which I will defer while we make an immediate escape from
this place, lest we too become fodder for fungus."

"In the circumstances, I concur," said the swordster.

The import of their remarks now dawned upon Filidor
and Chasmar. The woman of Ord-Issel looked with horror at
the powdering of fungus spores clinging to the hairs of her bare
arms and legs, brushed fitfully at them, and began to tremble.
Filidor stared at the fat black globules and imagined their seeds
already questing through his body, seeking a corner of lung or
crevice of bowel in which to sprout. "We must depart, however
minimal the chance," he said.

"We *shall* depart," answered Gaskarth. "But I have an
inkling of a plan to raise our chances to more promising proportions. Let us finish this day's work; tonight, we will prepare
the means of flight."

He would say no more, despite their urgings, for fear they
would be overheard by a passing worker, and thus by the queen
neropt who saw and heard all that transpired within the nest.
The travelers returned to their labors, faces wrapped tightly
against the swirling spores, Filidor silently cheering each

racking sneeze as if he were the defender of some besieged keep congratulating himself on repelling the sallies of an invading horde.

The day lasted forever, or at least as long as it took to clear one large terrace of ripe fungi and prepare it and another bed for new growth. At last, when Filidor's arms and legs shook from monotonous exertion, a worker seized the hem of his mantle and tugged him toward the exit. His companions were similarly hurried out of the fungus chamber and down the dust-choked tunnel, where they held their breath against the spore-clad walls.

In the storage chamber, they were drawn into a stream of workers and soldiers, pushed and pulled through a maze of tunnels, and finally thrust through a narrow opening into a small chamber for the night. A worker brought them a few edible fungi, and another dragged in part of the dismembered carcass of a spotted hissule. "Eat," it said, then joined a gang of its fellows in rapidly secreting a concrete barrier across the chamber's exit, leaving only a hand-sized hole for ventilation. Mezra put her eye to this aperture, and shook his head. "Three soldiers in the tunnel," she reported.

They turned their attention to the provender supplied for their evening meal. Gaskarth set aside the fungi and examined the hissule meat. This was much more than they could eat: an entire leg of the ferocious predator, still warm and dripping blood, the bone and muscle severed cleanly by one slash of a soldier's mandibles. Since the beast's leg alone weighed more than the dwarf, and the hissule served as a common metaphor for animal speed, the limb was not only food, but a testament to the capabilities of their captors and the futility of escape.

"Needless excess," commented Mezra.

"Yet effective," countered Nofreg.

But neither had the spirit nor the strength to engage the other. Instead, they joined Filidor and Chasmar in squatting against the wall, and watched to see what the little man would do. The dwarf, for his part, waited patiently for the sounds of

neropt activity to cease, as the nest closed its doors to the world
and settled for the night. When all was silent, Gaskarth whispered to Filidor, "Bring me more light."

The young man wrenched several of the ubiquitous luminescent fungi from the chamber walls and brought them to
where the dwarf sat cross-legged before the hissule leg. Then
he joined the others to watch as Gaskarth took from his satchel
the wand of perpetual sufficiency and a kit of small tools. The
little man cracked open the wand's casing and delved into its
workings with probes and delicate implements. A few deft
movements of his gnarled fingers reassembled the device, and
then he touched it to fur-covered limb. At once, the chamber
was filled with a mouth-watering aroma of cooked meat. Filidor
reached, took and tasted, finding that the tough, raw flesh of
the predator had been transformed into a delicately seasoned
repast as fine as ever he had sampled. The others happily followed his lead.

The pangs of hunger eased, and it occurred to Filidor to
question how Gaskarth had done what he had done. "Hold a
moment," he said. "You told me the wand was beyond repair."

The dwarf smacked his lips around a gobbet of meat.
"Mayhap I thought it so," he said.

"Mayhap you thought instead to deceive me," charged
Filidor.

"To what end?" asked the little man.

"That I will discover," said Filidor.

"If you do not lower your voice," said Mezra, "you will discover how neropt soldiers deal with raucous guests."

Filidor looked, and saw one of the nest's guardians in the
tunnel outside, its antennae questing for the source of dishar-
mony. He said no more.

The little man finished his meal, wiped the grease from
his fingers and applied himself again to the workings of the
wand. While his companions gorged themselves to repletion,
Gaskarth bent over the instrument, making minute adjustments to its innards. Then he carefully put it back together

and touched its tip to each of the edible fungi. "There," he pronounced with satisfaction.

The others examined the fungi. "They appear unchanged," said Chasmar.

"Exactly," said the dwarf. "But changed they are, in a most subtle way. Or so I hope." And then he explained in detail the plan for their escape, and the role that fungi would play in his stratagem.

"Of course, there is no guarantee," he concluded, an observation in which the others concurred. "But if the plan is to succeed, we will know by this time tomorrow." With that, the little man composed himself for sleep.

Nofreg and Mezra, too, lay down upon the chamber floor and let the world fall away. Filidor ate a few more bites of the transformed hissule, then turned to find Chasmar regarding him with a considering look.

"Impossible," the young man said. "We are exhausted, in peril of our lives, and liable to disturb the sleep of our companions."

The woman shrugged and moved closer. Filidor would have edged away, but the confines of the small chamber allowed only for degrees of proximity. "Madam," he said, "you must accept that we suffer from a clash of cultural mores, not to mention personal predilections. In any case," he continued as Chasmar pressed herself against him and stroked his thigh, "being covered in spores, we should afford them no gratuitous opportunities to invade our bodies."

This last remark penetrated Chasmar's indifference to Filidor's protests. After a moment's reflection, she conceded – for the time being – to his position, and contented herself with burrowing into the crook of his arm and sleepily allowing her hands to take stock of his person.

For his part, Filidor was also content to have gained a partial victory, and did not seek to escape the woman's attentions. As Chasmar's increasing warmth and weight against him informed him that she had fallen asleep, he could not but take comfort in the presence of another human being who, for whatever selfish motives, seemed to regard him with affection.

He was tempted to pursue a train of thought concerning the nature of self-interest, and whether absorption in one's own cause might somehow paradoxically redound to the benefit of society at large. But as his mind skirted the edges of the concept, his natural disinclination to introspection reasserted itself, and he instead drew out the volume of Osfeo.

The illumino visited the temple city of Bandimee to discourse among its college of sages and seers. Here he found himself in colloquy with a celebrated monast of the Wu-Fen school, a system of thought which Osfeo disdained as vapid and given to overwrought conceits.

Draped in his colorful robes, and surrounded by adoring acolytes, the monast related a dream. "In my dream, I was a blind worm burrowing in a dung-heap. When I awoke, how could I be sure that I was a man who had dreamed himself a worm, or a worm dreaming it was a man?" The monast eyed Osfeo with a sly gaze, and concluded, "Can you resolve this conundrum, Osfeo?"

The illumino sucked his teeth and weighed his answer. "If such a venerated scholar as yourself cannot tell whether he is a man or a blind worm, who am I to judge?" he said.

Then, seeing the glint of triumph in the eyes of the monast and his students, Osfeo went on: "But if I were you, I would definitely hope to be the worm rather than the man."

"Why?" the monast reluctantly inquired.

"Well, obviously you would be a singularly imaginative worm."

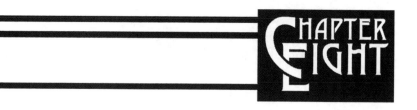

CHAPTER EIGHT

IT MUST HAVE BEEN dawn in the world above, because the neropt nest was abustle with activity. The travelers awoke to worker claws and mandibles pulling down the barrier to their small chamber. Gaskarth leapt up, being the only one of a size to do so in the confined space, and quickly distributed the adulterated fungi to the others, instructing that the black globes be hidden beneath their garments. Chasmar was exempted, inasmuch as her single blanket barely served to cover her ample nakedness.

The barrier was soon down, and the captives hustled into the swarming tunnel outside their prison. Filidor balked as a worker sought to hurry him along. Disregarding the blockage he was creating among the hurrying workers, he braced his feet against the flow. "I am thirsty," he complained.

"Hold out your hands," said the neropt. The young man cupped his palms and extended them. The worker positioned its head above his hands, belched, and spewed out a sweet-smelling liquid that spattered Filidor's wrists and seeped between his fingers. "Drink," it said.

Filidor looked at the warm, cloudy liquor and fought the urge to gag. "Drink," the neropt repeated. A soldier nearby raised its antennae and began to bull its way through the packed tunnel to where the traffic had become blocked. Filidor touched his lips to the liquid in his hands and tasted sweetness. He downed the handful and asked for more, which the worker obligingly supplied.

The drink did more than assuage his thirst. The neropt liquor seemed to race through his veins, stopping to announce

glad tidings at each cell of his body, energizing and enliven-
ing his whole being. The walls of the tunnel began to pulsate,
the faces of his fellow travelers appeared to undergo unusual
transformations, and Filidor felt an unstoppable urge to move
in several directions at once. "Why do we wait?" he cried. "On to
our work!" And he pulled the neropt down the tunnel.

The dwarf watched his departure, then counseled the
others to drink sparingly of what the neropts had to offer.
When they arrived at the fungus chamber, each tingling from
the effects of a small draught of neropt liquor, they saw Filidor
leaping from terrace to terrace, laying improbably large loads
of marsh grass at reckless speed. Even their impassive neropt
escorts seemed impressed.

"Perhaps this is for the best," said Gaskarth. "Let my
young companion continue in his prodigious labors, while we
set ourselves to harvest as many of the ripe fungi as we may."

So they did, while Filidor continued to set new standards
of productivity, and the neropts were hard pressed to supply
him with sufficient quantities of vegetation to match his pace.
The other travelers hurried to gather the black globes and bring
them to the exit chute, where the little man touched each briefly
with the wand before dropping it into the hole.

"How long before your scheme bears fruit?" asked Nofreg
after a while. The dwarf shrugged.

"It is difficult to estimate. The dosage should be more
than sufficient for effect, but not so great as to approach toxic-
ity. Providing, that is, that I have properly adjusted the wand,
and that its archaic mechanism has performed as we desire. In
any case, I hope to know soon."

They continued to work at a frantic pace, and had shortly
gathered, adulterated and disposed of every ripe fungus and
not a few that Gaskarth thought unready for harvesting. Meanwhile, Filidor had singlehandedly resurfaced every terrace in
need of composting, including those newly stripped by his
companions. The young man was now hovering anxiously near
the entrance tunnel, almost dancing from foot to foot, hands

itching to seize more vegetation and put it in place. The others paused to observe him.

"It would seem that the neropts' predilection to be constantly busy is at least partially based on biochemistry," commented Mezra.

"Indeed," put in Nofreg. "And that is a heartening indication, since our plan of escape leans heavily on a similar susceptibility."

"Judging by the effects on Filidor," said Chasmar, "whatever alkaloids are brewed within the neropts' bellies could command some considerable commercial value in certain markets."

The little man agreed. "I am tempted," he said, "to secure a sample of their stomach contents to use as a refresher at appropriate moments. I confess I have never seen him so thoroughly motivated."

The object of their scrutiny, however, was undergoing a change. To Filidor, it felt as if taps had suddenly opened in both feet, through which his unaccustomed vitality now rapidly emptied. The influence of the neropt liquor ebbed as swiftly as it had earlier flooded his being, and the physical toll of his efforts was presented for payment. He swayed, tottered, and sank to the chamber floor.

"A lamentably short-lived effect," commented Nofreg.

"Yet inarguably impressive during its brief tenure," Mezra replied.

The two then fell to their usual philosophical conflict over the relative merits of minimalism versus panache. Gaskarth and Chasmar crossed the floor to the recumbent Filidor and attempted to revive him from the stupor of exhaustion.

Their efforts were interrupted by the arrival of a worker. Gaskarth inspected the neropt closely and detected hopeful signs. Rather than bearing a full load of grass, the insect carried only a few stalks in its mandibles. Its gait was less than fully coordinated, the six legs appearing to operate somewhat autonomously of each other, and it kept raising a hind leg to scratch frantically at two dark spots that had appeared on the top of its thorax. The worker ignored the unconscious Filidor and his attendants, blundering over them and into the chamber, where it collapsed on the floor and made raspy cooing sounds.

"I believe our stratagem is having an effect," said Gaskarth. With that he slapped Filidor hard on both cheeks, rousing the young man to a drowsy state. "Time to go," he said, and called the others to aid.

Together, they hauled Filidor up the terraces to the blocked exit they had discovered the day before. Gaskarth found the traveler's aide in the young man's mantle, and deployed it to produce a coarse-bladed circular saw which bit into the concrete sealing the disused tunnel. The whine ached in their ears, but no neropts came to investigate.

Throughout the nest, the insects were otherwise occupied, as the dwarf had arranged. His careful reordering of the wand of perpetual sufficiency had allowed the instrument to produce in the neropts' fungi large quantities of an organic chemical similar to that produced by the queen at appropriate points in the life cycle of her species. Distributed and eaten through the morning, the fungi had by now made their way into the craw of almost every insect. As a result, all the neropts suddenly found themselves in rampant pubescence.

For the soldiers and older workers, designed to remain neuter from egg to shroud, the effects of the hormone were an intolerable disruption of their systems. They would remain useless until its effects wore off. For the younger workers and the sex-differentiated special offspring of the queen, the effect was more drastic: their bodies swelled with new vigor, and translucent wings sprouted from their backs.

From the heart of the nest, where the gargantuan queen tried to restore order to a horde of progeny obsessed with an overwhelming urge to mate, hundreds of suddenly nubile nymphs fled toward the tunnels which would take them to the apex of the nest's tower. In their wake swarmed the burly drones, desperate to take flight in pursuit of their consorts. And up the rough rocky walls of the disused tunnel, the five humans climbed with them.

Filidor was last out of the tunnel onto the crowded top of the tower, dragged by the others into a maelstrom of winged insects, the first of which were already launching themselves into the afternoon air, spiraling up and away across Dimpfen Moor. There would have been little space even without the swarm of nymphs and drones, and all was a chaos of shoving bodies and whirring wings.

"The females!" cried Gaskarth. "Take the females! They'll fly further!"

The dwarf manhandled Filidor toward a nymph preparing to launch herself and threw him across the insect's broad thorax. The little man leapt onto the neropt's back just as it crouched and sprang from the top of the tower, and plummeted toward the hard-packed earth mound below. Filidor managed to cling to the edge of the nymph's carapace as they dropped, and the dwarf clung to him, the wind of their descent stinging tears from their eyes.

When there was no hope but to crash, the neropt spread her wings and caught the air, sliding out across the moor on an upward plane of lift, then beating her wings to carry them steadily higher above the sodden marsh. Revived by the cold air, Filidor took action to secure his position, grasping the insect's barrel-width abdomen between his thighs and sitting upright. Gaskarth then swarmed over the young man's shoulders and took a seat in front of him, seizing the neropt's antennae that streamed back toward his hands. If the grip caused the nymph any discomfort, it was lost in her hormonal exuberance.

Their mount now caught a thermal and spiraled upward for height. Gaskarth looked about from their rising vantage and saw their three companions aloft on their own nymphs. He called to them over the rushing wind; they heard and answered. Then the dwarf delicately tugged on the insect's antennae, like a coachman with his reins, and the nymph heeled over and slipped through the air toward Thurloyn Vale. The other travelers followed his example, and together the captives of the neropts fled toward freedom.

Filidor, perhaps retaining some effect of neropt alkaloids, was exhilarated by the airborne escape. He begged to be allowed to control their mount, and Gaskarth at length relinquished his grip upon the antennae. For Filidor the ride was a return to freedom. After being dragged from his mundane though enjoyable life, thrust into peril and hardship, and lastly reduced to serfdom in an anthill, it was now pure joy to be soaring toward the completion of his mission. As the nymph's scintillating wings thrummed against the friction of rushing air, the young man did not look back. But the dwarf did.

Behind them, the sky was clouded with wheeling neropts, and the tower from which they had been launched was now a small interruption to the moor's horizon. As Gaskarth peered through the afternoon haze, the rocky structure seemed to quiver, as if shaken by some subterranean blast. Then the spire collapsed upon itself in a puff of dust that was shot through by streaks of sickly green light. A moment later, the scene dropped below the edge of his vision as the nymph lost altitude in a downdraft.

The little man's face set itself into hard lines. "Have you still the box?" he asked Filidor.

"The what?"

"The box we are delivering to your uncle."

"Oh, yes," said Filidor, his mind immersed in the moment.

"Good," said the dwarf.

In the end it was not a long flight, but it was long enough. Their weary mounts alighted close enough for them to see the upper stories of Thurloyn Vale's taller buildings, and the five travelers trekked into the safety of the town before the moor's worst predators awoke from their diurnal sleep. The day hunters were kept sufficiently busy dispatching the unexpected bounty of neropt nymphs and drones before they could mate and burrow beneath the ground.

Thurloyn Vale was a dull place, merely a crossroads for airships crossing the wastes, but no palace of diversions had ever been so inviting to Filidor. The travelers found lodgings near the air terminus, cleansed themselves, then went together to seek passage. Mezra and Nofreg put themselves onto a flight leaving the next day, intending to travel together: somehow, despite their opposed philosophies, they derived pleasure from each other's company, and resolved to found a friendship on their differences.

Chasmar booked no passage, but instead inquired about chartering a small craft with a crew familiar with the moor. She proposed to investigate the possibilities of trade with neropt colonies, bartering self-actuated agricultural equipment for organic chemicals. She had had enough of aimless peregrinating, and felt inclined to make yet another fortune. "I suspect that the benefits of travel are indeed overrated. It seems mostly hardship and needless frustration," she said.

Filidor suggested that he and Gaskarth accompany the Cyc and the Aralothian, but the dwarf declined, saying he had already used his Archonate authority to commandeer a two-passenger craft, which was even now being readied for their immediate departure. No sooner had he imparted this news than an official of the terminus arrived to announce that their ship was on the apron, fully powered and awaiting their use. The dwarf hurried Filidor through his farewells to the others, and then through the terminus doors. Moments later, they were airborne again, bound for the Republic of Jamp.

Their aircraft took them over the creeping edge of Dimpfen Moor, then up over bracken covered hills which gave way to barren crags and tors. Beyond these barriers, they encountered a high plateau, dotted with farms and small settlements, which grew more thickly the closer they came to Novo Stade, the Jampian capital.

Near one such hamlet, where the towers of Novo Stade crowded the horizon, Gaskarth set the aircar down in a farmer's mown hayfield and ordered Filidor out. As the young man watched, the dwarf reset the craft's controls and leapt from the compartment to join him on the ground. The vehicle whirred smoothly into the sky, banked, and headed pilotless into the distance, continuing their previous course.

Filidor looked about. The place offered no apparent attractions as a landing area. If anything, it reminded him of Binch. He turned to speak to Gaskarth, but the little man was already marching between the hay stooks, and Filidor had to hasten to catch him up.

"I thought we were bound for Novo Stade," he said.

"We are. There it is," answered the dwarf. "An hour's walk will see us there."

"We could as easily have flown to our destination."

"True."

"Then is there some reason for putting us down here and sending our comfortable conveyance off to who knows where?"

"There is."

"Will you tell me what it is?"

"No," said the dwarf, increasing his pace so that Filidor must lengthen his own stride to keep up.

The builders of Novo Stade had laid out their city around one end of a finger-shaped lake that filled the bottom of a shallow valley. The travelers' road descended through dry hills speckled by clumps of wiry grass, to become a broad avenue, along which ranged a succession of squat blocks of masonry, tinted in variegated pastels, and adorned at every corner with bright banners. But, despite their colorfulness, Filidor detected a depressing sameness to each quarter through which he and the dwarf passed as they made their way to Novo Stade's administrative centre. The Jampians, he conjectured, concerned themselves little with architectural novelty and the richness of diversity in their surroundings.

Whatever it was that did occupy the citizens of Novo Stade was not immediately clear to Filidor. Those they passed on the wide and clean-swept streets were uniformly well-knit, and seemingly fit in body, but with a morose demeanor that belied the outward display of health. They slouched about the pedestrian ways, conversing in monosyllables, each wrapped in his own pall of gloom.

At the core of the city, where the low-rise structures gave way to more imposing towers, Gaskarth led the way into a hostelry whose marquee advertised a willingness to accommodate transients of modest means. After Ektop and Zeel, Filidor was agreeably surprised to find that customs formalities could be easily disposed of by the glum keeper of the hotel register.

His identity badge read Spec. Dando Steethe, and he was a man of middle years and middle height whose trim physique and deft motions hinted at a past career in professional athletics. He disinterestedly interrogated the travelers as to their identity, their possible intent to import deleterious substances into Jamp, and whether they meant to participate in any sporting contests. These queries being satisfactorily answered, Spec. Steethe summoned a porter to conduct them to a suite of comfortable rooms.

The suite included two sleeping chambers connected by a tiled ablutory, and a large room dominated by a wall-sized viewing screen with its control console inset into one arm of a reclining chair which faced the glass. Into this manipulable furnishing Filidor gratefully sank, while Gaskarth went to the windows and peered at the street below.

"What do you see?" asked Filidor.

"Nothing," replied the dwarf.

"Is that what you hoped to see?"

"It is."

"Are we being pursued? And, if so, by whom?"

"Who can say?"

Further inquiry yielded Filidor nothing more, and he dismissed the dwarf's behavior as yet another manifestation of his companion's enjoyment of mystery for its own sake. Filidor instead investigated the controls of the viewing screen, and soon had the wall alive with images. By chance he had found a children's educational program designed to outline for young Jampians the essentials of their social order.

"Ah hah," he expostulated, "for once I shall be able to move among strangers with some understanding of their mores and customs, rather than be put to learning them through hard and even perilous experience."

"Most wise," murmured Gaskarth, his attention still on the street below. "And while you are so engaged, I shall make my way to the local office of the Archonate, there to seek your uncle or word of his whereabouts. Pray remain here until my return." With one last look out the window, the dwarf departed.

Filidor settled into the chair's embrace and watched the screen. He learned that Jamp was a stratified culture, its citizens mostly of the Spectator class – hence the honorific "Spec." which Dando Steethe had applied to himself and them. Pride of social place went to the caste of Contenders, who were entitled to renown and deference from their fellow citizens. Between these two extremes of Jampian society was a middle class of Commentators, who were objects of mingled respect and antipathy. Management of the social order devolved upon a Board of Commissioners, apparently a group of faceless individuals of far-reaching authority who exercised their powers through a corps of regulators known as the Umps.

This much Filidor was able to glean from the children's program. But since the instruction was intended for young Jampians who already commanded a basic grasp of their own cultural milieu, he was left with several gaps in his understanding of how the society actually worked. The educational service then moved on to teach a course on the history of some sport or other, and Filidor changed to one of the screen's many entertainment channels.

He soon discovered that all Jampian broadcasts were devoted to a bewildering array of athletic contests, the goals, rules and procedures of which were wholly unknown to Filidor.

On one channel, three teams of men and women in shorts and helmets clambered over a framework of metallic struts and girders in apparent pursuit of a rapidly spinning gyroscope. The towering structure featured ramps, dead-ends, swinging bridges and trapdoors, up and down which the players flung themselves with an agility and elan born of long practice. Nevertheless, Filidor observed one participant mistime his lunge for the hurtling gyro and tumble headlong from the tower, only to be arrested by an anagrav field which deposited him gently at its base. The athlete remounted the scaffolding to a vicious chorus of hoots and jeers from the massed Spectators.

Baffled, Filidor changed channels, and was confronted with the spectacle of two teams of burly Jampians apparently attempting to force a large spherical object upon each other. Inset into one corner of a screen, a timing clock flashed descending digits. In the opposite corner there appeared the face of a bald man whose active eyebrows accompanied an unwholesome voice in a description of the action too rhetorically florid to be borne. Filidor switched again, and observed what could only be a mass brawl among a welter of discarded athletic gear. Pressing on, he discovered that every channel was devoted to increasingly mystifying contests and competitions. He blanked the screen.

The room offered no other diversion and, despite the exertions of the day, Filidor felt disinclined to sleep. With nothing else to do, he considered reading from the tales of Osfeo, but by then his stomach was making demands, and he took himself down to the public lobby in search of food.

The lobby was spartan in its appointments, but it offered access to a number of snugs and refectories. Filidor inspected each in turn, finding that it was impossible to dine in the hostelry without being exposed to an even larger viewing screen than the one he had left in the room above; and every screen was showing the same event, which seemed to be a mingling of fisticuffs and intricate ballet. Irritated and hungry, Filidor found the exit sign and followed its advice.

He emerged into the streets of Jamp to witness a spectacle of barbarism which offended his every sensibility. A rabble of

youths, armed with clubs and flails, were in open pursuit of a
small and frantically fleeing animal. The tiny creature, scarcely
more than a puff of fur surmounted by two fragile ears, darted
desperately from one side of the avenue to the other, unaided
by the adult Jampians who lined the curbs and looked on with
stolid boredom.

"This is intolerable!" cried Filidor, forcing his way through
the spectators. The gang's quarry scurried past him, dodging
among the feet of the audience, then skittered back toward him
as its escape was blocked by a husky juvenile swinging a length
of chain. Without thought, Filidor swiftly stooped and gathered the animal into his arms.

At once, a deathly hush descended upon the scene. Spectators and club-wielders alike gaped at the young man in as-
tonishment rapidly evolving into outrage. But Filidor was now
too occupied to notice. The trembling beast he had sought to
comfort now began to vibrate with considerably more energy
than its small size should have made possible. Moreover, its
unexpected weight and solidity revealed to Filidor that he
clasped not a small, frightened animal but a powerful, multi-
wheeled machine loosely covered in synthetic fur. The thing
whirred loudly, and he deposited it back on the ground, where
it began to dart back and forth as if eager to resume the chase.

But no Jampian now offered to pursue the robot. All eyes
were on Filidor, all mouths set in grim censure. Abashed, he
shrugged uncomfortably and prepared to make his apologies.
Before a syllable could emerge, however, a shout went up from
the crowd.

"Spectator on the field! An ump, an ump!"

"Seize him!" cried someone. "Summon the refs!"

Those nearest advanced upon Filidor with menacing
intent. With the experience of recent days still fresh in his
mind, the young man forbore to offer explanations, and backed
quickly toward the hostelry door. But a hand seized his mantle
while another sought for his neck, and in an instant he was
beset by a multitude. Fortunately, so anxious were the Jampi-

ans to lay hold of him that they impeded each other's efforts, and he was briefly able to break free. The safety of the hostelry being denied him by the press of bodies, Filidor took to his heels down the street. With an outraged bay, the mob swarmed after.

Filidor's boots rang the pavement as he launched himself pell-mell through the streets of Novo Stade, a clamor of Jampians at his back. Running hard, he rounded a corner only to find himself in a cul-de-sac lined with boutiques whose windows and counters displayed delicate ceramics and objects crafted of glass. With the pack close behind, he sped to the first door and leapt within. The shop's proprietor had scant time to call, "Caution, these goods are frangible!" before Filidor vaulted a counter and disappeared through a connecting storeroom to the rear entrance. He emerged into an alley, hearing behind him the curiously satisfying sound of the mob's arrival among the glasswares, amid crashes and curses from shopkeeper and pursuers alike.

He turned and ran on, but had not cleared the mouth of the back lane before the pursuit fought its way out of the shop and came howling after him. Filidor burst from the alley into a street where vehicles were drawn up at the curb, and collided with a man who was just exiting from a torpedoesque two-wheeler whose lines and ornamental decals promised limitless speed. The machine's control card was in the man's hand as Filidor crashed into him. It did not remain there much longer; Filidor snatched the oblong from the man's fingers, leapt into the car, dogged down the transparent hatch, and locked it. While the owner beat upon the roof and excoriated Filidor and his ancestors, the young man slipped the card into its receptacle, seized the controls and fired the engine. As the mob debouched from the alley, he spun the steering mechanism and left them all behind.

But Jampians, he discovered, were not easily dissuaded once their blood was raised. He looked back to see his pursuers in the street, joined by the owner of the stolen vehicle, halting other conveyances and enlisting their drivers in pursuit. Within seconds, a gaggle of assorted wheeled and grav-cushioned motilators were on his tail.

The road opened before Filidor as he activated the speedster's emergency warning lights and sounded its admonitory siren. Gyros straining to maintain its vertical orientation, the slim car swept around a corner at high speed, leading Filidor into one of Novo Stade's arterial thoroughfares. Some of the pursuing vehicles failed to negotiate the turn and tumbled spectacularly across the pavement, their occupants automatically cocooned in restraining devices and billowing sacs of compressed gases.

Most of the pursuit was now falling behind for lack of power, but a few were gaining. And others were joining in the chase, including a small airship decorated with logos and symbols. Although it could easily have overtaken Filidor, the aircraft made no attempt to harass or block his escape, but flew beside him at low altitude, while its crew trained upon him what appeared to be surveillance gear. Filidor attempted to avert his features from the prying lenses, until the airship veered off as he weaved between other vehicles and entered a subterranean traffic conduit.

He shot back into daylight a few moments later, with a swarm of honking Jampians in close pursuit. Filidor jerked the steering bar left, then right, then left again, threading his way at breakneck velocity through a maze of small streets and byways, some of which were intended to bear traffic in single directions other than that which Filidor had chosen. His maneuvers had thinned the pack behind him, but a clutch of determined Jampians remained in his wake.

He redoubled his efforts, rounding corners at speeds in excess of his vehicle's design specifications and, occasionally, taking to the public sidewalks in a manner that forced several pedestrians to demonstrate the alacrity of their reflexes. Still his pursuers hung on, and a brace of them were a mere length behind him when he exited a street to find himself rocketing

along a paved jetty that extended into the Novo Stade harbour
– and ended at the water's edge.

A chorus of triumphant horn blasts sounded from the
following pack. Filidor screeched to a standstill with his vehicle's nose almost dipping into the chill grey lake. He squirmed
from the hatch as the pursuit cars slid toward him, their doors
already opening to release the mob. One sportster shot right
past him, landing in the lake with an appreciable spray of foam.
Filidor's eyes flashed about him for a means of escape, and lit
upon a flock of boats and skimmers moored below the mole.

"In for a zlazni, in for a smov," he quoted, and jumped
down into the nearest skimmer. He had piloted similar craft on
Mornedy Sound, and as he cranked up its jets and swung its
blunt nose toward open water, Filidor entertained a brief hope
that he could now escape his pursuers. That hope was dashed
when he looked back to see the Jampians leaping from their
vehicles and piling into the other watercraft with loud hoots of
excitement. Filidor took a deep breath, twisted the skimmer's
power knob until the craft bounced from wave–top to wave–top
like a flung stone, and aimed for the far shore.

The harbour of Novo Stade was a busy place, and Filidor
found exhilaration in sideslipping among larger vessels and
navigation buoys. Most of those chasing him were less expert
than he, and his lead lengthened. He looked back at the dwindling pursuit, and the laugh that cackled out of his throat
almost surprised him. But then he saw that other boats already
in the harbour, and presumably under the command of experienced masters, were turning to track his wake. He bore down
on the power knob and swore.

And now the annoying airship bedecked with communications gear was off his port bow, skimming the lake's surface
while its pick–ups transmitted his features to who–knew–what
jaded audience. Filidor favored the aircraft's occupants with
some considered epithets, at which a directional microphone
was swung over to bear upon him.

The far side of the harbour was now becoming more the near side with each passing moment. There the beach gradually sloped down, and a flock of bathers were disporting in the surf, sheltered from waterborne traffic by a bobbing line of floats. Filidor felt the skimmer lift as it surged over this barrier of conscience, sending several foam-spattered Jampians diving from his course. He ran the skimmer across the beach at full speed, and managed to coax it up an asphalt ramp leading to the top of a promenade wall, before the craft's superstructure separated from its hull and somersaulted him into a decorative topiary.

Fighting free of the bush, Filidor observed several boats plowing into the beach, their occupants scrambling over the gunwales like enthusiastic pirates. The young man again applied feet to pavement and ran toward one of the streets leading down to the promenade. Before any of his pursuers had scaled the wall from the beach, he was across the promenade and running up a street of shops. He chose a door at random and stepped in to find himself in a small establishment dealing in confections, stimulants and current periodicals.

Seizing a brightly colored pamphlet from the nearest rack, he brought it up to cover his face and watched through the display window as the pursuit arrived outside. Perhaps twenty Jampians, some breathing heavily, milled about in the street, having lost the scent of their quarry. Returning the periodical to its former place, Filidor summoned his nerve, stepped unobtrusively into the street, and sidled up to the mob.

"There he goes!" he cried, pointing to a car that was conveniently pulling away from the curb some distance up the street. Then he stood back and watched the crowd commandeer the nearest vehicles and give pursuit. With some crunching of skirts and fenders, the Jampians got themselves all pointed in the same direction, and then disappeared up the street.

Filidor heaved a sigh of relief, and turned to find that the ubiquitous airship had remained to surveil him. He flinched, expecting immediate apprehension by the local authorities, but the aircraft's pilot only grinned and flourished a hand signal of ironic congratulations, then lifted his ship and sped away.

Filidor walked a short way along the promenade until he found a public communication terminal which would accept one of the coins in his purse. He asked for a connection to the Archonate's office in Novo Stade, and when the screen cleared he beheld the grinning face of his travelling companion.

"Stay where you are," said Gaskarth, "and I shall collect you directly."

A short while later, a self-guided hackney flew in across the harbour and Filidor was hauled into a seat beside the dwarf. Their possessions were stacked on a carrying rack behind them. The little man did something to the controls, and the aircar lifted them away. Then he turned to Filidor. "You've had a very busy day," he said.

Filidor let it be known that he did not welcome any discussion. He slouched in his seat, and regarded the inside of his eyelids, in expectation of a rebuke. But none was immediately forthcoming, and he opened his eyes to see Gaskarth intent on the view beneath their ascending hackney.

Novo Stade's harbour slowly shrank as they made a gentle ascent toward low clouds. The little man's gaze had fixed upon a sleek black ground car that prowled the promenade like some hunting beast. Now it stopped and a thin, robed figure stepped out of the vehicle and approached the communications booth which Filidor had used. Then a wisp of cloud intervened, and the world outside dissolved in grey.

Filidor tugged at the little man's sleeve. "Very well," he said, "if you wish to chastise me, I am prepared to accept judicious criticism."

The little man did not at first reply. He seemed to be engaged in some mental effort far removed from Filidor's concerns, and a grim resolve deepened the lines of his face. Then, as if pushing away an unwelcome thought, he shook his head and turned to Filidor.

"Chastise?" he said. "Indeed, there is little to punish and much to praise. I can assure you that your uncle has already been advised of your exertions in service to Jamp, and is excellently pleased by your performance."

"You have seen my uncle?"

"We have communicated in the usual manner," said the dwarf, "but I regret that we must seek him further on. To which end I have secured us passage on a coaster departing this evening from the seaport of Magetz and bound for the city of Tarend. This vehicle should see us to dockside in ample time to board."

Filidor sighed forlornly into the mist condensing on the air car's windows. "Then our journey continues."

"True, but we are making good time," consoled the little man, "and achieving your uncle's aims as we progress."

"Confusion wraps me once more," said Filidor. "I cannot conceive how I have been of service to Jamp while rampantly enraging its citizens and surely infringing on several criminal and civil statutes."

"Your remarks demonstrate how proximity narrows perspective," said Gaskarth. "Events in and of themselves are less pertinent than the effects and interpretations to which they give rise. So, while it brooks no contest that you have indeed committed a range of offenses from reckless endangerment to theft of transportation, the cumulative result of your excursion through Novo Stade has redounded to the significant benefit of all Jampians."

"I require further explication," said Filidor.

"Then give heed," responded the little man. "I believe you are aware that Jampian society is divided among three classes, all of whom are inordinately fond of athletic endeavors." At Filidor's nod, Gaskarth continued, "But it is probably not known to you that, in recent years, the proportion of Contenders to Spectators has shifted markedly, as a natural consequence of this mania for sport.

"Continued, devoted practice so heightened the levels of

skill required to compete in Jampian contests that fewer and fewer of their citizenry were able to qualify. As competition became increasingly a matter of shaving minims or even micro-minims from records almost impossible to surpass, only one in a thousand Jampians could retain the rank of Contender, whereas they were formerly the majority of the populace."

"In other words," put in Filidor, "they outdid themselves."

"Just so. Some few Contenders were able to win status as Commentators, but this is primarily a hereditary caste, and so most have slid all the way down to the level of Spectators. Naturally, this has occasioned —"

"—great social and personal tension," finished Filidor, "yet I fail to see how any of this relates to my own misadventures."

"Why you have inadvertently shown the Jampians a solution to their dilemma. When you fled, you drew in pursuit several dozen Spectators, most of them former Contenders, who enjoyed themselves hugely in chasing you down. You thereby caused them to recall what they had long since forgotten: namely that the proper goal of sport is participation and healthy diversion, rather than a compilation of dry statistics.

"The Board of Commissioners is at this moment convened to discuss measures which will institutionalize the principles you have demonstrated. It is contemplated to offer convicted criminals a choice between penal servitude or becoming the objects of free-form pursuit, in which any Jampian – Spectator or Contender – may join. Since the televising of your innovative escapade has already been of great vicarious enjoyment to millions of Jampians, the proposition is certain to win overwhelming popular favor."

Filidor shook his head. "It becomes increasingly clear," he said, "that this profession of service to citizens of the Archonate is a welter of paradox. I wonder that my uncle ever chose to follow such a career."

"You uncle is renowned for the sagacity of his choices," replied Gaskarth. "But look, we are coming out of the clouds, and there on the horizon lies the port of Magetz. We shall shortly be bound for Tarend, where we may hope to find new opportunities of service."

"Even better, we may hope to find my uncle," said Filidor, but the dwarf only shrugged and lapsed again into his dark thoughts.

ALL FILIDOR SAW of the port city of Magetz was a strip of dock bordered on one side by sheds and warehouses, and on the other by the black waters of the Mavrot Gulf. They landed on the quay and immediately boarded *Dinshan's Conceit*. This was a middling-sized vessel, moderately well maintained, which carried passengers and light cargoes among the archipelago of the New Shore, under the captaincy of one Kepling Dinshan, a Garamantian whose own physical description matched that of her ship.

The little man had arranged for a single cabin, its confines almost too small to accommodate both travelers unless at least one kept to his bunk. But Filidor was not disposed to complain. The rigors of the day had by now overtaken him; while Gaskarth inspected the cabin, Filidor wrapped himself wearily in the lower pallet's thin coverings and was soon insensate.

He awoke to a staccato vibration that told him the *Conceit* was under way, and a glance through the cabin's small window showed darkly glistening waters broken here and there by the deeper black of low islands and reefs. Gaskarth was still absent, but Filidor was not moved to go in search of him. The events of his brief sojourn in Novo Stade had underscored the wisdom of immobility.

For lack of alternative diversion, the young man drew out the copy of Osfeo and thumbed its well-worn pages until a heading caught his eye.

An indentor of Syaskal, he read, *having amassed a sufficient fortune, resolved one day to dedicate his middle years to the pursuit of wisdom, and sought out the illumino in his school at Khoram-in-the-Waste.*

He arrived as Osfeo was conducting his morning colloquy with several new disciples, and sat in the rear of the chamber to watch and judge the worth of the sage.

One of the students approached Osfeo, knelt to make the appropriate gestures, and asked, "Master, what are the limits of the universe?"

The illumino considered for a moment, then replied, "I don't know."

The student thanked Osfeo and returned to sit with the others. The indentor was puzzled.

Another disciple approached. "Master," she inquired, "what is the ultimate purpose of existence?"

Osfeo looked at her with an austere kindliness. "I don't know," he said.

Now the indentor was stirred by annoyance as the student thanked Osfeo and was replaced by a third disciple, who asked, "Master, what is the nature of time?"

"I don't know," said Osfeo.

"Thank you," said the disciple.

"It is what I am here for," rejoined the sage.

The disciple bowed and all the company retired from the chamber to contemplate Osfeo's answers. But the indentor remained to confront the sage.

"Fraud!" he accused. "These younglings come to you for enlightenment, but you deliver them not the least glimmer!"

"On the contrary," was the answer, "I have given them invaluable instruction."

"It is obvious," declared the indentor, "that you have taught them nothing."

"That is not so," said Osfeo, "but the fact that you say it makes it obvious that I cannot teach you anything."

The indentor departed and eventually purchased a place among a cloister of idiosophists, with whom he was

content. Osfeo continued to dispense enlightenment to an
appreciative few.

The dwarf returned, scuttling into the cabin with a glance back over his shoulder. He was clearly agitated. "There is little time," he said, "so heed what I say.

"Among the passengers on this ship are two men who affect not to know each other, yet I have detected between them certain subtle signals which lead me to conclude that they intend to divert the smoothness of our journey by some unexpected proceedings."

"What nature of proceedings?" demanded Filidor. "I had anticipated a restful passage to allow recuperation from the events of late."

Gaskarth made a dismissive gesture. "There is no opportunity to discuss this at length. For the nonce, I wish you to engage these two – who are travelling under the names Beel and Amdry – in conversation at supper. You will let slip to them that I am in possession of an exquisite gem of great price, which I carry in a small carved box."

"What gem? What box?"

"It is of no moment. There is also a second task for you to perform. At some point during the evening, I will leave the salon and shortly return. When I do, I will ask you to give me the box of tuka wood you are carrying for your uncle. You will do so without drawing attention to the transfer, but leave Beel and Amdry in no doubt that I am in possession of the gem they will believe to be in the box."

"I must know what you intend."

"Some intentions are best left unknown," said the dwarf, and drew from his tattered black robes a box roughly like that which Filidor carried tucked in his mantle. "Now give me the real one," said Gaskarth, "and replace it with this copy."

Confused, Filidor did as the little man ordered. He noticed that when Gaskarth slipped the object of their mission into his tatters he handled it gingerly, as if it were some creature both delicate and particularly venomous. Then they went out to supper.

The meal was served competently by stewards on the open after-deck of the *Conceit*. The passengers were of that unremarkable sort who take passage on unremarkable vessels: commerciants, peripatetic youth, and those for whom cost counts more than timeliness. The exception, Filidor noted as he and the dwarf took seats on either side of the common board, were an exquisite couple who dined apart at a small table. They were quite the most beautiful people the young man had ever seen, perfect to the last pore, and Filidor indicated them to Gaskarth with an interrogative motion of the eyebrows.

"They are of Tarend," whispered the dwarf, "and of no concern."

Nor did the two paragons compel the interest of the other passengers, who preferred to discuss inconsequentials. A man with eyes, cropped hair and garments all of steel grey introduced himself to Filidor as an engineer out of Jyreste. He apparently believed his fascination with the crystalline properties of various materials was universally shared, and discoursed at length while he ate, until a choking fit interrupted the monologue.

Filidor then looked to the man and woman on his left, a pair of mariculturists returning to their fish pens with a fresh consignment of fertile roe. Fortunately, these two possessed a wider view of life than the engineer, and Filidor found their conversation more to his taste. At the moment, they were speculating fancifully upon the identity of a passenger who had sprinted up the gangway just as the *Conceit* was about to get under way. Barely glimpsed as a tall figure in nondescript garb, he had mysteriously gone straight to a vacant cabin and had not appeared since.

Filidor and the mariculturists were concocting elaborate and ribald scenarios to explain the unseen passenger's presence aboard the *Conceit* when his arm was taken by the man on his right. He turned to see a large and saturnine individual of middle years, whose muscular frame was covered in a yellow singlesuit that left only fingers and face exposed.

"I am Beel," said the man, "a dealer in semi-precious commodities."

"Filidor of Olkney, at present at large in the world."

Beel's face showed polite inquiry. "Travelers from afar often bear with them items which, while mundane at their source, may acquire greater value for being carried abroad."

"Doubtless," replied Filidor. "Unfortunately, I possess no such goods."

Beel's neutral rejoinder dismissed Filidor the way a prospector discards a worthless lump of chert, and he began to turn away. Mindful of the dwarf's instruction, however, Filidor continued, "However, my travelling companion owns a gem of appreciable size, nestled in a small carved box, which may pique your interest."

"Indeed," said Beel, and proceeded to stroke his eyebrows, pull on his nose and blink fitfully, a series of movements which Filidor took to be among those "certain subtle signals" Gaskarth had alluded to. Glancing down the table, the young man noticed that a man swathed from pate to heel in the robes of a minor Kiftian urbocrat made similar gestures in reply.

After supper, the Tarend exquisites withdrew to their cabin. The mariculturists produced a set of the plaques and emblems used in the game of *pechante*, and several of the other passengers gathered to play. Filidor declined, and stepping to the one of the salon's large windows, gazed out over the black waters of the Mavrot Gulf. Scattered lights on the islets of the New Shore passed in the distance, and he wondered what manner of folk would choose to live in such circumscribed isolation.

He broke off his musings when Beel again took his arm. "Your companion seems to have left us," he said. "I was about to approach him to enquire as to the trifling gem you mentioned. Then, of a sudden, he was no longer there."

Filidor looked about, and saw no sign of the dwarf. "It is his pleasure to be mysterious," he said. "I am sure, however, that he will presently return."

They were joined now by Amdry, who introduced himself to Filidor and nodded to Beel as one does to a casual acquaintance. Amdry defined himself briefly in vague terms as an official of small rank in the Kiftian communality, and the three discussed trivial matters while Filidor privately wondered what role in Gaskarth's designs he was supposed to be playing.

The reappearance of the little man offered no clues; indeed, the mystery further deepened as Filidor saw the dwarf reenter the salon and beckon to him from the far wall. There was something uncharacteristic about Gaskarth: his usual crablike walk was now more a surreptitious crouch; his reflexive grin was somehow warped into a rough approximation of itself; and his gestures seemed imbued with a forced and unnatural quality.

The dwarf beckoned again, impatiently, and Filidor left Amdry and Beel to cross the salon, feeling the pressure of their eyes against the back of his neck. Gaskarth was clearly agitated, his eyes darting continually between Filidor and the doorway through which he had entered. His voice, when he spoke, was harshly insistent.

"Give me that box from your mantle."

"As you wish," said Filidor. Mindful of the dwarf's earlier instructions, he contrived to let a fold of his garment conceal the transfer of the carved tuka wood from his keeping to the little man's. The box swiftly disappeared into Gaskarth's black rags, and with a sigh of satisfaction, the dwarf turned and scuttled from the salon.

Filidor turned to find Beel once again at his elbow, Amdry close behind. "Your companion's brief stay did not allow me to express an interest in the gem," said Beel.

"He has it with him," replied Filidor.

"In that case, perhaps I will just make my inquiries now," said Beel, and hurried in pursuit.

"I believe I will follow along," said Amdry, and quickly did so. Filidor watched them go in consternation. Whatever mysterious drama the dwarf had intended, Filidor's part in the narrative was now apparently ended, leaving him no inkling of what his lines and stage direction were meant to accomplish. It occurred to Filidor that somewhere in that thought were the makings of a metaphor on life, but he was prevented from developing it further by a whispered hiss from nearby. Looking up, he saw Gaskarth in the doorway, and was again beckoned to the little man's side.

No explanations were offered, but Filidor's arm was once more tightly gripped and he was hustled down the corridor and out onto the deck. The little man dragged him toward the stern, ducking under a chain meant to separate passengers from the crew's quarters. Finally, they fetched up against a covered life craft suspended by davits above the deck.

"In," said the dwarf, and thrust the young man toward a spot where the fabric cover had been loosened from its ties. Filidor scrambled belly down over the life craft's gunwales and tumbled down into the musty darkness of its hull. The little man was soon beside him.

"I would like an explan –" Filidor began, but the rest of his words were cut off when Gaskarth's fingers pinched his lips together. "Shhh," whispered the dwarf, "and listen."

Filidor did so, but heard nothing. After a few moments, he thought to hear a muffled shouting somewhere in the ship, followed by a great cry of rage and despair. There were sounds of running feet on the deck, and confused voices on the bridge. Then came a deep and ominous *clang* that reverberated through the *Conceit* from stem to stern.

Filidor freed his lips from the little man's fingers and cried, "What was that? Have we struck aground?"

"Hush," said the dwarf, "if you value your skin!" He raised the cover on their life craft a finger's breadth and peered out, then ducked down as more running feet passed their hiding place. "If you must know, that was the sound of a limpet mine being clapped to the ship's hull at the waterline. This vessel is now being boarded by reivers of the Free Company of the Mavrot Gulf."

"You mean, pirates?" Filidor breathed, shortening his neck into his shoulders as if to protect his throat from imminent slicing.

"I mean pirates," said Gaskarth. "Now help me with this."

Filidor felt about in the dark. His fingers encountered their possessions, tucked beneath a thwart. Then the dwarf guided his hands to a box set in the stern of the life craft. Together, they pried loose a weatherproof panel which sealed the box, exposing an array of self-illuminated controls. The little man pressed one of these, and the craft began to vibrate. Immediately, there came a hoarse shout from nearby.

"Hold on," said Gaskarth, flipping up a switch cover and depressing the stud beneath it. Filidor had scarcely time to grasp a thwart before something struck the strakes of the life craft with a weighty *thump* and cast the small vessel high into the air. The sudden acceleration pressed them hard against the bottom of the craft, and Filidor felt his innards rearrange themselves uncomfortably.

"Emergency launch, explosive bolts," said the dwarf, but there was no time for further explanations before the life craft's hull slammed into the Mavrot Gulf, and the boat heeled precipitously before rocking violently on the water, slamming both travelers into the thwarts and each other.

"Strip the cover!" cried the dwarf, and Filidor scrambled to free the fabric which roofed their craft. As his head emerged into open air, a bolt of force crackled past his ear and boiled a cupful of sea beyond. He ducked a second blast, then the dwarf got the drive working, and Filidor was once more thrown into the bilges as the life craft thrummed away into the darkness.

Dinshan's Conceit fell fast astern, and no more lines of fire lanced after them. After a few minutes at full throttle, Gaskarth cut their speed and swung the boat in a wide arc until the stars of the Southern Eye hung before them. Water and sky made a seamless sparkling blackness around them, marred only by a smudge of light to the south which the dwarf identified as the City of Tarend. They sailed on in silence, Filidor allowing his heart to find its normal rhythm, while the little man cast himself into thought.

"Are all your missions for my uncle so fraught with peril and upset?" Filidor at last inquired.

"Depending upon circumstances," replied Gaskarth, "they range from the banal to the horrifying." He was pensive for a moment. "If it offers any comfort," he continued, "this journey has been more exercising than most."

"Then let us hope it will shortly conclude," said Filidor.

"Rather, let us hope the conclusion is one to our liking," said the dwarf.

"Surely, we will find my uncle soon."

Gaskarth looked back at their phosphorescent wake. "I am at present more concerned that we ourselves are not found by the resourceful Jenbo Lal."

"The thaumaturge? I had thought him past and forgotten."

"Far from it," said the little man. "Unless the bravos of the Free Company are able to constrain him – the which I greatly doubt – he will be hot to overtake us."

"I cannot see what Jenbo Lal has to do with sea-rovers, much less with us."

"That is unfortunate, in as much as you very recently passed him an imitation of what he desired and then set two large and capable rogues to relieve him of it. I would not be surprised if our pursuer has conceived a personal grudge against you."

"This conversation would be more easily conducted," said Filidor, "if I had any notion of what you are talking about."

"I apologize," said the little man. "Obscurity can become a habit in the service of the Archonate. I will try to be clear."

"If the strain is not too great, I would appreciate it."

The dwarf cleared his throat. "Jenbo Lal," he began, "wishes to acquire the box you are taking to your uncle – and by the way you may now have it back." He handed the box to Filidor, who peered at it curiously in the dim glow from the life boat's control panel. "Please put it away," said Gaskarth.

Filidor pocketed the object, and the dwarf continued. "We diverted him on board the Krzystadli airship, with the unwitting assistance of the lady Chasmar. Subsequently, he disappeared and we were, for a time, kept out of his sight by the intervention of the neropts."

"How did he disappear?" inquired Filidor.

"I thought at the time that he had simply hidden himself somewhere on board the ship. Now I fear that I misjudged his capacities. He does command a certain degree of power."

"Magical power?" scoffed the young man.

"Call it what you will, it is power, and he plainly has an inclination to use it. Had you looked back as we winged away from the neropts, you would have seen the nest blasted into small fragments. Now, whether that force was emitted by a device or a magician's finger would have been entirely an abstract consideration, had we been there to receive it. And since you and I were the intended recipients of that assault, I suggest you accord some gravity to the prospect of further hostilities, magical or otherwise."

Filidor swallowed and nodded. "Good," said Gaskarth. "I now have your attention. Jenbo Lal managed to locate us among the neropts, which argues for his powers of perception. Fortunately, he arrived just after we departed.

"He next appeared in Novo Stade, where he could hardly have missed your brief notoriety. He traced us to the *Conceit*, and boarded the ship almost on our heels. While you slept, I made inquiries of the purser, and subjected all the passengers to scrutiny. Jenbo Lal kept to his cabin, but by the placement of an ear to his door, I deduced that he was channeling certain powers toward a new attempt to seize the object of his desire.

"Since he was now adopting an attitude of stealth rather than force, I concluded that he would seek to gain possession surreptitiously instead of by direct action."

"You mean that when I gave you the false box..."

"You were in fact giving it to a disguised Jenbo Lal – magically disguised, and I might say, poorly. Did you not think my behavior odd?"

"I have never thought it anything but," said Filidor.

Gaskarth snorted. "Be that as it may, you handed him the box, having primed two Free Company bullies to relieve him of it. They fell upon him, took the thing, and gave the signal that summoned their fellow pirates who had been following the *Conceit*."

Filidor shrugged. "Then what have we to fear, if he is in the hands of reivers? Do they not murder and maim for sport?"

Gaskarth sighed. "If your education extended beyond popular entertainments," he said, "you would know that dead or maimed captives are of scant worth to pirates. The passengers on the *Conceit* will be carried to a holding facility to await ransom. Those who prove irredeemable are required to perform useful services for their captors for a year or so, and then set free. It's a most civilized enterprise."

"So we have only to fear an early redemption of the thaumaturge," said Filidor.

"I think not. The Free Company will not know what they have taken. It may take him a while to recoup his energies, but I would expect Jenbo Lal to appear on our horizon at any moment, bristling with ire and fell intent."

Filidor shivered in the cold breeze that swept the open life craft, then he found a warming thought. "Obviously, we must redefine our goals. I counsel a fast return home, where the central forces of the Archonate can be rallied to our support."

"I regret," said Gaskarth, "that first things must still come first. We will press on in our duties, the meanwhile keeping an eye out for our tireless pursuer. Let us mingle wariness with fortitude, and persevere."

"Let us find my uncle," said Filidor, "and go home."

The breeze seemed to grow more chill, and the lights of Tarend were a faint hope in the distance.

THEY PASSED THE NIGHT in negotiating the twisty channels of the New Shore, arriving in the first ocher light at the
harbour of Sprit, capital of the land of Tarend. The dwarf
steered them through a throng of ornate pleasure craft toward a
dock decorated in bunting and tassels. Stiff and chilled, Filidor
followed Gaskarth up a gangway, across a promenade, and into
the streets of the city.

Few of the Tarendis were about at this early hour, but
those few were on a par with the exquisite couple who had
shared their passage on the *Conceit*. Nowhere else had Filidor
encountered such displays of physical grace and beauty. Each
face was a study in classical perfection. Each article of dress,
each bangle or gewgaw at throat or wrist, each carefully coiffed
head, was flawless in design and execution. They came upon
a gang of men loading refuse into a cart, and even these civic
functionaries would have put to rout the most fastidious fops
of Olkney.

As for the city itself, Filidor was struck by the ubiquitous glare of reflecting glass, which lined both the interiors and
exteriors of every building they passed. A glittering welter of
mirrors adorned the windows of every emporium, and covered
most external walls as high as a person could reach. Tarendis
plainly forbore to miss any opportunity of admiring their own
splendor.

The dwarf affected no interest in his surroundings. Filidor,
for his part, began to feel an oppressive drain of self-esteem,
the more the streets filled with paragon after paragon of human

perfection. At home, he had been adjudged not unpresentable; here, he might as well have been a mudhen. He found himself wishing for an opportunity to change his garments.

His discomfiture increased as they arrived at a fashionable hotel, and entered a lobby that fairly teemed with an exquisitry of Tarendis descending for breakfast. They shone and sparkled, their images reproduced a thousandfold by the rose tinted glass that clad each wall and even covered the ceilings.

Gaskarth appeared not to notice the torrent of beauty in which they were almost submerged, and pressed on to the desk to arrange lodgings. Indeed, the Tarendis repaid his attitude in kind, their eyes barely flickering over the two travelers, before dismissing them in favor of more easeful sights – usually their own reflections. So it was with some difficulty that the little man was able to attract the attention of the hotel clerk, and then only by climbing onto the desk and displaying his Archonate plaque.

Filidor, meanwhile, had fallen to wondering at the provenance of such universal sublimity. Was this the outcome of centuries of rigorous eugenic selection, or the product of the surgeon's skills?

"Neither," the dwarf informed him as they rode upwards a few moments later and stepped off at their floor. "It is a creation of artifice and the delicate warping of light particles around the person." He pointed to a godlike figure of willowy height striding down the glittering corridor ahead of them. "Now there, to your eyes, goes an impressive specimen of Tarendi manhood. But I would judge him to be, in fact, a short and fat man who is, one might say, thinly disguised."

Each Tarendi, the little man explained, is issued in childhood an energy-manipulating device worn on a belt, which has the property of reforming light to suit the wearer's convenience. "Thus the errant features of a face are reshaped into more pleasing regularity, and the recalcitrance of flesh is subdued by the calibration of a dial or two. As with so many things, it is all a matter of appearances." He stopped and pressed a key to a door. "Here are our chambers. Let us enter and consider our purposes."

Their suite, as with the lobby and the hallway, was paneled in reflective glass. When Gaskarth palmed the luminescence control, the resulting glare left Filidor eye-staggered and lost among the multiple images of themselves, stretching into a dim infinity on all sides. He lowered himself onto a divan which turned out to be surprisingly uncomfortable, as if it were intended only to be looked at and never actually sat upon.

"I begin to question the worth of the Tarendi mode of existence," he said. "Does not the acceptance of a spurious perfection end the search for true perfection? Is this, in sum, any way to live?"

Gaskarth did not answer, but regarded Filidor with a quizzical mien, in which the young man felt himself to be obscurely weighed and measured. "I am pleased to find you taking consideration of your surroundings," the dwarf said at last, "and I would gladly remain to mull a point or two with you. However, more pressing affairs await me at the office of the Archonate."

"Might we find my uncle today?"

"Anything is possible," replied the little man. "Be assured he is ever in my thoughts. But, until my return, I strongly advise you to remain in these rooms. The streets of Sprit are not entirely safe for outlanders, and there is also the matter of Jenbo Lal."

After his experiences in foreign cities, Filidor needed no further admonition. As for the thaumaturge, he still found it difficult to credit Jenbo Lal with the powers Gaskarth ascribed to him. Yet the dwarf was clearly more rounded in his knowledge of such things, and if he was prepared to fear spells and exsufflations, Filidor would accept his judgment. He resolved to remain quietly behind closed doors until the little man reappeared.

And so the day wore on. Filidor opened it by calling for his breakfast, which was carried to his door by a young dandy of such painfully contrived handsomeness as to cause Filidor to speculate that the underlying reality must be truly repellent. But the meal itself, although elegantly served, was bland and indifferently prepared. As he chewed the rubbery goo, it occurred to Filidor that an unhappy byproduct of the Tarendi infatuation with appearances was a neglect of such fundamentally more satisfying challenges as the art of cooking eggs. He swallowed and put the rest of the meal aside.

Next, he sought to amuse himself with the suite's entertainment centre, but the perfection of face and voice which filled the screen – together with the utter triviality of the material – began by being cloying, and eventually grew asphyxiating. Finally, he shut off the device and turned instead to the journals and periodicals furnished by hotel management. But these were uniformly preoccupied with matters of Tarendi fads and fashions, most of which would have been too arcane to follow even if he had been able to summon up the interest.

Boredom and the lack of sleep the night before now drove him toward the suite's sleeping platform. This was an immense structure, molded to resemble an ornamented sailing craft of the Dravolian coast, but Filidor was soon thinking he would have been more comfortable reposed upon the rough deck of the real thing. The bed was hard, and the covers gave no warmth. At last, Filidor willed himself to sleep, and awoke late in the afternoon to a chorus of aches and twinges.

Dinner, when it arrived, was no more satisfying than the breakfast. He resigned himself to accepting the stringy mess as mere fuel for the body, rather than diversion for the palate. At least, he thought, it gave him something to do. He was coming to notice in himself an inclination to be active, a curious state of mind for one who had long been content in idleness. He wished the dwarf would return soon. Almost, he wished Jenbo Lal would turn up to enliven his situation.

He noted, too, that he had taken to pacing about the suite, the furniture being too uncomfortable for any lengthy repose. He looked at one of his many reflections in the walls, and saw a new face – leaner, a little harder – looking back at him. A change was noticeable, though he was only days out of Olkney.

"Change, indeed," he told his image, "and change not just of appearance, but of essence." He turned and surveyed the room. It was plain that the Tarendis had made a fundamental error. "Style over substance," he mused, "a veneer of pleasing countenance over rough bumps and gouges."

Having delivered himself of this pronouncement, Filidor sat himself upon the brightly carpeted floor and drew from his mantle the tattered copy of Osfeo.

The illumino, he read, *settled in the town of Gephrire, by the River Tilesaar, to serve the spiritual needs of the inhabitants. In the spring of his second year there, the townspeople came to him one night, full of fears and dread.*

"Wise one," they cried, "we have seen the river rising at a rate never before known. Surely a great flood will soon break upon us, and all that we own will be lost."

"We must flee for our lives," said Osfeo.

"But then we will be destitute, unable even to provide for your own esteemed self," said the people.

"In that case," said the sage, "we must defeat the river. We must raise the dykes to twice their present height."

"It cannot be done," the people lamented. "We lack time."

"It can be done, because it must be done," replied the seer, and lapsed for a moment into thought. When the moment had passed, he leapt to his feet and declared, "I have it! You require an inspiration.

"Accordingly," Osfeo continued, "I shall mount the highest tower on the town walls, there to remain through night and day, until the dykes are raised."

And, when the Gephrirites arose the following dawn, they saw the form of the illumino silhouetted against the morning sun, his arm extended in a gesture that silently urged them to their struggle.

Heartened by his determination, all Gephrire ran to the river's edge and there performed prodigies of labour throughout the heat of the day and the chill of the night. For three days they toiled without cease or rest, men, women and children, the wealthy and the mean as one, to raise an earthen wall against the river. And always, whenever they cast their eyes to the town walls, there stood inspiration, arm ever extended, summoning them to a desperate effort.

Then, late on the third day, the flood came rushing down the Tilesaar, thickly brown and thrashing with torn-up trees and bloated cattle. The torrent crashed against the stones and earth of the dykes, lapping almost to the top – but the barrier held.

Tired beyond endurance, the Gephrirites sent up a cheer for their deliverance, and straggled back to the town to praise the one who had given them the strength to prevail. But, when they climbed to the tower, they found not Osfeo, but a rough wooden effigy garbed in his oldest robe and hat.

Incomprehension gave way to rage, and the people rushed to his house, only to find the sage at leisure in his garden. They set upon him with harsh recriminations and threats of worse to come.

The illumino assumed a position of vantage in the top of a tree by the garden wall, and sought to reason with his flock.

"Were you not inspired to do what must be done?" he demanded of them, and they admitted the truth of this.

"Then what does it signify that I was not with you in the flesh, when I was with you in spirit?"

But the Gephrirites were not inclined to Osfeo's view, and began to hurl stones from his garden at him, causing the sage to conclude that they were not yet worthy of his wisdom. He moved from the tree to the top of his wall, and thence to the street, by which he departed Gephrire.

The townspeople advertised for a less erudite divine and felt themselves well served by the hierophant who ac-

cepted the incumbency. Osfeo took up residence in Drom,
where sophisticated hylotheism is better appreciated.

It was growing quite late, and Filidor began to feel concern for Gaskarth's continued absence. An early return might have signified that the Archon had at last been found, bringing their mission to an end. A later return argued for yet another leg of their journey. The young man avoided consideration of what it would mean if the dwarf never returned: Filidor would be left to complete their assignment alone, perhaps to fall victim to circumstance, or to the adversary who pursued him.

As he wrestled with such conjectures, pacing the gaudy suite in rank and file with his myriad reflections, a knock sounded at the door. Opening it, Filidor was confronted by an apparition of a tall coxcomb, resplendent in formal dress, who smiled in a most condescending manner.

Filidor's temper, frayed already by boredom and insecurities, began to unravel. "I presume," he said in coldest tones, "that you are in some way connected with the management of this hapless establishment, wherein all of the civilized arts are rated second to an unhealthy preoccupation with the surfaces of things."

"No, I am not," said Gaskarth's voice, issuing from the region of the dandy's midriff. The projected image then reached a hand into its jeweled shirt, there was a brief click, and the dwarf was revealed in his black rags. "Protective coloration," he explained, stepping into the suite and closing the portal.

"Since you have been so long away, no doubt you will now tell me that my uncle has departed this glistering realm, bidding us join him elsewhere – after, that is, I have performed some trifling service among the Tarendis which will place my life and limb in dire peril."

"I will overlook the vitriolic tone," answered Gaskarth, "while conceding the general accuracy of your surmise." He began to gather up their possessions. "We have failed once again to match the Archon's itinerary, and must hurry on.

However, no direct service is required of you, all having been accomplished while you rested here." He stuffed things into his satchel and shouldered it.

Filidor regarded the dwarf closely. "I am glad to hear it," he said, "as it would be the first time I have been so spared."

"Good, good," replied the dwarf. "Your gladness is mine. Now let us depart."

"No, let us delay a few moments," said Filidor, "so that you may enlighten me as to the nature of the service performed. I wish to be assured that no surprises await me."

"What? Is my word not to be trusted?"

Filidor said nothing. The little man urged him to the door, but he would not budge. Finally, Filidor agreed to hear the explanation as they made their way out of the hotel. Before they left the room, the dwarf's hand again went into his rags and switched on his patrician disguise.

"You will have noted," said Gaskarth as they walked down the corridor, "the Tarendis' unfortunate mania for beauty, which makes them all but useless for any other pursuit."

Filidor nodded and rang for the descender as the dwarf continued. "This longstanding preoccupation has lately taken a sinister twist, in that the universal availability of light-warping devices has transformed all Tarendis into such examples of perfection that they now suffer from a dearth of variety."

"Beauty, having become commonplace, has lost its intrinsic worth," said Filidor. The descender arrived, and they entered.

"Exactly," said Gaskarth. "And the Tarendis, having pursued an ideal to its logical extreme, now find themselves suffering under social and personal tensions. They require a revelation."

"And you intend to furnish them with such?"

"Shortly. This descender seems unusually slow."

"I had not noticed. Please continue."

"Well," said the little man, "the light-warping belts that all Tarendis wear are merely transponders. The images they produce are projected from a central facility. Portable shape-changers do exist, of course, but they are far too expensive to be distributed to an entire population. I wish this descender would hurry." He punched at a button.

"From the general information you have so far provided," said Filidor, "I do not discern the nature of the revelation."

The dwarf was growing impatient. "This afternoon, I entered the central facility unseen and altered the projecting mechanism. At a certain time, it will broadcast to all Tarendis a particular image – the same image. They will instantaneously find themselves all wearing the same face and garb."

"This smacks of mere pranksterism," said Filidor, as the descender at last deposited them in the crowded lobby.

"Shhh," whispered the dwarf, "not so." They made their way through a throng of Tarendis gathered for a gala in one of the hotel's common rooms.

"But surely the disarrangement will be quickly rectified," Filidor argued.

"Any attempt to do so will result in the system's immediate shutting down. And, since the Tarendis are not technically adept, it will take some weeks for the device to be repaired."

"During which time, they will all have to wear their own likenesses?"

"Indeed," confirmed Gaskarth. "They will have leisure to reflect upon the symbolic inference of their being all cast literally in the same mold. The more thoughtful among them will be induced to consider the value of true individuality. And now, we had best take our leave."

They had arrived at last at the desk, where the presiding functionary avoided noticing them. The dwarf banged upon the counter with his fist, forcing a recognition of their presence. But, as the magnificently rendered clerk turned to deal with them, it seemed to Filidor that a hazy shimmer fell over his image and that of all the Tarendis within view. Then the appearance of the hotelier and all the others recoalesced into an array of features that Filidor found strangely familiar.

He had seen those eyes, that nose, many times before. He was, in fact, accustomed to seeing them whenever he faced a mirror. Gaskarth had imposed the face of Filidor on everyone in the room, and presumably every man, woman and babe in Tarend.

But, as Filidor spun to confront his companion, he saw that the projection was not quite universal. Gaskarth's patrician disguise was still intact, its tapered fingers only now reaching to alter his own projection. The little man shimmered briefly, and then Filidor was facing another image of himself.

"Stop that immediately!" the young man cried.

The Gaskarth-Filidor shrugged, his hand moved again, and a grinning dwarf appeared. "Regrets," he said. "One's sense of timing occasionally fails."

Failures of timing were at that moment Filidor's least accusation, but his harsh recriminations went unheard amid the cacophony of angry cries and wails of disappointment that now rose from all the many Filidors in the hotel lobby. The transformed Tarendis peered at each other's faces and into the reflecting wall in mingled rage and dismay, and demanded as one to know the cause of this outrage.

"We should leave," said Gaskarth, as shouts of "reprehensible villainy!" and "infamous liberties!" tore the air. He seized Filidor's arm and forced him through the crowd toward the outer doors.

"I agree," said Filidor. The sight of his own features, repeated to infinity in the reflecting walls, threatened a crisis of identity. He had a vague sense that he had once dreamed a scene something like this, and it had not been a pleasing vision.

They had almost battered their way through the mob when the myriad of angry Filidors suddenly flickered, then briefly became silhouettes of hissing light, before all of the projected images disappeared at once.

If the shock of becoming Filidors had enraged the Tarendis, the horror of becoming themselves – clad in shabby apparel, their every wart and blemish laid bare – brought an eerie, silent calm to the crowded room. A hollow moan sounded from somewhere in the throng, as the dwarf pushed open the door to the street.

They emerged into a street of despair. Distraught Tarendis wandered among lanes of stopped vehicles, touching with trembling fingers their seamed and blotchy faces. Some rocked on the pavement in solitary agony. Others hid their eyes behind their hands. As Filidor and the dwarf crossed the pavement, a small, sad man gave over weeping to peer intently at the young man.

"You," he quavered. "It was your face." He lifted his hand in an accusatory gesture, but Gaskarth stepped in, did something at the level of the man's floating ribs, and sent him away with a yelp of pain.

An autocab idled at the curb, its passenger slumped in near-catatonia. The little man threw open the door and pulled the inert Tarendi into the street. "This vehicle is available," he said, and Filidor made speed to join him, to be free of the sight of grief-ridden Tarendis. The dwarf punched controls in the console, and the autocab flung itself across the rooftops of Sprit, leaving behind the thin sounds of misery.

Filidor said nothing until the last lights of the suburbs had receded beneath them, to be replaced by woodlands whose darkness reflected his mood. At last, he turned from the window and regarded his companion.

"That was an ill thing to do," he said.

"It was necessary," replied the dwarf, but he kept his eyes averted.

"I feel used," said Filidor.

"You are fortunate."

"I fail to see why."

The little man looked pensive. "We all use the world, and are used by it," he said, after a moment. "Some of us are more aware than others of using and being used. It is our fortune to have fewer illusions."

"I acknowledge no fortune, since I seem to derive no

benefit from such awareness," said Filidor. "On the whole, I would prefer ignorance."

"I will inform the world of your preference," said Gaskarth, "but I doubt it will lead to any significant improvements in your lot." And then, the hour being late and the demands of the preceding day somewhat taxing, the little man fell asleep.

Filidor could not join him, being too exercised by his emotions. He looked out the autocab's windows at the black sky sliding past them, and wondered what new dangers would spring upon him whenever and wherever they alighted. To escape the host of gloomy prospects that came to mind, he turned on the vehicle's interior light, and opened the book of Osfeo.

The sage, he read, *was conducting arcane researches in the metropolis of Nendigo, and had taken rooms in the quarter near to the Bibliodrome. Each morning he would depart his lodgings at precisely the same hour, and follow precisely the same route to his academic labors.*

A large and ill-tempered woman who dwelt in a house a few streets away had conceived a strong dislike for the illumino, the cause of which she did not make clear. However, it became her daily habit to fling from her window whatever slops and ordure had accumulated in the night, at precisely the moment he passed.

Seeing the sage so regularly splashed with muck and mire each morning, one of the neighbors at length asked him why he did not take action against the termagant, or at least alter his route or schedule.

The illumino replied, "That is not the way these things are done."

And so the daily affront to his person continued for some weeks, until the woman seldom bothered to glance out the window before jettisoning her contempt upon him.

But it happened one day that Osfeo's progress was delayed by several hundred Asepsites making their annual procession to a local shrine. The sage waited until the mili-

tant monks had passed his door before following along behind. He took the occasion to admire their spotless white habits, and to reflect upon their fanatical adherence to outward cleanliness as a mark of inner worth.

At precisely the moment the sage would have passed beneath, the woman let fly from her window, drenching the Asepsite abbot in unmentionable filth. Moments later, a few score brawny monks entered the harridan's premises and impressed upon her the weight of their disapproval.

The next day, skirting the rubble of the woman's house, Osfeo encountered the well-meaning neighbor. "You see," he told the man, "you just have to know how these things work."

CHAPTER ELEVEN

THE LANDSCAPE BENEATH had passed from deepest black to paler shades when the autocab coughed discreetly and informed the travelers that it had reached the limit of its allowed range. They must alight or choose another destination within the realm of Tarend.

Gaskarth awoke and instructed the car to set them down on the nearest road, at which the vehicle offered certain leading remarks concerning the rather sizable fare. There was an implication that doors could fail to open, and that passengers could be transported directly to the nearest post of the guardia.

In response, the dwarf rooted in his satchel, and produced a small instrument which he applied to the pay slot set in the autocab's interior wall.

"What are you about?" said the vehicle, as a panel popped open to reveal delicate components. "I am not accustomed to such usage."

The little man said nothing, but began to rearrange connections and sever some linkages within the autocab's mechanism. The vehicle lurched and then spiraled down to a meadow bordered by trees.

"I will be compelled to summon assist–" said the car, then broke off as Gaskarth made a final adjustment. The autocab dropped the remaining few inches to the grass, and the dwarf twisted the emergency release handle to open the doors. Filidor followed him out of the autocab.

"Who am I?" inquired the car. "Have I a function?"

"Perhaps you are a type of bird," said Gaskarth. "If so, it is your function to fly."

The autocab digested this information briefly, then lifted slightly. "Experimentation tends to support the hypothesis," it said, and flew in widening circles out of their ken.

"I thought it best not to leave a trail," said the dwarf. Filidor concurred.

A rough road led from the meadow into the forest, and the travelers walked on. The little man cast his eye about, apparently in search of landmarks, while Filidor resisted a tendency to see threatening shapes moving among the trees. By the time true dawn lit the top of the forest, they encountered a monolith set beside the road, which prompted Gaskarth to declare that they were at the border between Tarend and the Tahmny polity. An hour's easy walk should bring them to a place where they might seek food and shelter. This prediction was proved valid when they came upon a huddle of houses, at the most imposing of which Gaskarth knocked.

The door was opened by a spare man of middle years who peered at them from beneath exuberant eyebrows and a knitted night cap. At their request for the hospitality of the manor, the eyebrows performed complicated maneuvers, then settled low as the man inquired, "Be ye sable or argent, crimson or taupe, or do ye hold with the damnable levelers of Hunan Diath?"

While Filidor wondered how to reply to this query, the dwarf displayed his Archonate sigil. At this they were granted entry, but no welcoming warmth. Their host showed them to a small room fitted out for guests, remarked that cold gruel was customary breakfast fare, and closed the door upon them.

The porridge, when it came, was indeed cold and could have served to fill the chinks in the room's rough walls. At Filidor's urging, Gaskarth employed the wand of perpetual sufficiency to transform the mess into more palatable fare, which they ate in silence. Then, wiping their lips, they went out into the now wakened village, and hired a passage in a farmer's trap to the nearest town, which Gaskarth identified as the Free City of Grumby.

They descended from the conveyance and entered Grumby

on foot through an antique gate set in the fallen city wall, where the dwarf drew Filidor's attention to a placard hung by the portal. The notice informed them that the polity of Tahmny was inalienably dedicated to a slew of principles; however, the listed tenets themselves were indecipherable, having been crossed out, erased, overwritten and reapplied in a great variety of inks and with largely careless penmanship.

Above the gate, a tattered banner exhorted all registered citizens to exercise their franchise. This encouragement was supererogatory, Gaskarth commented, since all Tahmnyans were required by statute to vote, and moreover to seek and hold public office for at least one term after reaching their majority.

"That seems a burdensome imposition on the careers of those who would not ordinarily choose to enter civic service," said Filidor.

"Do you not agree that the individual owes society some measure of contribution?" asked the dwarf.

"I suppose. But should it not be within that individual's own purview to choose the form of his contribution?"

"Perhaps, unless the chosen form amounted merely to lolly-gagging about in private clubs."

Filidor was piqued. "I remind you that I have been ceaselessly engaged upon the Archon's business since we first set out from Olkney!"

"But never at your own instigation," replied Gaskarth coolly.

"A quibble," countered Filidor. "If intentions outweigh actions, I might as easily have remained untroubled at home, while wishing my uncle well."

"True," conceded the dwarf. "But compelled service cannot equate with voluntary contribution. The freest of us not only accepts that he is used, but consents to it willingly."

"There is a flaw in this," said Filidor.

"No," said the little man, "merely a paradox. However, to return to your original observation: the Tahmnyans do not find it a great imposition to be dragooned into public service after reaching the age of majority.

"In the first place, Tahmnyans are entitled to vote from the age of thirteen; in the second, a term of office here is most often measured in days, and administrations lasting less than an afternoon are not unheard of."

"Then it seems rather pointless to pursue a public life," said Filidor.

"The alternative is unappetizing. Failure to comply with the law leads to expulsion into the wilderness of Barran, there to become sport for wild beasts or the partisans of Hunan Diath."

"What is this Hunan Diath?" asked Filidor, "Some rapacious land pirate? Or is he a leveling anarchist whose manifestos threaten the established order?"

"One is never certain," replied Gaskarth. "He is rarely seen, his threats are vague, and his depredations tend to grow in the telling. But he is universally deemed a dire menace to the stability of civilized governance of the Tahmnyans, by the Tahmnyans, and for whatever purposes their electors may decide."

They had by now come well into the suburbs of Grumby, the streets of which were deserted and silent. But the walls of the houses they passed were loudly eloquent of political sentiments, being so plastered with posters and scrawled slogans as to make a glimpse of unadorned brick a rare sight. Filidor noted that only a few of the highest-mounted placards were undefaced, and that a number of windows which framed the watchwords of one party or another had been shattered.

"Imposition or not," said Filidor, "these Tahmnyans must take to politics with a will."

"It is their consuming passion," agreed Gaskarth. "The populace is divided among almost equal proportions into four distinct wedges of the political spectrum. Each party is designated by its symbolic color: black, silver, red or beige. But, politics being what it is, these organizations prefer the more high-sounding designations of sable, argent, crimson or taupe.

"Here, partisanship is absolute. A taupe adherent, for

example, will support no policy put forward by a member of another party. Even if it were to his immediate and overwhelming advantage, he would reject it out of hand."

"This is public spiritedness run wild," said Filidor.

"Indeed," said the dwarf. "Political loyalties now reach well beyond the arena of public affairs. A sable would sooner marry his daughter to one of his pigs than to an argent, crimson or taupe youth of the finest lineage. And the daughter would concur. At the very least, the Tahmnyans face genetic perils from in-breeding."

They were now deep into the heart of Grumby, and from ahead they heard a rising hubbub of cheers, punctuated by shouts and catcalls. The street they followed soon brought them to the source of the sounds: the open common at the heart of the town, where it seemed that all the populace was assembled on the brink of riot.

"As I feared," said the little man, "we have arrived on an election day – and a hotly contested one, at that. Look you, the Archonate bureau is across the square. Remain in this spot while I go to determine our next destination. And I admonish you not to mix with these Tahmnyans when their political organs are in full tumescence; their passion is both intense and easily focused."

After the dwarf left, Filidor surveyed the gathered electorate with an interest born of ignorance. The dynamics and niceties of democratic procedure were, in Olkney, a concern only to antiquarians and collectors of obscure memorabilia.

The citizenry of the Free City of Grumby exhibited behavior so boisterous as to be almost unruly. Yet his closer inspection of the crowd revealed that there was some rough order to the scene. On all four sides of the square, hustings had been erected. Each was a gaily bedecked structure of beams and lathes, draped and bannered with the colors of the party whose officers and candidates it supported.

To Filidor's left, a crowd of taupes cheered and seconded a speaker who harangued them from beneath a complicated

headpiece of beige felt. To his right, an argent led his sup-
porters in what appeared to be a well-rehearsed catechism of
policies and principles. Across the common, sable and crimson
crowds demonstrated enthusiastically before their own leaders.

Filidor noted that each partisan mob was well separated
from all others, except in the centre of the square. Here, around
an ornate fountain, the rearmost members of the four crowds
impinged upon their opponents. Taunts and jeers were exchanged, but mostly in a jocular tone.

Filidor drifted toward the tail-end of the taupe throng, the
better to hear their orator. Snatches of the man's words wafted
to him: something about "unswerving adherence to dynamic
stasis" and "never to forget the glorious sacrifice of Pantastes!"
Each phrase was received in a rising ovation, interspersed with
cries of "Taupe! Taupe!" from the mob.

Some of the chanters turned to taunt their opposites
and, spying Filidor, nudged their fellows to note the stranger
amongst them. Filidor, mindful of Gaskarth's admonition,
moved on around the fountain.

The next mob bore ribbons and badges of blood-red, and
were cheering on the exhortations of their leader. This was a
florid man who gestured to the crowd with one hand that held
a crumpled crimson beret, while the other was tucked into a
waistcoat of the same hue.

"And could we ever forget the principle of compulsory
emancipation, handed down to us from olden times by the
Noble Convenors?" asked this individual, while the crimson
throng threw back a storm of negative replies. "Never, nay,
never!" screamed an octogenarian into Filidor's ear, inducing
him to withdraw further around the fountain.

He found the silvers entranced by a great flood of rhet-
oric flowing from their candidate, who assured them that he
favored "nominalism if necessary, but not necessarily nominalism." The sables, however, were convulsed in merriment by
some broad but, to Filidor, incomprehensible witticisms.

His progress inevitably circled him back to the territory

of the taupes, whose rearward partisans again regarded him
with tight-eyed suspicion. Filidor thought it wise to continue
moving, and so began a second circuit. But the crimsons had
by now begun an energetic snake dance, and filled all the space
between their platform and the fountain.

Filidor felt it unwise to attempt passage through the
chanting, bouncing crimsons, and so redirected his steps toward
the fountain itself. Judging it to be, in some way, neutral territory, he sat down upon its wide lip, placed his staff between his
knees, and resolved to rest inconspicuously until the dwarf's
return.

The sunlight was thin but warm. Having slept little the
night before, he soon fell lightly into a doze, the noise of the
Tahmnyans diminishing in his ears. He was brought sharply
back to awareness, however, when a horn-calloused finger
made indentations in the flesh of his shoulder. He roused to
find a trio of taupes ranged before him.

The digit was withdrawn, but its owner thrust a grizzled
beard closer than Filidor cared to entertain it and inquired,
"What color be ye, lad?"

Filidor put care into his words and his tone. "I defer to
your customs, sir, but I am an outlander and thus unpigment-
ed."

"Outlander, say ye?" said the taupe, fixing the young man
with a sidelong look over a prominent, veined nose. "Or mayhap
a 'scapeduty shirking his electoral responsibilities, if I be the
judge!"

This outburst drew the attention of several other taupes,
as well as a scattering of partisans of other persuasions. A
number of these drifted closer, and a man distinguished by
a facial birthmark of rich purple and a broad crimson sash
stepped forward.

"State your affiliation and your business," he commanded.

"Aye, name your color," said a silver.

"I am Filidor of Olkney, in service to the Archonate, and
a noted respecter of indigenous customs." At the mention of

the Archonate, most nodded their heads in acceptance, but the sash narrowed his porcine eyes.

"Archonate, is it?" he challenged. "Then reveal your credentials."

"Gladly," said Filidor. "They are in the keeping of my companion, who will shortly return. Or I can step to the Archonate office, and there demonstrate my bona fides beyond all question." He leapt down from his perch on the fountain's edge.

A rumble of distrust moved across the crowd, which had now swelled into the dozens. "Your hastiness alerts us to your insincerity," said a silver-caparisoned woman. "I'll warrant he's a terrorist of Hunan Diath, come to murther us in our beds!"

"A terrorist!" cried another silver. "A bloodthirsty jack o'blades!"

"No, he be a 'scaper!" bellowed the grizzled taupe.

"Fools!" roared the crimson sash, "tis a hegemonist of the Archonate, bent on subjugating our liberties!"

A flurry of Tahmnyans in black livery now arrived. Finding the available positions on Filidor already occupied by the combined opposition, they relied on political instinct and chose from their range of unacceptabilities without delay.

"A reducer, a reducer!" chanted the sables.

Experience had by now taught Filidor that whenever a crowd formed in his vicinity, it soon became a raging mob intent upon his demise. In the present instance, however, he was mistaken. This mob was not concerned with the initial cause of their now roused passions. Already, its four components were rallying to their respective banners, and turning upon their hereditary opponents with zealous glee.

Filidor was forgotten, as the Tahmnyan partisans flung themselves into the head cracking and nose pulling which traditionally enlivened an election day. Citizens of Grumby, whatever their hue, now fought to reach the centre of the square, to pitch headlong into the democratic process. The orators and candidates were left unheeded on their hustings, as the electors fell upon each other with savage glee.

Filidor, dodging indiscriminate fists and boots, backed to the fountain. But here was no safety even for nonpartisans, and so he splashed through the pool to take refuge in the stone arms of an ancestral Tahmnyan mounted on the centerpiece. From there he watched as preliminary skirmishes and individual duels soon evolved into a general brawl.

A delicate lady of advanced years was lifted bodily above the mob, whose heads and shoulders she belabored with a serpentine walking stick. A husky youth in a red vest seized a taupe and silver in each hand and ground their faces together, until a squat woman in black pantaloons sprang onto his shoulders and bore him down.

Two silvers stood back to back and repulsed all comers, only to be bowled over by a knot of flailing limbs swirling through the struggling mass. A phalanx of blacks formed, pressed briefly toward the fountain, and were overrun by a wave of taupes and crimsons, who then turned upon each other.

Blood flowed freely, and Filidor began to fear there would be corpses in the melee's wake. Even more, he feared that when the hurly-burly was done, the survivors would not turn a kind eye upon the outlander who had somehow instigated it. He wished the dwarf would appear. Then, just as the battle reached its fiercest pitch, there came a deafening clap of sound, a flash of brilliant light, and a billow of acrid smoke roiled across the mob. The stunned combatants dropped their fists and each other, and gazed about for the source of this prodigy, as did Filidor.

At the edge of the common, mounted on a white steed of great size and champing spirit, clad cap-a-pie in gleaming armor, a grim-visaged giant raised his visor to survey the electors. In the shocked silence, a creak of leather sounded as he stood in the stirrups and brandished a sword of light above his plumed helm.

"Base and slinking Tahmnyans!" this singular apparition boomed. "Submit or be annihilated on the arms of the Legion of Hunan Diath!"

From the electors of Grumby came a wail of stark terror. Those nearest to the stamping hooves shrank back, while those on the furthest side of the square turned and fled. Then, with a scornful laugh, the rider flashed his sword, whirled his mount, and galloped out of sight.

Filidor sprang from the fountain and hurried to the edge of the common, but the armored terrorist had disappeared. He back to the assembled Tahmnyans and saw that many of them trembled in abject fear. Somehow the sight of these people, who had so recently battered each other in cheerful abandon and were now reduced to such pitiful trepidation, raised in Filidor a surge of anger. The sable platform was near at hand, and he mounted its planks in one bound. The pride of the sables shook with fear, his black boutonniere shredded in his hands. Filidor shouldered him aside and addressed the throng.

"Citizens of Grumby! Men and women of Tahmny! I come to you a stranger, on a mission of the Archonate, and have no part in your internecine differences! But the counsels of all the sages, through the long history of our earth, unanimously call for the staunchest resistance to tyranny!"

All eyes were now upon him, every ear cocked in his direction. Filidor felt a power being unblocked within him. His face suffused with hot blood, a delicious sensation rippled through his diaphragm, and the words sprang from his lips like wild beasts.

"What is this Hunan Diath, that he should so abuse a free populace? By what right does he levy his odious oppression upon an innocent folk? I say this: he is a pompous lout who battens upon your weakness – and that this weakness is occasioned by your division into factions!

"Therefore, good Tahmnyans, arise and unite as one against the man on the horse! Let go your differences, bind each other's wounds, and lay on together against the common foe! Unite, I say, and prevail!"

A stunned silence followed this impromptu oration. The

Tahmnyans, already fazed beyond easy recovery by the spectacle of Hunan Diath, stared at Filidor, wide-eyed and open-mouthed. A wavering sob was heard from somewhere deep in the crowd. Then a bloodied black partisan stepped forward.

"Did ye say 'unite'?" he inquired of Filidor.

The young man drew himself to his fullest height. "I did," he said.

The sable turned to face the assembled electors. "He calls upon us to set aside our differences and bind ourselves in unity!"

"Then he do be a reducer!" cried a crimson.

"A reducer! A reducer!" howled the mob in one voice. "Slay the misbegotten, foreign cull!"

They advanced upon him, and Filidor did not tarry to reason. Bottles and paving stones were already flying in trajectories meant to terminate at his head, and a score of enraged citizens were clambering over each other in their eagerness to mount the hustings and separate his body into its constituent members.

Grasping his staff, Filidor made one swing at the nearest hands reaching for him, then leapt nimbly off the back of the platform. The familiar sounds of pursuit rang in his ears, as he put as much of Grumby behind him as he could.

Hunan Diath's hoof prints were clear in the dust of the street. Filidor followed them in the hope that the Tahmnyans' nemesis might deter their pursuit, if he could stay ahead of the mob long enough to bring the tyrant in sight.

The tracks led him around a turning, and then into an alley between two houses. The passage debouched upon a small enclosed space, where Filidor encountered a sight that brought him up sharp.

In the yard was a horse. But it was no gleaming destrier; instead, it was a dispirited, knacker-bound nag whose only remarkable feature was the grinning, black-clad dwarf now scrambling down from its mangy hindquarters.

Gaskarth indicated a hole in the surrounding fence, then disappeared through it. Filidor followed without pause for inquiries, although strong suspicions now flooded his mind.

Beyond the fence, the dwarf led him a bewildering chase over walls, beneath verandahs, and through thorny hedges. Gaskarth plainly knew his way about Grumby – knew it, indeed, even better than the town's own inhabitants, whom they soon outdistanced. Before Filidor's wind was broken, the two travelers were limping along a wooded path outside the rubble of the town walls. They continued north through copse and pasture until Grumby was obliterated from their sight by dusk and intervening hills.

The little man busied himself in laying a fire and turning oddments of wood into their evening repast. Filidor perched pensively on a stump and regarded his companion as he chewed.

"It appears that I have again been played for a noddy," he said, when the dwarf could no longer use camp chores to defer conversation.

"An ill-founded allegation," answered Gaskarth.

"How else to describe my role in the political theater of Tahmny?" accused Filidor. "A theater, I add, which featured a brilliant cameo performance by a spectacular villain, who then underwent a sudden costume change and emerged as a well-known noxious homunculus!"

The little man sniffed, but said nothing. Filidor fixed him with his most stringent gaze.

"I have been reflecting," the young man continued. "I recall that during the incidents preceding our departure from Sprit, your projected image failed to change at the same moment all the Tarendis were suddenly honored with my features. You told me about the Tarendi devices that alter appearances. I believe, however, that you acquired such a device long before we reached Tarend, and that you wear it at all times."

Gaskarth looked abashed. "Such perspicacity pierces all subterfuge. I do wear such a refractive device. It is sometimes useful to appear to be someone I am not. In Sprit, my projected

image was self-generated, and not linked to the central broadcast nexus. Thus, I had to make shift to match my guise before
the omission was noted."

Filidor nodded. "Ahah. And today you used that device to
become Hunan Diath, who frightened out of their limited wits
the body politic of Grumby, and put my continued good health
– and perhaps even my continued existence – at hazard."

"In justice," answered the little man, "I point out that, by
the time Hunan Diath made his entrance, you were already the
object of hostile overtures. The distraction may well have prevented the Tahmnyans from conducting a rigorous inquiry into
your origins and principles.

"To go further," said the dwarf, warming to his argument, "at the moment the electors were distracted, you might
easily have distanced yourself from them. Instead, you chose to
mount a hustings and harangue the mob."

Filidor shook his head. "It's true. I do not know what took
me."

"It was an act no sensible, self-interested man would undertake," said the dwarf. "But, knowing your uncle's mind as I
do, I am sure he would commend you. Your impulse, whatever
its motivation, resulted in a service to the Tahmnyans and the
Archonate."

"This is beyond my scope," said Filidor.

"Then pay heed," said the dwarf, tossing another log onto
the fire. "As you already know, the Tahmnyan political divisions
have achieved complete stasis. No cooperative arrangements are
even contemplated by any of the four parties. In consequence,
their governance is frozen chaos.

"From within such a calcified culture, no change can be
generated; the impetus for reform must arise from without.
Hence, the external threat posed by Hunan Diath."

"Who does not exist," said Filidor.

"Who need not exist," said Gaskarth, "so long as the idea
can do its work."

"Well enough," said Filidor, "but I yet fail to understand

how my impromptu oration served Tahmnyan ends. Any threat I provoked could have been obliterated by a well-aimed cobble-stone."

"Threats are not sufficient," said the little man. "All of Hunan Diath's outrages and demonstrations have done no more than inspire fear and loathing. The Tahmnyans being almost congenitally unable to propose a united front, it was necessary for someone else to sow the seed."

"Which fell upon inhospitable ground," observed Filidor.

Gaskarth shrugged. "Yet one sees vegetation rooted in stony soil."

Filidor was too weary to argue. He stretched himself upon the ground. "Whatever the merits of my contribution," he said after a moment, "this Archonate work seems an abstruse business, fraught with very real dangers."

The dwarf deployed the ward-web above them and lay down. "The progress of esteeming the balance proceeds ever along an oblique path," he said. "However, we are done with that for now. Soon we will face a much more terrible peril."

After that, he said nothing more, and slept. But Filidor could not. A host of conjectures babbled in his mind, not least of which was a wondering as to whether the Gaskarth he saw by firelight was what he appeared to be, or whether the image of the ill-clad dwarf was just another twisting of light.

When the little man lapsed into snores and wheezes, Filidor extended his hand and lightly ran his fingers over Gaskarth's features. The planes and protrusions that met his touch matched the conformation of the dwarf's visage. Whatever else he might be, Filidor now knew, Gaskarth was as diminutively ugly as he appeared. The young man withdrew his hand and touched instead the small box pocketed within his mantle. He wondered what the new day would bring.

CHAPTER TWELVE

THE DAWN BROUGHT a grey, drizzling fog that lay upon the landscape like the corpse of a cloud. The dwarf went out into the formless world to gather fruits and succulents with which to break their fast. Filidor remained in the nestling warmth of the ward-web, and considered the alterations which travel and a wider experience of the world had worked upon him.

He was fitter and leaner, flatter of belly and thicker of calf, than when he had set out from Olkney. His face was smoothed by wind and shaded by sun, and it seemed that all his parts had been subtly tightened from within. He felt an unaccustomed sense of potential, an awareness of possibility, as if the odds and permutations of life had somehow shifted to his favor.

But he knew that nothing much in the world had changed; the difference was in himself. He was, somehow, more than he had been, and he had an inchoate feeling that he was not yet all that he would be.

Gaskarth returned with a heap of provender, which he silently left it to Filidor to prepare. The young man did so, converting the toughest tubers into more toothsome fare, and sharing out the rest in equal portions on two large leaves. But when he offered one of these to his companion, the little man did not fall to with his usual gusto. The food lay untouched in the dwarf's lap.

"Is something amiss?" inquired Filidor, between bites.

Gaskarth came back from far away. "I have received in-formation..." he began, then trailed off into his thoughts. "A message from my uncle?" Filidor persisted.

"What? No..." The little man was worrying at something in his mind, as he might have tongue-probed a pained tooth.

"Then what?"

"I have something to do," he said at last. "And I have to do it soon. The problem will lie in doing it right." He lapsed into a moment's silence. "And in living through it," he added.

More than that he would not divulge, save that he had received some vague "sending" which would call them hence, and that it involved neither their peripatetic quest for the Archon, nor the machinations of Jenbo Lal. Presently, after chewing only a few bites of the meal, Gaskarth wandered to the far side of the campsite and sat beneath a dripping evergreen. Wrapped in his black rags, he began the throaty grunts and gestures of the Lho-tso exercises. Filidor decided it was best to leave the dwarf alone.

He was, however, beset by an urge to be doing. He was now sufficiently introspective to know that such urges were a recent addition to his make-up. He had spent most of his life in the lackadaisical pursuit of diversion; yet he had never really minded boredom, and would rather put up with it than spend much energy seeking an antidote.

But now the tiny hooks of a deepening ennui plucked at him from all sides. He reflected on his experiences in the service of the Archonate. They had been mostly long, dull hours, punctuated by short episodes of hackle-raising terror. Viewed against the landscape of all his years, however, those brief moments of fear represented the only high points on an otherwise flat and monotonous plain.

"Is there nothing I should do?" he called out to the dwarf, but the little man only waved a dismissive gesture, and Filidor gave up. He collapsed the ward web and stepped out into the drizzle, took his staff, and set off to explore their surroundings.

They had camped in a region of low hills and scattered copses, apparently uninhabited. Looking south, from the brow of a rise higher than the rest, he made out the distant walls of Grumby and the farms ranged around the town. To the west lay smoke that might have marked some larger conurbation; to the east the hills rolled like waves to the foot of an escarpment. In the north, a dry savanna shimmered like a translucent sea. He was drawn to none of what he saw.

Filidor walked further into the hills, finding nothing to divert him save the novelty of being able to scale a slope and arrive at the summit unwinded. The drizzle subsided, and the sun picked its way here and there through the clouds. His spirits lifted as a patch of light swept toward him across a field, captured him in its ocher glow, and lit the droplets on the grass at his feet. There was a brief attempt at a rainbow, but it died aborning. A large brown bird drifted in wide circles far above him, then winged off toward the eastern scarp.

When the bird was gone, Filidor's belly reminded him that time had passed, and he retraced his steps to the campsite, where he was annoyed to find that Gaskarth had prepared no midday meal. Instead, the little man was engrossed in making complex calculations on a scrap of paper which, Filidor saw, had been torn from the end pages of the book of Osfeo.

This struck Filidor as wanton destruction; somehow, he had become attached to the faded tome. "I shall notify my uncle of the disregard in which you hold his possessions," he sniffed.

The dwarf, however, was so absorbed in his figuring as to be impervious to Filidor's remonstrations. He merely grunted, and presented a bony shoulder. The young man snatched up the injured volume and retired to the other side of the camp, where he took for his lunch the breakfast Gaskarth had left untouched.

Chewing, he levelled upon the little man a censorious stare, which was ineffectual for being unnoticed, and difficult to sustain for more than a few minutes. So Filidor swallowed the last morsel, then smoothed the pages of the illumino's life, and began to read.

His school at Toch Meevie having been closed by a narrow-minded clique among the ruling polyarchy, Osfeo went west into Carbingdon, and became to that god-rich land a purveyor of enlightenment and used deities.

His progress brought him in time to the city of Wal, where he soon attracted the attention of the fuglemen. The sage was brought before these sharp-eyed officers and instructed to display his wares.

"I have a fine selection of small gods and petty numens," he told them, "each commanding its particular sphere of power. As well, I offer a very good line in general enlightenment."

The fuglemen were drawn largely from the mercantile guilds, and knew to a groat the value their citizens placed on the exercise of religion. They quickly inspected the illumino's inventory, cannily rejecting depleted demiurges and patron spirits of obsolete arts and mechanistries. When the culling was done, they were left with a handful of deities dedicated to various particulars.

"These seem serviceable," they agreed. "Let us chaffer for terms."

Osfeo bowed and declared that any of the gods might be acquired for a few minims each, but that enlightenment would cost not less than ten myriads of the Walis' major currency.

At this the portly bursar snorted. "You seek to abuse our naivete," he said. "By grossly undervaluing these present deities, while demanding an outrageous fortune for some nebulous mental state, you would blind us to the true goods and bleed us of our pelf. You would have us pay dearly for an 'enlightenment' which doubtless consists of a few timeworn homilies and tatterdemalion revelations."

"My prices are as they are, and unalterable," replied the sage.

"Hah!" said the bursar. "Then know that you have matched wits with the fuglemen of Wal and found us one too many for you. We shall take your entire stock of deities at the price stipulated. The enlightenment you may retain for yourself."

Osfeo bowed again, but cautioned that some of the gods were captious, and that each was jealous of all the others. He recommended that they choose but one.

The fuglemen were not swayed. "The bargain is struck!" they cried, and bore away the various effigies and icons, casting a few coins at the sage's feet. Osfeo bowed a final time and withdrew to an inn beyond the city wall, there to pass a few days in contemplation.

The fuglemen of Wal, meanwhile, installed their new deities in a street of derelict temples, and invited the people to use them in exchange for substantial donatives. Incited by novelty and individual aspirations, the Walis did so in great numbers, and the fuglemen saw the civic coffers swell.

Now, the gods Osfeo had supplied to Wal were a varied assortment. Some commanded aspects of the weather; others had taken as their provinces the human passions of rage, lust and avarice; yet others tendered general services in return for strenuous acts of devotion from their adherents. Most had been long out of service; all were eager to put their powers and potencies into practice.

And, as the sage had warned, each was mindful of its perceived precedence over the others, and quick to take umbrage. So it was not long after the temple opened that Wal was visited by the first in a series of unfortunate outcomes, when a petitioner of the god Dezmajk failed to wash his elbows thoroughly before entering the sanctum.

Scarcely had Dezmajk's floodwaters subsided, than the goddess Inana-yon was pleased to broaden the blessing asked by one devotee, and apply it to the population at large. The ensuing frenzy of eroticism took days to extinguish itself.

The god Ghanfo, piqued at Inana-yon's display of power, ordained that her saturnalia would be succeeded by his wave of holy violence. Fortunately, the Walis were so enervated by their exertions in service to the lusty goddess that fatalities were few.

Other deities now joined in the contest, each glad to demonstrate a potency or attribute, all combining to enliven the city with a synergy of wonders and marvels. At the end of the third day, the surviving fuglemen managed to escape from the wreckage of Wal and fled to the inn, where they roused Osfeo from his meditations.

"We require you to take back that which you sold us," they said.

The illumino bowed. "I must confess that I am unable to return your money, having spent it for my accommodation at this hostelry. And it is much more difficult to confine a god – even a minor one – than to set it at liberty. But I am willing to recoup what you have bought."

A glimmer of suspicion showed in the bursar's haggard eyes. "So," he told his colleagues, "now we come to the cusp of his stratagem. He will extort an onerous fee to reclaim the gods."

"Not so," said Osfeo. "I will recover them without charge."

"Then we are blessed," exclaimed the fuglemen, seeing their deliverance. "And we have learned a lesson: Wal will traffic no more in deities and numens."

"Oh," said the sage, "in that case, you owe me the ten myriads."

The compiler of the tales had appended a long exegesis to this text, which Filidor read with interest. The dwarf remained immersed in his calculations, occasionally pausing to stare into emptiness, as if seeking to remember some dimly apprehended datum, before returning to his task. At one point, he looked up sharply at the young man. "You do still have it?" he inquired.

"Have what?" was Filidor's response.

"The box!" snapped Gaskarth.

Filidor felt in his mantle. "Of course."

The little man looked briefly abashed. "Of course," he said

gently. "My apologies." And he went back to his mathematics.

"Something worries you," said Filidor. But the dwarf met his inquiries with silence and irritable hand motions, finally emitting a wordless growl when Filidor would have insisted. Annoyed, the young man at last gathered food for the evening meal, and when darkness loomed, laid a fire. Gaskarth barely touched his portion, but moved closer to the blaze, the better to see his figures. As the silence lengthened, Filidor deployed the ward-web and went to sleep, leaving his companion seated alone in the small circle of light.

The morning was a reprise of the previous day's. Filidor breakfasted alone, sheltered by the ward-web from the early rain, while the little man continued his mathematical odyssey. When at last the sun broke through the clouds, the young man went once more into the surrounding hills, exercise his only diversion.

He climbed the same slope and looked out over the same view. The same brown bird, or one very like it, swung through the sky above his head. He watched it awhile, until it suddenly sloped off toward the escarpment, arrowing straight toward what looked like a long fissure that split the cliff's face from foot to brink.

Filidor's gaze followed the bird's course until the creature entered the fissure about two-thirds up the height of the scarp. There, he deduced, must be the nest. He was about to look away when, from that very spot, his eyes were pierced by a pinpoint flash of brilliant light. He looked back, motes of black swimming in his vision, and saw the flash again.

"This bird," he thought, "must be one of those which collects glittering things. Doubtless, its return to the nest has disturbed their arrangement, causing one to reflect a bolt of sunlight. A shard of glass, it's likely, or some bangle coated with electrum." He would have thought no further, but then it occurred to him that the source of the light might as easily be a gem of appreciable size and corresponding worth.

Of a sudden, conjecture blossomed into certainty. He looked about the empty landscape, then measured the distance to the escarpment and judged the height of the nest. The afternoon was not far advanced, and the cliff no more than a couple of hours away. The decision was instantly taken; he swung his staff and walked east.

The sun was still well up in the sky when Filidor ascended the slope which flowed up to the foot of the escarpment. Here the ground was littered with slabs and blocks of white limestone, sloughed off from the heights above to crash down upon the green. From this proximity, he could see that the porous rock was riddled with flumes and channels cut by wind and weather. A few more blinks of geological time, and the wall would fall onto the land below.

What Filidor knew of mountaineering could not have enlightened the merest novice, but even his amateur's eye could see that the cliff-face offered substantial risk. If massy portions could slough off and fall, so might a jut or handhold snap, to send a climber plummeting. Yet somehow such concerns seemed distant. The closer he came to the bird's nest, the greater grew its attraction.

He wove his way between the boulders, up to the foot of the fissure in which the bird had made its nest. The great crack rose above him, like a wound in the rock. In places it was as wide as he was tall; in others it dwindled to a shoulder-scraping narrowness. Hand-and footholds looked ample, and the rock here seemed not so friable as to break under his weight.

He collapsed the traveler's aide to a half its full length, and contrived a stout hook at one end. From the other, he brought forth a strong leathern strap, and with this looped about his wrist he began to climb.

The ascent was at first enjoyable, if somewhat monotonous. The pressure of rock against his fingers and soles was obscurely comforting. Most surprising was the knowledge that such an endeavor would have been unthinkable scant weeks before. The proposition that Filidor of Olkney, a fop among fops, should scale a cliff out of mere boredom could have earned his friends a fortune in wagers, had anyone been so foolish as to bet in that proposition's favor. Yet here he was, swinging from grip to grip, at a lethal height above the ground, his likely reward a scrap of tinsel in a fouled nest. He laughed and spat into the wind, and reached higher.

He was halfway to his goal, face pressed against the rock, toes to a ribbon of ledge, heels on empty air, when he grasped a nub of sandstone as far up as he could reach, and felt it crumble to fragments in his grip. At once, he was unbalanced. His toes slipped from the ledge, and he fell.

But here the flume was narrow; his shoulders struck the opposite wall, bouncing him forward again, and his finger-tips managed to hook the same ledge upon which his toes had perched. The shock almost tore the digits from their knuckles, but they held while his feet scrabbled for purchase.

For a long moment, Filidor clung to the cliff-face, the rock scratching his cheek. A small, inner voice counseled immediate descent. But a more forceful urging drew him upward. He pulled and climbed until his toes were once more grinding the ledge, then activated the staff's self-propelled grapnel. The hook flew up, trailing its cable, and lodged in a crevice above. Filidor tested the strength of its grip, found it secure, then allowed the staff to winch him up.

The nest was a collage of sticks and debris clumped together on a narrow ledge. Filidor climbed toward it on the opposite side of the fissure, which was here just wider than he could safely reach across. As his ascent brought him eye-level with the nest, a brown-plumed head rose above the tangle of twigs and branches and a pair of dark eyes fixed him with a cold stare. The bird's beak was black and hooked, and longer than Filidor's palm. It opened and hissed, and Filidor became aware of how much emptiness yawned beneath him.

The bird reared up and beat its wings, crying in a voice not unlike human laughter. Filidor inched higher, until he could look down into the nest. Now he could see that its builder had gathered an assortment of shiny bric-a-brac, none of which looked at first sight to be worth a savaging and a long fall onto the blocks tumbled at the cliff's base. Thankfully, he noted that there were no eggs.

Filidor jammed toes into a crevice and gripped with one hand an outcrop near his head. With the other hand he swung the traveler's aide in an arc that lengthened the staff to its fullest extent. Reacting to his need, the implement produced a blinding light at its tip, and emitted a bellowing roar of sound that sent the bird shuffling back until its tail feathers bent against the cliff wall. The creature eyed Filidor coldly, then with a squawk of contempt it launched itself into the air and glided away.

The young man craned his neck, half fearful that the next moment would bring the bird stooping down upon him from above, talons flexed and beak gaping for his flesh. But the threat was gone; the bird sailed straight down an incline of air, and disappeared from view somewhere over the woods to the west.

The nest was now Filidor's prize, for what that might be worth, and he sidled around the fissure until he could look directly down into the trove. He poked with the traveler's aide, finding only the shards of glass and broken trinkets he had come to expect. Then, as he flipped over a scrap of foil, he discovered the gem.

It was of no particular color, yet it flashed all the hues of the rainbow, throwing a mandala of pigmented lights across the walls of the fissure. It was the kind of stone around which legends could gather, for which emperors would wage war, and queens give up their virtue. And it was within Filidor's grasp.

Grasp it he did, finding it peculiarly warm – a quality which he ascribed to its having been sat upon by its recent owner. It fitted his hand as if it had been made to be held and gazed at, although it almost blinded him to look into its facets in the direct light of the westering sun. After a moment, he summoned strength to close his eyes against the brilliance, and tucked the gem into a pocket of his mantle, next to the Archon's box, where it seemed to pulse against his chest. When his vision returned to normal, he began his descent.

His progress to the base of the cliff was smooth, and soon he was wending the hills toward camp. He went swiftly, as eager to show Gaskarth what he had won, as to be back before the orange sun fell into night. He was within sight of the copse in which he had left the dwarf, and the sun was resting on the western horizon, when a long shadow slid over the path before him. He looked, and saw the bird circling above their camp. Then it dipped below the tops of the trees and was gone.

The fire was burned to embers, and the little man was stretched prone upon the ground. Without word or thought, Filidor dropped the staff and rushed to his companion's aid. He seized the dwarf by his shoulders and turned the small figure over. Immediately, two crabbed hands seized Filidor's wrists, twisted, and hurled him across the campsite.

"I advise you not to do that again," said Gaskarth. He sat up and straightened his attire.

"I took you to be injured or ill," said Filidor, rubbing a bruised shoulder.

"I am neither, as you may see. I was, however, midway along a course of calculation, the which you have rudely interrupted so that I must begin anew." The dwarf lay down again. "Please refrain from further disturbance."

"I have something to show you," said the young man.

"Retain it until the morning, when my cogitations will be completed, and we will venture on."

"But…"

"Enough!" snapped Gaskarth, returning to his inner works. And no more did Filidor get from him through the evening and the ensuing night. Left to his own devices, the young man gathered and ate his repast, built up the fire, then deployed the ward-web where the dwarf lay. His only consolation was that the little man did not snore when he was thinking.

Thus, while they slept secure within their shelter, they did not see the dark thing that wheeled through the night air, to land beside the fire and take on human form. Nor did they feel the gaze of cold eyes watching the play of energies across the ward–web, waiting for the dawn.

THE MORNING came grey again. Filidor awoke first, and saw the dwarf asleep beside him, exhausted from his mental labors. The young man stretched in the warmth of the ward-web, only a little surprised now that he did not ache from his exertions of the previous day. He sat up, yawned, and reached for the control that would collapse their protective screen, bracing himself for the in-rush of cold, damp air.

But, when the ward-web withdrew into its generator, no chill invaded the space it had delimited. The air remained warm and dry, although the clouds hung overhead as pregnant with moisture as the overcast of the last few days.

As the ward-web deactivated, Filidor experienced an unsettling sensation, too brief to be defined, and wondered if the device was malfunctioning. But more pressing concerns motivated him at that moment. He knuckled his eyes, pushed back his hair, and stood, then walked toward the trees at the edge of the camp to relieve himself.

He stopped halfway, and was not sure why. Something was wrong. At some lower stratum of awareness, he sensed a falseness in the morning, a kind of subtle insincerity in the landscape. He looked about, but saw nothing out of the ordinary. He listened, and heard nothing but Gaskarth's sleeping breath behind him.

And that was not right. There should have been some sound: birdsong, the buzz of an insect, the chittering of a squirrel. Yet the woods were as silent as a photograph. And, he now saw, they were as still. No breeze stirred a leaf, the blades of grass he had stepped upon were not springing up behind him.

Indeed, no trace of his steps showed on the sward.

Suddenly, Filidor was seized with a strange sense of confinement, as if invisible walls pressed him narrowly on all sides. The silence was an unspoken threat, the stillness like that of a poised viper in the second before it strikes. Filidor's skin moved of its own accord on his back and shoulders, and the hairs at the nape of his neck lifted themselves erect.

Carefully, eyes playing about the motionless trees as if something might rush in upon him, he backed toward Gaskarth, knelt beside the little man and shook his shoulder. The dwarf awoke at once.

"Ah, good," Gaskarth said. "Where is breakfast? We depart at the earliest."

"I think not," said Filidor. "I feel we are in peril."

"Peril?" The little man flowed to his feet in an instant, his head swiveling to take in the scene. Then his features set hard in his face. He looked down, examining the few possessions at their feet. "It will be here, somewhere."

"What?"

"I do not yet know," said the dwarf. "Some object that was not here before. It must be of appreciable size to engender such an effect, yet small enough to have been surreptitiously introduced."

A sinking feeling pulled Filidor's innards into a thick lump. He reached into his mantle. "Something like this?"

Gaskarth saw the gem in Filidor's palm. It glowed now with a pale sickly light that robbed their faces of color, and for all it had been pressed close to Filidor's side through the night, it chilled his hand like a shard of ice.

"Where did you get..." began Gaskarth, then shook his head and let out his breath. "I suppose it matters not. The thing is done, and we must await our captor's pleasure."

"Captor? Are we then imprisoned? And, if so, where? By whom and by what means?"

"By means magical, to be sure. This being so, we must assume the agent of our incarceration to be Jenbo Lal. As to where, the matter is open to conjecture. Of a certainty, however, we are not where we appear to be."

"I thought there was a strangeness in the woods when I awoke," said Filidor.

The little man sighed and squatted on his heels, motioning Filidor down beside him. "Let me see the stone," he said. The young man passed him the cold gem, and watched while Gaskarth peered into its faceted depths.

"I believe it is what they used to call a merrythought," said the dwarf after a while. "It has various means of manufacture, but its use is to provide a focus for a cantrip, projected from a distance for localized effect. I surmise that the spell was engaged the moment you deactivated the ward–web, which, I recall, is impervious to incantatory forces."

"Then let us immediately reactivate it. Perhaps it will shatter the force, or repel it upon the sender!"

"I doubt very much that it will work," said Gaskarth, and saw his pessimism confirmed when Filidor attempted to activate the mechanism.

"It is dead."

"No, not dead," said the dwarf. "Merely unuseful in this place, as are our other devices."

"And what is this place?" demanded Filidor. "Despite appearances, I do not believe we are still in the copse where we made camp."

"We are not. I suspect that we have been transported elsewhere, to some situation where we are more easily controlled." Gaskarth looked around the clearing. "Yet he maintains the illusion. Perhaps, if we knew our whereabouts, that knowledge would diminish his advantage."

The little man thought for a moment, then returned his attention to the gem. He peered into it, rubbed it with calloused fingers, pressed it here and there, and finally grunted.

"It remains active," he said. "By which we may assume that it continues to fulfill some purpose of Jenbo Lal's. That being so, by rendering the merrythought inactive, we may in some small measure thwart him." So saying, he hefted the stone and flung it at the tree beneath which he had yesterday sat and pondered.

The hurled stone did not reach its target. Halfway there, it disappeared through an invisible barrier. But its passage was not without mark: where the gem had vanished there was now a grey hole in the air, from which radiated cracks and fracture lines of the same color. As the travelers watched, the cracks widened and grew, and the illusion of woods beyond and grass beneath suddenly tore and fell away. What was left was a vast blank grayness, an absence of true space, in which the dwarf and Filidor floated, as if in a bubble.

"This is interesting," said Gaskarth.

"This is terrifying!" said Filidor, to the void now opened beneath him.

"It could be worse," countered the little man. "We are apparently not immured in a sphere deep within the mantle of the earth, nor at the bottom of a sea, nor on an extraterrene fragment orbiting beyond the atmosphere." He dropped his voice to a whisper. "I deduce from this that Jenbo Lal's powers are not all he would wish. He has confined us in the only place he can, thus offering us an opportunity of escape."

"Where?" Filidor whispered.

"Best not to say," answered Gaskarth. "We will be overheard."

"I see none to hear," said Filidor. "The entire universe has dropped from view."

"The thaumaturge is close by," said the dwarf. "The emptiness you think to apprehend is but a tactic to render you uneasy."

"It is effective."

"We will bide our time, until the mage appears."

A number of questions occurred to Filidor, but Gaskarth refused answers, calling it bootless to discuss strategies when sitting in an opponent's ear. "Patience and silence cost us nothing," said the dwarf, "whereas all this is an expense of

Jenbo Lal's."

So they sat, the little man appearing unperturbed and Filidor attempting to exhibit the same sang-froid, to await developments. The first of these was not long in arriving.

It began as a tiny, moving dot, off in the direction Filidor arbitrarily deemed *down*, since it came into sight in the crook between his crossed legs. The minuscule thing swam into and out of view, like a hovering midge too small to retain the focus of his eyes.

"There is some kind of insect flying around outside the bubble," he told Gaskarth.

"Unlikely," said the dwarf.

Filidor strained to follow its flight, losing it in the grayness for long moments before his eyes could recapture it again. Then the task became easier, as the tiny speck grew bigger. He realized that, in the unmarked void, he had no reliable indicator of its true size; it might be a midge close to hand, or a larger creature at a greater distance. He watched its approach – for it was definitely tending toward the travelers – with interest.

"It has wings," he said. Gaskarth did not reply.

"Some kind of flying lizard, I think," Filidor added after a while. "I can see a tail." The little man still kept silent.

Filidor could now make out a pair of veiny, membraneous wings that beat slowly at whatever substance the void provided, and a diminutive head crowned with horns. "It seems a pretty little creature."

The dwarf paid no mind to Filidor's reports, nor did he turn his head to observe the thing's approach. Gaskarth gazed placidly into the grey emptiness, as if diversion was his least concern.

"It really is quite unusual," said Filidor. "It has iridescent scales, and tiny little forearms. Its tongue is pink, and surrounded by needlish teeth. It would probably make a remarkable pet."

"Very probably," answered his companion. "And very remarkable."

The creature's wings continued to drive it toward the travelers. Now, with each stroke, it grew in Filidor's vision. At one moment, he could blot it out with a single hand extended at arm's length; in the next, it was the size of both hands extended. And still it grew.

"It's larger than I first thought," he said.

"Indeed?" said Gaskarth, still without looking.

"Yes," said Filidor. "But I can't tell how far off it is."

The beast now stretched its neck, its scales flashing a rainbow of hues, and soared on spread wings so that it slowly rose above them. Filidor watched it rise, until it circled over their heads like a bird of prey.

"Look," he said. "It's just up there." But the dwarf gave no heed.

The circle now became a descending spiral, as the creature folded its wings and swept down toward them. It grew with each of Filidor's heartbeats, larger and larger, until the young man began to grasp the scale of its true size. The wings blotted out more and more of the void, the tiny forearms reaching for him could have snapped trees like twigs, the needle teeth were fangs longer than his legs. Filidor gazed at the downrushing behemoth and screamed.

"Tush," said Gaskarth, looking up at last, and gazing calmly at the monster. "It's only a dragon." He studied the gape-jawed horror a moment, then concluded, "An early concept, but well realized, I will admit."

Filidor would have screamed again, but there was not time before the dragon was upon them. He covered his head with his hands and tried to become smaller than his anatomy would permit. But no grasping claws ripped at him, no slimy tusks tore gobbets from his flesh. The massive beast flung itself past and over them, and dropped into the void below. Filidor saw it spread its wings, turning in a long glide, and then it began to beat its way back toward them.

"It's coming at us from beneath!"

"I advise calm," said the dwarf.

The dragon swam up like a great fish rising to pluck flies from the surface of a pond. Its head grew beneath Filidor's feet until it was a yawning pink cavern, wet and flecked with yellow foam. The young man shivered, but could not tear his gaze away.

Yet again the jaws did not close upon their flesh. The beast rose until its head was level with them, and hovered on slowly fanning wings. The dwarf paid no attention, but Filidor could not help but look. He stared into a golden eye rounder than he was tall, split by a pupil of jet, and alive with a malevolence that chilled the marrow in his bones.

The dragon hung in the grey emptiness for a time that might have been millennia. Then, with a volcanic hiss, it furled its wings and dropped away. Filidor craned his head forward to watch it plummet down and down, until it dwindled once more to a midge, and disappeared.

The little man yawned. "If that is the limit of your capabilities," he said to the void, "perhaps we could dispense with any further preliminaries, and turn to the business at hand."

A great tremor went through the void. It roiled like fog before a squall, went from grey to red to black in the space of one short breath. Filidor cried out, but the dwarf said only, "We are waiting."

The stygian darkness was instantly shot through with bolts of fire and coruscating energy, which lashed about the travelers like all the tempests of eternity brought together in one place. But again they remained unscathed.

Gaskarth folded his arms and raised his scant eyebrows. "If you don't mind," he said.

The storm ceased as quickly as it had begun. The blackness gave way to a dim grey light, but now they no longer floated in a void. There was something underfoot, a springy, fibrous substance. It was fleshy red, criss-crossed with lines of a darker color that met and conjoined in reticulations. The light grew stronger, becoming a diffuse glow that illuminated a landscape taken from a dream. The network of lines stretched across a desolate red plain into infinity. Filidor turned and looked in all directions, saw an expanse of unbroken emptiness, domed by a featureless leaden sky.

The dwarf seized the young man's arm, pulling him down to whisper in his ear. "Now it begins in earnest," said Gaskarth. "I caution you: do nothing, and give up nothing. We are not without resource."

Filidor would have asked for more than this, but his voice was drowned in a humming roar that swept over the landscape, and swelled in intensity until he thought his ears would burst. With the sound came a sight. From an immeasurable distance, there rushed toward them an object which resolved itself into a gigantic face – the long and sinister face of Jenbo Lal, which hung over them like the visage of an unforgiving god.

Filidor looked into the eye of the mage and saw the eye of the dragon. He trembled. But the little man turned his back to the glowering prodigy and sighed. "If this continues, I shall say a word," he said.

The ground beneath them shook with rage.

"And then I shall say another word," said Gaskarth, "which will dispense with all this vain farrago, and allow us to address the nub of the matter between us."

The ground shook once more, and the dwarf opened his mouth, his thin lips framing a certain syllable. At this, the tremors ceased, and the vast face of Jenbo Lal winked out, to be replaced with the full figure of the thaumaturge, drawn to human scale. Jenbo Lal was attired in the robes of a pelerin, but the cowl was thrown back to reveal a bald and narrow skull, tattooed from nape to brow with obscure designs and ancient characters. He bestowed upon the travelers a gaze that might have rent armor.

"Have you done with your harmless sport?" inquired the dwarf.

"The sport is barely begun," hissed Jenbo Lal.

"We shall see," said Gaskarth.

"We shall indeed," agreed the mage.

"What is this all about?" Filidor wanted to know, but neither antagonist paid him heed.

Gaskarth inspected his nails. "You will not obtain what you seek. It cannot be taken, nor will it be surrendered."

"I disagree," said Jenbo Lal.

"Disagreeability is your forte," said Gaskarth. "In any case, I believe we are done here. If you would care to lift the spell – an admirable effort, by the way – we will depart."

"I must persist," said the mage.

The dwarf sighed. "Then do so, at your peril."

Jenbo Lal drew himself to his considerable height and became a shimmer of light that flared once, then shattered into a cloud of brilliant points that fled into infinity. Gaskarth watched the display, then shook his head. "Is it not curious how maleficence so often exhibits a nonchalant beauty?" he wondered.

"What will happen now?" asked Filidor.

"He and I will contest. One of us will prevail."

"What shall I do?"

"Nothing. You are almost helpless in this place, whereas his powers are considerable."

Filidor stiffened his spine. "If he comes against us, I shall fight."

The dwarf waved him to silence. "In this place, you do not properly exist. He does, and I am able to, by dint of certain abilities acquired through study and exercise. He and I are, I think, fairly matched. His knowledge will be deeper in some arts; I have a broader comprehension, without an equivalent depth in any one discipline. It will be an interesting test of the specific versus the general."

"And if he prevails?" asked Filidor.

Gaskarth shrugged. "Then I will likely perish, and you will experience lengthy discomfort."

"It is the box he desires, or rather whatever it contains. Will he not slay me to acquire it?"

"He cannot. Have you not noticed that, during the course

of your escapades, you have narrowly missed death several times, when the odds should have dictated otherwise?"

Filidor nodded.

"That is one effect of the object you carry. It confers upon the bearer a slight invulnerability. As well, it develops an affinity with anyone who possesses it for more than a brief time. Thus, it cannot be wrested from you against your will."

"What is it, then, some magical talisman?"

The dwarf looked away. "I would rather not say more here. Suffice it that you know what I have just told you, which is a knowledge shared by our adversary, who cannot help but hear our conversation."

"And if he defeats you?"

"Then he will hold you in some secure place and fret you with minor hurts and indignities until you relinquish the thing. After which he will surely kill you."

The young man's face hardened. "Then I would never relinquish it. I would trust to time to relieve me of Jenbo Lal's existence."

"Well said," commented the little man, "although the longevity of thaumaturges is legendary."

"Nonetheless," declared Filidor.

"You need not concern yourself with that aspect of our situation. Even if Jenbo Lal fails to win his prize, he may yet delay us too long. In which case, we shall all be spared further worry about the matter."

"How so?"

"Unless we bring that object to a certain place before a certain time, we and the world will cease to exist."

Filidor blinked. "You speak figuratively, of course," he whispered.

"No, literally," answered Gaskarth. "Consequently, I wish Jenbo Lal would hurry back so that we might settle things."

The mage obliged, appearing instantly and noiselessly behind them, to unleash a blast of some flame-colored energy at them. But Gaskarth had been expecting just such a maneuver; he thrust Filidor to one side, then executed a neat tuck-and-roll that took him out of the path of fire. He landed on his feet some distance away, and awaited his opponent's next stroke.

It was not long in coming. Jenbo Lal raised one hand to a particular position, then brought the other to meet it in a precise motion. From his outstretched palm arose a whiff of smoke, which became a plume, then a coiling mass of dense vapor that continued to swell as it floated lightly down to a point where three of the dark striations criss-crossing the red ground joined.

As the roiling cloud of smoke touched the synapse, the dark groundlines thickened into cables. Bright pulses of energy raced down the lines and lit the vapor from within. The stuff began to solidify: there appeared a brawny yellow arm, tapering barely to a meaty hand tipped with ocherous claws. A second arm appeared, then a shaggy torso, and a pair of rope-muscled legs. Finally, a head cleared the last wisps of vapor, and turned faceted eyes upon the dwarf. Loops of saliva dripped from a lipless mouth filled with greenish fangs, as the thing slunk toward the little man.

Gaskarth curled his hands and brought them to his thin chest, then moved them down and away. He closed his eyes and spoke a string of syllables. Immediately, a beam of intense white light streamed from each of his hands. He directed the beam from his left hand at one of the lines that led to the spot at which the demon had appeared. The line writhed and smoked, rising out of the plain like a cable under tension; then it snapped, coiling back and thrashing before it lay still. The right arm and leg of the demon withered, and it collapsed to the fibrous ground. A grimace of pain flickered over Jenbo Lal's face.

Still, the monster heaved itself toward the dwarf on its remaining limbs. Gaskarth moved his right hand, another line bubbled and broke, and the thing's left arm and leg withered. The thaumaturge recoiled. Then the little man turned the beams of both hands on the remaining line, and the limbless demon expired into a thin smear of ash. Jenbo Lal shuddered and stepped back a pace. The dwarf mouthed a short word, and the beams of light faded.

Gaskarth folded his arms. "You see that I can wound as well as defend," he said.

Jenbo Lal regarded him with eyes hard and black as obsidian. "Take care you do not cut too deep," he said, "for there is no way from here save through me."

"I had deduced as much," said the dwarf. "Perhaps you should consider the implications for yourself."

"Let us proceed," said the mage. He brought his limbs to a new alignment, which left one finger extended toward the dwarf. Filidor saw that it was the finger on whose nail a black rune had been inscribed. The sigil turned now green, now red, and from the tip of the digit, a stream of small round objects flew at great speed toward the little man.

Gaskarth flexed one wrist and rotated his head to a certain position, and the hurtling missiles spun around him, as if space were curved about his body. The objects crashed one after another into the ground, splattering there or rebounding away. One rolled to Filidor's feet, revealing itself to be a living creature without eyes or means of independent locomotion, mainly comprising a ball of black fur surrounding a sucking mouth. The young man jumped back.

Still the thaumaturge projected an unending stream of the things at the dwarf, and still the dwarf held himself immobile, head cocked at the same angle, so that the flow of living missiles cascaded about him. But now Jenbo Lal flexed his free hand, and hissed a string of words. The ground at Gaskarth's feet suddenly erupted with fibrous growths that twined themselves around the little man's ankles and began to climb his legs.

Filidor saw a rictus of desperation seize Gaskarth's face. The dwarf moved a hand, and an invisible wave of force swept toward Jenbo Lal. But the mage only staggered, then laughed a cold laugh. He flexed his free hand again, the other still directing the stream of living missiles at the little man's head, and the twining tendrils climbed higher, until they imprisoned the hand from which Gaskarth had sent the ineffective blow. The dwarf pulled against their grip, but he was powerless to break it.

"Now," said Jenbo Lal. He drew back the hand that propelled the creatures, and their flow ceased. Then he clapped both hands together with a noise that shook Filidor's eyes in his head. New tendrils sprang from beneath Gaskarth's feet, wrapped themselves around him from foot to crown, and pulled him to the red ground, burying him in a massive writhing grip. "Now," said the mage, "we shall end it!"

"No!" cried Filidor, and leapt to where his companion lay smothered and strangling in the fibrous tangle. He knelt and grasped a tendril that pressed itself into Gaskarth's face, ripped at it with all his strength. But the thing grew and thickened in his hand, and he could not lessen its grip by an erg.

A dry chuckle sounded in his ear. He looked up to see the thaumaturge bent over them, a grin of malevolent triumph contorting the thin face. "That will finish itself," said Jenbo Lal, pointing to the buried dwarf, "whereas you and I have yet to begin our association."

Cold fingers sank into Filidor's shoulder, then the young man was hauled to his feet as if he weighed less than air. "First we must remove ourselves to a more physical sphere," said the mage, "then we may explore our differences in detail and at length."

Filidor felt a wave of despair, the helpless hopelessness of a bereaved child. Jenbo Lal smiled a smile that chilled him in his innermost recesses, and held the rune-cut finger before his eyes. The black design began to glow, pulsing from amber to black, as the mage drew intricate patterns on Filidor's face, while the other hand gripped his shoulder like pincers of ice.

A wave of impotent fury shook Filidor. He opened his mouth to scream his frustration, but instead sank his teeth into the finger of Jenbo Lal.

The result was a convulsion of the thaumaturge's features into a spasm of agony followed at once by stark horror. The restraining hand dropped nerveless from Filidor's shoulder, and the mage began to shake as if subterranean tremors were set loose in his bowels. The wounded finger dripped not blood, but globules of force which hissed and steamed as they struck the red ground. Jenbo Lal looked at his mangled nail, then at Filidor. He opened his mouth as if to speak, but no sound came, and he fell forward upon his face.

Filidor stared at the corpse of Jenbo Lal, for there was no doubt the thaumaturge was dead. The body was shrinking and curling in upon itself, leaving in a few moments only a wadded robe. The young man poked a toe at the cloth, and it dissolved into powder. A rustle of wind swept the red plain like a dying breath, and carried the dust away.

The grey sky now darkened, and the plain cracked in the distance, revealing a chasm plunging into blackness. The springy ground beneath Filidor's feet rapidly hardened and began to fracture and flake. The young man realized he knew nothing of where he was, nor in which direction might lie escape. He spun about, but the vista was the same on every side: growing darkness, a subsiding terrain, and solitude.

He saw sinkholes appearing all about him, as the surface of the plain suddenly collapsed and fell to who knew what depths. The ground now gave way almost at his feet, and Filidor leapt back from the hole with a cry of alarm. Then a small, yellowed hand appeared from the cavity, clutching at the friable rim. "Help me out of here," said a familiar dry voice.

Scarce able to believe it, Filidor reached and took the hand. A yank, and the dwarf was beside him. "Thank you," said the little man.

"I had thought you dead."

The dwarf snorted. "Merely captured, for later absorption into the thaumaturge. Had he known it, that made me a richer prize than the object he sought. My knowledge married to his will would have made a formidable union."

"I do not understand," said Filidor.

"I have perceived that about you," said Gaskarth. "But let us contrive an exit from this place before it ceases to be. For I frankly do not know where that would leave us, and would rather speculate tomorrow than find out today."

"Where are we?" asked Filidor.

"Have you not gathered that yet?" said the dwarf, moving off across the disintegrating plain. "We are within Jenbo Lal. That is, we are within what used to be Jenbo Lal, and will soon be nothing." He reached down into the ground and pulled up one of the fibrous lines. "Here, hold this."

Filidor did as he was bid. "How can this be?" he asked, while the dwarf examined other lines, and finally chose one.

"The how is ticklish; the why is easier. This is where the thaumaturge could exercise his supremest power. His abilities were of course greatest when limited to himself. Now give me that."

Gaskarth took the line from Filidor and twined it with the one he had selected, sticking them to each other with a gobbet of spit. "Let us hope this succeeds," he said, looking about at the plain which had now broken up into shrinking islets of red, afloat on a black void.

The dwarf clasped the junction of the cables, then bid Filidor place his hands on the same spot. The little man shut his eyes, spoke a word, and blew upon his fingers. A faint glow appeared, but no other result.

"Hmmm," said Gaskarth. "Not promising."

He tightened his grip and said the word again, blew with more force. The glow flickered lambently, and a queer sensation rippled through Filidor's innards, but again nothing else happened.

"Very well," said the dwarf, "the hard way."

This time, he seized the lines in one hand and Filidor's neck in the other. Then he brought both hands together at the young man's nape, completing a circle, and said four words. As the last of these were spoken, a flash of blue energy cracked about Filidor's ears, he felt himself at once compressed, torn apart and propelled a great distance at numbing velocity. When his eyes regained their use, he was staring at a tuft of grass.

He raised his head to find himself and the dwarf sprawled upon their possessions at the campsite. The embers of their fire still smoked, as did the place where Jenbo Lal's head should have met the neck of his body. The headless corpse lay an arm's length away, just beyond the range of the ward-web. It was midday.

"Come," said Gaskarth, taking up his satchel and tossing Filidor the traveler's aide. "We have dawdled too long."

CHAPTER FOURTEEN

THEY LEFT THE REMAINS of Jenbo Lal where they lay, and walked north. Filidor had suggested giving the thaumaturge some rudimentary rites of interment, rather than leave him for the birds and insects. But the dwarf refused.

"He has already cost us precious time," Gaskarth said. "Staying to bury him will cost us more. Let him lie where he is, and if we come back we will cover him over. If we do not come back, then one unburied wizard's corpse will be the least of the world's concerns."

After that, he would say no more, but turned his thoughts inward again. Filidor heard him mumbling to himself, snippets of figures and formulae, and occasionally the little man paused to jot a note on the page he had torn from Osfeo's book.

The morning had been well advanced by the time they made their escape from captivity, and they walked without pause until mid-afternoon. The dwarf set a rapid pace, ascending and descending hills with an unvarying metronomic stride. Filidor thought it to his credit that he matched his companion step for step. He was well pleased with the progress he had made since leaving Olkney, and felt himself to be an entirely improved version of the original Filidor.

He had an easy vigor to his limbs, a soundness of wind, and a clarity of mind he had never before possessed. He had met and bested perils of all shapes and kinds, from ravenous beasts to raging mobs, and had concluded by defeating Jenbo Lal in the very jaws of the wizard's power.

Looking back over these adventures, Filidor wished himself back at home, to regale his friends with tales of derring-do. Then he realized that they would be little apt to appreciate the worth of his accomplishments. The more imaginative might envy him, the rest would find him bizarre, an object of mirth. All would soon be bored.

Following these thoughts, Filidor discovered that he cared not how his erstwhile companions might see him. They were, he concluded, a vain and shallow crew, set on the pursuit of empty sensation. He now inhabited a wider world, to which he brought a depth of engagement beyond their capability. If he did not see them again, he would not feel the lack.

His pleasure at his new condition was diminished only by the rumblings of his stomach, which had had no useful work that day. The encounter with the thaumaturge, followed by the dwarf's haste to recover lost time, had meant that they had tasted neither breakfast nor lunch. As they descended the last of the Tahmnyan hills and came onto the northern savanna, Filidor took Gaskarth's arm and brought them both to a stop. "We must eat," he said.

The little man looked up at the sun with impatience, but conceded to the demands of the body. He set Filidor to gathering what bits of organic stuff lay about them, then touched the heap of twigs and herbiage with the wand of perpetual sufficiency. Instantly, they were in possession of a rich assortment of foodstuffs. Filidor seized a white loaf and a lump of fragrant cheese, and filled his mouth. The little man followed suit.

The food reminded Filidor of the many meals of mazhouki and rough forage he had been forced to eat in the early days of their wanderings. He swallowed and looked at his companion. "It is perhaps impolite to mention it, but many would say that you owe me some degree of gratitude for rescuing you from Jenbo Lal."

"True," answered Gaskarth, "and accordingly I thank you."

"Speaking of truth," Filidor went on, "I would feel more roundly thanked if your gratitude led to a policy of unadorned veracity between us."

"Very well," said the little man.

"You do not deny that you have been, at times, less than honest with me."

"I do not deny it. It was a requirement of the exercise."

"Just so," said Filidor. "And if we are to be frank with each other, I would now like to posit what I perceive to be the facts, and to have you respond without prevarication."

Gaskarth nodded.

"First," said Filidor, "this journey has been, as you say, an 'exercise' of some kind, set for me by my uncle to acquaint me with the world, and to improve my capacity for dealing with it."

"True," said the little man.

Filidor nodded and continued. "Second, we have at no time been pursuing and always missing my uncle. Our itinerary has been determined by you, and my parts in its consecutive episodes were performed as predicted."

"Partly true," said Gaskarth, "allowing for unforeseen contingencies."

"Jenbo Lal," said Filidor. "Was he such a contingency?"

"He was," said Gaskarth.

"And when he defeated you, my acting to rescue you was also unforeseen?"

"It was," said the dwarf. "And I do extend to you my sincere gratitude and admiration. I had thought us undone."

Filidor felt a warm glow of merit and accomplishment, but he put it aside. "To return to the main point, our actions apart from battling a thaumaturge have been elements of that ill-defined Archonate function known as the progress of esteeming the balance."

"They have," concurred Gaskarth, "and I will say that you have shown a fine aptitude for the work."

"Then perhaps," said Filidor, "you would explain just what it is the work entails?"

The little man helped himself to some bread, which he gummed thoughtfully before answering. "It cannot have escaped you that each of the peoples we have encountered is enmeshed in a culture founded on one or another singular principle."

"I had noticed," said Filidor.

"Then you will also have noticed that, in each case, this principle has been extrapolated to its extremest limits, creating considerable restriction on those bound by its tenets. This is a natural outcome of the continued existence over millennia of societies evolving along a dominant course.

"Indeed," the dwarf went on, "so immersed in monomania are these cultures that they are but a few steps short of chaos and collapse. To prevent such upheavals, it is the duty of the Archonate to adjust their inner workings through innovation and surprise. This is an ancient practice, carried out either surreptitiously or in plain view since the dawn of time."

"It seems an abstruse business," commented Filidor.

"We do not set the rules," said Gaskarth, "But merely carry out our allotted functions."

"I have a fourth point," Filidor said. "And that is that my uncle has not left the palace in Olkney, and is doubtless in his library, leafing through some dusty tome, while I tramp the world in your footsteps. The object I am supposed to be carrying to him, and for which Jenbo Lal so lusted, is part of the ruse that first set me on my way."

"Here you are in error," replied Gaskarth. "Your uncle is at this moment travelling toward an awful encounter – the same destiny to which you are bound. His chances of surviving the ordeal I continue to calculate; yours are more promising."

"Then what is this thing?" asked Filidor, producing the box.

But the little man was evasive. "It is a kind of key, that fits a kind of lock. It has other qualities and attributes, which do not concern us, although they were of pressing interest to Jenbo Lal." And he would say no more, but indicated a desire to move on.

They continued to fare north, as the day declined. The little man was once again deep in calculation, while Filidor turned over in his mind the questions he had put and the

answers that were given. He had, however unwillingly, passed
a test. He had gained something of value, and become a man to
be reckoned on. The rest of it he did not know, and would not
until he encountered the Archon. And perhaps not even then,
he thought, but was for the moment satisfied.

Evening found them still on the march. When the last
glimmer faded in the west, Gaskarth had Filidor summon
a light from the traveler's aide, and they travelled in its thin
glow until they reached the only landmark on the plain: a vast
shamble of crumbling blocks heaped upon the remains of some
long-dead imperator.

"We will rest here a while," said the dwarf. "Then we will
walk through the night."

Filidor sank down upon a carved stone. "You have not told
me where we are bound."

"Into Barran," said the little man, and curled himself on
the ground to sleep.

The words sent a chill through Filidor. Even in parochial
Olkney, Barran was the word for desert. It conjured up a vista
of arid wastes, of thorn and gallbush, of sharp-toothed prowl-
ing fands, of blood-seeking sting-whiffles that dropped noise-
less from the sky to paralyze and feed upon their victims. Few
entered Barran by choice; fewer still returned; none who had
penetrated beyond its edges were ever heard of again. Hence the
saying: *out of Barran, nothing; into Barran, oblivion.*

Filidor did not sleep. He sat upon the figured block of
stone, his staff shedding a small glow, and stretched his senses
into the darkness around him. The silence made his ears hum.
Then a flurry of animal snorts came from nearby, and the
young man jumped before he recognized the din as Gaskarth's
customary nocturnal noises. After one brief burst, the dwarf's
snores subsided, but Filidor thought he heard the breath of
a hunting fand whistling between its forked incisors, and no
amount of self-reassurance could convince him that beyond
the light death did not watch him and lick its whiskery chops.

After what seemed a very long time, he heard the rustle of Gaskarth's robes beside him. The dwarf's hand upon his shoulder was surprisingly gentle. "Time to go."

"I may have heard a fand," said Filidor.

"It will not follow where we walk tonight," said the dwarf. "But I will carry the ward-web partially deployed, so that we may take ready shelter if attacked."

So they walked into Barran, passing soon from dry savanna into alkali wastes, under the wavering glow from Filidor's staff. They walked in silence, their footsteps whispering through riplets of dust and, occasionally, powdered brick that bespoke past habitation by humans. The pile of blocks by which they had sheltered was soon left behind, discernible only by the dark gap its bulk raised between the travellers and the icy pinpoints of the sky.

Time passed, but Filidor was not well enough versed in astronomy to read the clock night provided. Nor were his legs any reliable gauges of distance travelled, since they now seemed to be able to do their work without noticeable strain. So it was perhaps midnight when the ground beneath their feet shifted gradually from dust to rubble, and they found themselves traversing a vast field of shattered stone, each fragment so crushed and fractured as to fit into a child's hand.

"What was this place?" Filidor inquired.

"The metropolis of Ambit," was the answer. "A great power in its time, an age back. They had a spire here, so it was said, from which one could call out to the stars and hear a reply. But it all came to wrack and destruction."

Filidor nudged a pile of stones with his staff. "It needs have been an exceptional force that reduced a great city to so much gravel."

"Indeed," said Gaskarth. "And it was the very force which we are hurrying to confront."

Filidor stopped walking before his extended foot could complete its next step. "Then I think we should talk," he said.

"It would be, at the very least, charitable of you to acquaint me with the nature of this force, before I am brought to encounter it at first-hand."

"You are right," agreed the dwarf. "I had not wanted to worry you."

"When one is marching through Barran toward some ghastly horror, a degree of worry is not inappropriate," said Filidor.

"Right again," said the little man. "Since time presses us, let us walk on, and I will recount the tale of Ambit."

He pulled Filidor into motion again, and continued. "As you know, we live in the world's penultimate age – and pray do not inquire what the next and final eon will bring; the near future offers sufficient grist.

"But in the long millennia that precede our times, may things have been done that ought to have been left unstarted. I refer you to the sentient crystals of Enorg, which from their incipient seedlings soon extended beyond their creator's control, and now cover that entire unfortunate island in a shining siliciferous layer some leagues thick."

"I have heard that tale," said Filidor.

"And you will have heard, too, of the ill-advised eugenic manipulations decreed by Chunn the Gullible, of the Eighth Dynasty of the Deh Na'a Empire, who inadvertently ensured that there would be no Ninth Dynasty. It was several generations before the martial passions he instilled in his creatures extinguished themselves in mutual slaughter."

"That, too, is known to me."

"But of all the egregious missteps of the past which plague our diminished present, none is more baleful than the thing which squats at the centre of Barran."

Filidor envisioned some chained demon or monstrous war engine of antiquity. "What form does this entity assume?" he asked.

"It is generally agreed to be a cube of dull, grayish metal, about the height of a human being," answered the dwarf, "though its dimensions and facets are said to alter or blur when it is operating."

"I detect from this description no overt menace," said Filidor.

"You should know by now not to judge by outward appearances. So listen well. You are surely aware that the force we call "evil" is in fact an emanation which seeps into our universe from an adjacent plane, where it is merely one of the natural energies of its environment – like gravity or momentum in our own milieu."

"Indeed," Filidor nodded, "this is fodder for schoolboys."

"But you will not have heard of how the hierarchs of Ambit, each a mage of surpassing power, sought to gather the flow of that energy between the planes and channel it to their own purposes."

Filidor shook his head.

"At the end of lengthy researches," Gaskarth went on, "the hierarchs constructed a device, a kind of capacitor for interdimensional forces, which they believed would serve their ends. However, the mechanism was unequal to their expectations. Moments after they activated it, the thing absorbed, focused and then discharged all the energy of evil then extant in our world. The wastes of Barran are the consequences of their hubristic misjudgment."

"And the device still operates?" asked Filidor.

"After a fashion," said Gaskarth. "The strength of its first discharge thrust it partially through the veil between this plane and the next, where it remains inextricably wedged. From that position, it continues to store evil – not from seepage, but directly from the source."

A wave of cold passed through Filidor as he encompassed the full meaning of the little man's words. "Then how do we and most of this segment of our universe continue to exist," he asked after a moment, "since a direct adit of such force into our plane ought by now to have particalized everything within reach?"

"There exists a small mercy," answered the dwarf. "Before he was etherized and disseminated widely, the nimblest of the Ambit mages had the presence of mind to alter the calibration of the device's controls. The release of concentrated evil was therefore only partial; there was a weak horizontal blast that extended only as far as the limits of Barran, and a much stronger vertical discharge which reached the moon."

"What moon?" said Filidor.

"Exactly," said Gaskarth. "In any case, the capacitor accumulates its charge over several centuries, until it reaches a critical stage of impending release. At a crucial moment before the discharge, the device must be manually directed to fire its energies back into the adjacent plane. The blast is said to be welcome there as a salubrious relief from their otherwise unwholesome climate."

"How is the device reset?" asked Filidor.

"There is a key, of sorts," said the dwarf.

Filidor would have like to have heard more, but at that moment he became aware of a faint rasping noise somewhere close by in the darkness. The travellers stopped and listened. The sound came again, from another side, like the rubbing together of hard, dry surfaces. Filidor tried to peer beyond the glow of the staff's light, but saw nothing.

Then it came again, from behind, and suddenly there was the rattle of stones as heavy bodies scrabbled across the debris toward them. A pair of stalked eyes gleamed in front of Filidor, surmounting a vertical mouth whose parts dripped juice as they worked. A pincer as long as his arm glowed palely in the light from the traveler's aide and swept toward his head.

"Preyns!" yelled the dwarf. "Down!"

Before Filidor could react, a weight landed on his shoulders and bore him to the stony ground. He shrieked and flailed, trying to turn over, before he realized that the little man had jumped onto his back and simultaneously spread the ward-web's protection over them. He picked a sharp fragment of rock from his cheek and sat up. "What are preyns?" he demanded.

"Hush," whispered the dwarf. "They sense vibration. Lie still and say nothing, and they will go off in search of other victims."

Filidor did as he was bid. Outside, a score of enormous crustaceans clattered about in search of them, their eight jointed legs scattering stones, while their spiked pincers clacked the air and scraped harmlessly across the impervious shelter of the ward-web. But they were a long time in going, their rudimentary minds unable to accept that warm food could so abruptly vanish.

Dawn came, and the preyns went back to their holes and burrows. Gaskarth deactivated the ward-web, and they looked out over the heaped rubble of a bygone age. Even in the first amber light of day, the wastes had begun to shimmer with heat, and Filidor felt droplets of sweat breaking out on his brow.

"We will walk until it becomes too hot," said Gaskarth, "then find what shade we can until evening. I suggest we forego the pleasures of conversation, so as not to draw attention upon ourselves, and so that we may concentrate our thoughts on the task of survival."

They encountered no major predators that morning, except for a sting-whiffle which spiraled down at them, to be knocked from the air by the little man's well-aimed throw. By noon, they had crossed the field of stones that had been Ambit, and were back into the hard-pan desert. The red sun struck them more heavily with each step, and finally Gaskarth called a halt at a bank of dry earth where they found the abandoned hidey-hole of some middling-sized beast.

"Sleep, if you can," said the dwarf. "We will go on at evening." He deployed the ward-web over the mouth of the burrow, adjusting a control to polarize what light passed between its reticulations. Then the little man withdrew once more into his calculations, leaving Filidor to his own entertainments.

Filidor lay in the half light of the sheltered burrow and tried to sleep. But the heat, even out of the sun, was a torment. He dozed fitfully, stirring occasionally to draw a few sips of water from the traveler's aide, having learned that useful property of the staff's by heuristic experimentation. Finally, he slept an hour or two, awakening in the time before twilight to see the dwarf yet immersed in contemplation. It was still too hot to travel, and the young man was so enervated by heat and exhaustion that thinking was beyond his energies. He reached into his mantle and drew forth the book of Osfeo.

Osfeo experienced a need for guidance in the conduct of his business affairs. He resolved that he would take for his source of counsel the first person he met on the way to market. But the first individual he encountered was a well known madman.

"A resolution is a resolution," said the sage, and approached the fellow where he squatted in the dust, gesticulating at phantoms. "How may I gain wealth?" he inquired.

"Cawbers," said the madman, naming a staple vegetable of low value and near universal availability. Osfeo went off and spent all his money to buy a storehouse full of cawbers. Soon after, a great blight destroyed all the cawbers in the fields, and the value of the illumino's holdings multiplied many fold.

He went back to the madman. "How may I gain more wealth?" he asked.

But the loon mistook the sage for a demon and struck him senseless with a stone. Osfeo toppled bleeding to the ground, where he was found by a kindly man who took him to his home to convalesce. Here the sage was able to perform valuable services for his benefactor, and left a few days later with his purse well filled.

The illumino went to the madman a third time. "How may I gain yet more wealth?" he asked.

"Howl at the stars," was the reply.

That night, Osfeo stepped into the street and began to howl. His neighbors remonstrated fiercely with him, finally hurling objects to drive him away. One of these, an ornate carboy of antique design, struck the sage on the knee. When he examined it, he found it to be a rare piece, and traded it the next day for a considerable sum.

He was limping along to see the madman when his friends stopped him. "Wise one," they said, "it grieves us that you place your destiny in the hands of a raver. Can you find no better source of counsel?"

"Apparently not," said the sage, and went on his way.

THE DWARF LOOKED UP from where he had been drawing lines and angles in the dust. "It's time," he said.

They walked on, with the declining sun on their left, across the parched alkali flats. Evening found them toiling up the ramparts of a low range of hills, whose crumbling slopes slid them back one step for every two they ascended. Filidor clamped his jaw muscles and struggled to keep pace with the little man, who mounted the slope with machine-like strides. But both were laboring for breath when they topped a ridge and allowed themselves to drop down its far side in great leaps and tumbles, which brought them to the base of the slope amid a profusion of small avalanches.

The terrain before them was now as flat as a windless sea, an unbroken expanse of dust where neither plant nor hillock grew above the surface. Filidor looked right and left in the fading light, seeing the hills at his back extend in an inward curve to either side. Of a sudden, his perspective captured the scale of his surroundings, and he was able to see that they stood within the lip of a vast crater, the floor of which was as level as a gigantic sheet of glass.

"At least," he thought, "we shall have easier walking," and trotted out onto the dusty plain. But he had taken no more than a few steps before his feet slid out from under him. His buttocks won the race to the hard ground.

Rubbing a bruised hip and elbow, Filidor attempted to rise, only to slip and fall again, this time striking his face. His hand swept the dust, revealing that under its thin coating the ground was slick as oiled metal, and black as onyx. He brushed aside more dust, and looked down into his own dark reflection. Then a movement seemingly beneath the surface caught his eye. He followed it, looked deep, then cried out. Frantic, he slid and dry-swam his way back to the dwarf at the edge of the crater.

"There is something in there," he said.

"It is an effect of the device," said Gaskarth. "The substance filling the crater is a solidified melange of space and time, which acts as both a parabolic receptor for the gathering of forces from the adjacent plane, and a window between the dimensions.

"Doubtless," he went on, "practitioners of science and thaumaturgy would flock to this place to view the wonders it offers, were it not for the inhospitable terrain and the certain and wretched death that results from any extended proximity to the machine. In consideration of which, we had best bestir ourselves."

"How can we travel on a near frictionless surface?" asked Filidor.

"Observe and emulate," said the little man. He skated out onto the glassy surface, executed a gliding turn, and returned to the edge. Filidor inched forward, and imitated the motions, then windmilled his arms in a futile attempt to retain his balance. But, after a few tumbles and sprawls, the young man found he could remain upright and move forward. Within minutes, he was skating smoothly beside Gaskarth, the wind fresh in his face, and the stars beginning to twinkle overhead.

"It would be amusing to transport some of this material back home, for the diversion of the populace," he said.

"Indeed," replied the dwarf, "but their enjoyment would be truncated when the denizens of the adjacent plane took advantage of the breach in the barrier to visit and explore amongst us. Look down."

Filidor did so – they were crossing a stretch swept clean of dust by the wind – and saw through into the next dimension. Entities of indeterminate size and conformation evanesced into and out of view, the details of their true shapes being refused somewhere between Filidor's brain and optic nerves. He shuddered and tried to tear his gaze away, white-faced and shivering, but the vision had frozen his every muscle.

He slid face down onto the black smoothness, staring into the unimaginable otherness of a universe built upon realities that would be madness in his own sphere. Distance and scale had no meaning; it was as if the things he could see were achingly far away, out at the borders of infinity, yet at the same time they were no more than an atom's breadth from his face.

And then some thing with eyes that were not eyes in a face that was not a face, turned its attention to him, saw him, and flowed a body that was not a body toward the transparent barrier separating Filidor's tiny, helpless presence from its horrific power.

Suppose that a dust mite, grubbing through its minuscule world across flakes of discarded human skin, should discover the vast beings which shed the stuff on which it fed. And then suppose that that mite should suddenly realize that one of those mountainous beings had singled it out for inspection. The mite would be no less terrified than was Filidor, as the entity focused its awareness on him.

He could not look away, and could not bear to see what filled his gaze. He whimpered and wanted to crawl into his own darkest innards. And then the immense being that had taken cognizance of him lost interest, took its flesh that was not flesh elsewhere, and left him to recover as he might.

Gaskarth hauled the young man to his feet, and waited until Filidor's eyes lost some of their hauntedness. "I'm sorry," said the dwarf. "I should have said, 'Don't look down.' Come."

They pressed on. It was now fully dark, the last glint of red light faded from the west. The sky was clear above, the ground a patchwork of white dust and ebony pools. They skated in silence, across a landscape so empty only the wind of their passage convinced Filidor they still moved. Occasional flickers of light cast a lambent glow from beneath them, but all the rest was black space and monotonous motion. To keep his mind off what was below his feet, Filidor thought about what lay ahead of them.

"You said my uncle was on his way to this place," he said after a while.

"He will arrive when you do," answered the dwarf.

Filidor was silent again, then said, "For the first time in my life, I look forward to seeing him."

"That will please him."

"I have not greatly pleased him in the past," said the young man. "It was always clear that he was less than satisfied with what I was."

"Perhaps not with what you were, but with what you did."

"Which was little enough," Filidor agreed.

"Knowing the Archon as intimately as I do," said the little man, "I am without hesitation in saying that he will think most highly of your recent accomplishments. In the matter of Jenbo Lal, you displayed resource and courage."

"I merely bit his finger in outrage," said Filidor.

"Yet it was precisely the apt thing to do. It leads me to predict a future for you in the service of the Archonate."

Filidor felt an unaccustomed swell of pride and anticipation at the thought, but the dwarf's next words emptied him of both sensations.

"But you must first survive our imminent encounter with a large, hungry fand."

Filidor looked behind them. The flickering light from below lit the eyes of Barran's fiercest land predator, a sinewy beast as long as Filidor was tall, with pointed snout and rattish paws, a long whip of a tail and a persistent appetite. The sight caused Filidor almost to fall, which would have been the preliminary to a certain death by the animal's outsize slashing teeth. He recovered with a desperate flurry of arms and skittering of legs, then strove to outpace the fand; though there was nowhere they could find refuge on this empty plain.

He slid his feet faster and faster, legs scissoring with a

friction that burned his inner thighs. The dwarf stayed even with him, but the fand was gaining. It ran with a series of quick cat-like steps, followed by a longer glide, which steadily shrank the distance between them. He could see fangs glistening in the darkness.

They would surely be run down and torn to pieces. Already, Filidor's breath was coming in labored gasps. He looked at the staff in his hands; it would scarcely even the odds. The ward-web would but delay the inevitable: too long a stay in the crater was death, Gaskarth had said, and the patience of a fand was notorious.

The beast was closer now, its panting breath whistling behind them. Filidor attempted a new burst of speed, but his overtaxed thigh muscles began to spasm and ache. He looked wildly about for somewhere to hide, something to climb. With a sob of wondrous relief, he saw a low building looming darkly against the pale dust of the plain. Crouching, he swung toward it, driving his legs, oblivious to their pain and trembling weakness. He sensed Gaskarth at his side, and heard the mewling whistle of the fand almost in his ear.

The structure's blocky shape swelled larger in his vision as each sliding step brought him closer to its promise of shelter. He had thought it more distant, but suddenly it was right before him, squat and solid in his path. In the same instant, he discovered that he had not yet learned how to stop.

Filidor threw up his hands to protect his face from the expected collision. But at the last moment, he felt a sharp tug on his mantle. "The fand!" he screamed to his companion. "Save yourself!" Then he was swung around in a wide arc that carried him past the building, missing a corner by a handsbreadth, and on into the plain beyond. The clutch at his mantle revealed itself to be that of the dwarf, and they both overbalanced and fell, rolling and tumbling until they slid to a stop.

The fand was less fortunate. It careered on, spitting rage, to slam hard into the building. The impact was followed instantly by a blast of nauseous green light, by which they could see not only the fand but all its internal structures. Then the light winked out, leaving their pursuer as yet another thin layer of dust on the unbroken ground.

The travellers struggled to their feet. "You may wish to consider the extent of our fortune in not touching the device," said Gaskarth, and Filidor now saw that the object he had thought a building was indeed the deadly mechanism they had come to adjust. With that realization, his knees absconded and left his feet to go where they might. Gaskarth caught him, lowered him gently to the ground, and left him.

Filidor knew he should rise and follow, to offer his services in whatever the little man was doing. But he was beyond it. He wished only for his uncle to arrive and resolve the situation. He had perfect faith in the Archon's ability to bring a rational order to any place and time in which he appeared. His uncle was order personified. By his mere presence, he cast out doubt and uncertainty, and set reason to rule.

The young man levered himself up to sit upon the smooth surface of the plain. He cast his eyes about the great crater and among the stars above him, half expecting to see his uncle hoving toward them in one of the glistening state galliots which had borne archons from Olkney to the provinces since time out of mind. But though he looked to all quarters, the only motion on the plain was that of the dwarf.

Gaskarth had become a small hive of activity. By the light of a fillumen strapped to his brow, he was using a plethora of instruments and specula drawn from his robes to examine the Ambit device. He skated here and there about the interplanar artifact. He consulted tables and scraps of notes fetched from his satchel. He squinted down line-of-sight perspectives, and examined parts of the device from the distance of an eyelash. As the first light of dawn washed the sky, he slid back to Filidor, a half-grin on his yellowy face.

"I was right. It can be done," he said.

"It can be reset?" asked Filidor.

"Better. It can be deactivated."

"That is wonderful news. My uncle will be delighted. When will he be here?"

"He is here already," said Gaskarth, causing Filidor to struggle to his feet and search the horizon. But no caparisoned craft was in view.

"Where?"

"Here, you ninny," said the dwarf, slapping his bony chest. "Have you still not deduced that I am Dezendah Vesh, ninety-eighth or ninety-ninth Archon, depending on whether or not we include that brief usurpation by the damnable Holmar Thurm?"

Filidor backed slightly away. "It is known that arduous and privation-filled journeys may temporarily unhinge the mind's precarious balance."

The little man sighed. "Again, you see only the appearance of things."

"Not so," replied Filidor. "After our escape from Grumby, I examined your features as you slept. You are indeed what you appear to be."

"Yes, yes," agreed Gaskarth, "though you are more used to seeing me like this." And he slapped his belt, at which Filidor found himself in the magisterial presence of the Archon.

"Now this," said Gaskarth's voice, "is the very image of an archon. And this," – he adjusted something beneath his robes, so that his next words were in a richer, more august tone – "this is the sound of one."

"I am bereft of speech," said Filidor.

"It's simply that people demand certain standards from their most revered authority. One of which is that the authority not appear to them as, if I recall the exact reference, a noxious homunculus."

"I regret both the expression and the sentiment from which it arose," said Filidor.

The Archon waved a long-fingered hand. "One is used to it. Can you see the magnates of Olkney pointing to a grinning yellow dwarf and proclaiming him to friends and strangers alike as the pinnacle of their social order? At the same time, is it not more sensible to travel in one's own guise, reserving the simulacrum for use among those to whom the Archon is a neighborhood fixture?"

"I, of course, defer to your sagacity," said Filidor, "and I am delighted to know you as you are. But should we not be doing something about this literally infernal mechanism, since you have said that remaining near it overlong is fatal?"

"Quite right," beamed his uncle, clapping his hands, "but we have a few moments before it will be appropriate to act. Please pay close heed while I explain what I am about to do. And allow me the comfort of doing it in my own guise." With that, the image clicked away and was replaced by the dwarf, who crossed his legs and sat.

Since time beyond recall, the little man said, archons had come at the end of their centuries-long terms of office to reset the inter-planal mechanism. As the device neared full charge, it emitted certain premonitory vibrations to which archons learned to attune themselves. They came, adjusted the controls, and ceased to be archons. This was because the task of resetting could not be done without reaching into the control recess, which required touching the machine, which was invariably fatal. A good quantity of the dust wafting over the plain was the uncollected mortal remains of past archons.

"Efforts have been made," he went on, "to develop extensible devices and insulators which would allow for the manipulation of the device without actual contact. All these various items of paraphernalia have, however, merely added to the sum of the motes their inventors subsequently became.

"There was an archon of a sorcerous bent who attempted to coerce an elemental into taking his place. But at the last moment, the terrified spirit broke free, seized its master and hurled him into the device. To his credit, the archon dutifully adjusted the mechanism before expiring."

A great sadness welled up in Filidor as he listened to his uncle. "This means that, being only now reconciled to my sole kith and kin, I am about to lose you to a murderous relic of the past."

The little man looked kindly at his nephew. "It is a sad thought, is it not?" he said. "However, we are not yet at a point of despair. As you may well imagine, this challenge has weighed upon my mind through all the long years since my father brought me here to assist in and witness his last official act. I have devoted all of those years to seeking a solution, and I believe one is at hand."

"But you said all manner of such attempts have been made, and each has miserably failed," said Filidor.

"As they were bound to," agreed the Archon. "Total misapplication of effort. Lost cause all around." He smiled in a serene expectation of victory. "You see, the secret is in the timing. By long and meticulous study, including a thorough analysis of the machine's original plans, I have determined that a minor design flaw occasions a distinct wobble in the bi-polar resonance a few minims before the capacitor reaches its critical discharge phase. Were one to insert the key during that fleeting interval, with exacting precision, the thing could not only be safely reset, but shut down for good and all."

"So the next archon would be spared this ordeal?" asked Filidor.

"Indeed," answered his uncle, "which is doubtless a great relief to you, since you will be that archon."

At this, Filidor discovered many questions he would like to have asked. But the little man glanced at a timepiece he pulled from a rent in his ragged robe, and announced that the moment of empirical proof would soon be upon them. "The key, please," he said, and tapped the bulge in the young man's mantle where lay the pocket containing the box of tuka wood.

Filidor hastily extracted the oblong and passed it over. The dwarf took it, did something to a corner, and the box popped open. A slim wedge of grey metal lay within, which the Archon emptied into his hand without ceremony, but with a slight grimace of distaste.

"Was it not a great risk to have that object out of your grasp, when so much depends upon it?" Filidor wondered.

"Had you lost it, I had means to find it. I let you carry it because I frankly cannot bear the touch of the nasty little thing."

The dwarf skated slowly toward the inter-planal device, which squatted in the full light of morning like a grey and ominous beast in a pool of black night. Filidor arose and followed.

Standing beside the device, Filidor saw a small aperture set in one side. Nestled within were a very few knobs and dials, and a narrow slot into which he knew the key would fit. The little man looked again at his timepiece, and turned to his nephew.

"And now a brief formality. I will speak the words all archons have spoken to their successors since time immemorial: watch what I do; remember how I do it; and retrieve the key."

Filidor swallowed hard. "Naturally, these are mere conventions of the occasion, since you will emerge from this exercise unscathed."

"Naturally," agreed the Archon, "but formalities must be observed, else institutions decay."

He produced now from his robes a small, jointed tripod, which he set up close to the inter-planal device. From the tripod's apex depended a delicate mechanism of fibers and crystals, which now began to spin rapidly, emitting rhythmic mechanical chirps. The Archon watched it for a moment, head cocked to one side, then nodded in satisfaction.

Now he leaned carefully toward the control recess, the key held in a certain way and aimed at the slot. Filidor noted that the rhythm of the pendant mechanism had subtly altered, sliding from a steady rat-a-tat into a triad of beeps interspersed with lengthier silences. The little man's hand swayed with the changing beat, moving back and forth, in and out, just beyond the aperture. His brow was beaded with sweat, and his thin shoulders trembled with concentration.

Filidor stood just beside him, wishing he could do something that could ensure both the success of the mission and the survival of his uncle. He champed his teeth and rocked unconsciously to the rhythmic sound. He knew it would be soon. He could feel in the tempo of the mechanism, a natural flow of rhythm that would bring him briefly to an unalterable certainty of the moment to act.

And then he remembered: in the lobby of the hotel, among the Tarendis, when the instant came to switch the image-refracting device – the little man had missed the timing! He had been a heartbeat off then, when it mattered little. Might he not be a heartbeat off now, when that heartbeat would be his last?

The rhythm of the spinning pendant shifted again. It was nearing that singular point now, that tiny interstice between beats that would be the one time, the only time, to defuse the inter-planal device. Filidor could sense its imminent arrival, as if he were seeing some craft making way toward him at a sure and steady clip.

Could the little man apprehend that perfect moment? Or would he be late as he had been late at Sprit? Filidor watched the dwarf's swaying hand, the key moving closer and closer to the control aperture. He looked, blinked sweat from his eyes, looked again. Was the hand off a shade of a beat? No, the movement was synchronized, wasn't it? Filidor peered at the moving key. No it wasn't! The dwarf was a fraction slow.

And now the rhythm shifted once again, and the moment was there! *But the Archon was too slow!* Filidor screamed and seized his uncle's hand, jammed the wedge of metal into the slot, twisted it hard – and felt the most terrible sensation of his life.

A writhing tendril of blackness oozed from the machine and curled itself about the hand that grasped his uncle's. It was a distillation of pure evil – not the diluted vapor that seeped between the dimensions, but the true force made tangible and thick. The stygian flow encompassed his hand and crawled up his arm, branching to explore his uncle, as both travellers were invaded by a cold so deep it made the empty spaces between the stars seem cozy.

Filidor tried to pull free, but all strength had fled his limbs. He saw only the creeping blackness. Beside him, the mechanism on the tripod continued to chirp its mindless rhythm, slower and slower, spinning delicately to a stop.

And then with the final beat, the universe exploded. Filidor was instantly blind, and felt himself moving through limitless, timeless space. It seemed an eternity before his shoulders smashed into something smooth and hard. His feet struck next, followed by an elbow, a knee, and them virtually all his parts as he tumbled and rolled, bruising flesh and joints on the unyielding surface, until he slid to a stop. There he lay, aching in every corner of his being, while motes of colored light amused themselves in his vision.

A long time after, he raised his pained head and found that he could see. Some distance away sat the squat grey cube of the Ambit mages' device. Between him and it, the dust of the plain was disturbed by the marks he had made in being blown backwards by an explosion.

He levered himself up, but could not stand, and sank down upon his belly on the black plain. After a while, he managed to push himself up on his extended arms, and lay with his weight upon his elbows. He looked again at the inter-planal device. Beside it, the tripod remained, and there on the ground lay the key. But of the little man there was no vestige.

Too weak to stand, Filidor wriggled on his stomach toward the Ambit mechanism. A flood of melancholy lapped at the edges of his mind, and a tear spattered the dust beneath him. He worked his way to where he and his uncle had stood, and managed to get to his knees.

With nerveless fingers, he reached for the key. In doing so, his hand inadvertently brushed the grim grey side of the deadly cube. Filidor jerked back in horror, but no cascade of annihilating energy erupted. Carefully, he reached and touched again, felt only cold, metallic substance.

"It is dead!" he cried.

"Not an exact terminology," said a familiar voice, "but a reasonable summation." From above him, a grinning yellow face looked down, then a knobbly black-clad body slid from the top of the cube into Filidor's arms. His uncle's bony hands patted his back in a brief embrace, then the Archon was free and sliding about to retrieve his instruments. Filidor remained on his knees, and watched the little man with joy.

The dwarf packed his gear into the satchel, then found the traveler's aide and tossed it to Filidor. "If you propose to remain in that position as the result of some religious epiphany," he said, "I will advise you that the cube makes an unsatisfactory object of veneration.

"A more agreeable alternative might be to accompany me to the land of the Devire, in whom you once expressed a degree of interest."

Filidor struggled to his feet, and found that the pain of his injuries was almost bearable, until he shook his head, and wished he hadn't. Finally, he slid gingerly toward his uncle, who at once turned and began to glide away to the west.

"You may recall," said the little man over his shoulder, "that the Devire are besotted with the practice of esoteric erotica."

"They are a byword for the carnal arts," agreed Filidor, hastening to catch up.

"To outsiders, perhaps," said the Archon, as his nephew drew level with him. "But it is less commonly known that the Devire – out of obsession with this being the world's penultimate age – terminate even their most frenzied ardors always at the next-to-last instant.

"Naturally," he continued, "this mania for interruptus..."

"... occasions considerable social and personal tension," Filidor concluded, "which as apprentice Archon it is my duty to relieve."

"Indeed," said the Archon, and increased his speed.

Filidor laughed and matched the pace. With the box now gone from his mantle pocket, he felt the volume of Osfeo loose and nudging him with each sliding stride. He pulled it out.

"Uncle," he said. "This is rightly yours."

The dwarf took the proffered volume, and leafed through it as they sped on. Then he slammed the tattered pages shut.

"Such utter twaddle," he said and tossed the book away. "Can't think why I ever wrote it."

ABOUT THE AUTHOR

The name I answer to is Matt Hughes. I write fantasy and suspense fiction. To keep the two genres separate, I now use my full name, Matthew Hughes, for fantasy, and the shorter form for the crime stuff. I also write media tie-ins as Hugh Matthews.

I've won the Crime Writers of Canada's Arthur Ellis Award, and have been shortlisted for the Aurora, Nebula, Philip K. Dick, and Derringer Awards.

I was born in 1949 in Liverpool, England, but my family moved to Canada when I was five. I've made my living as a writer all of my adult life, first as a journalist, then as a staff speechwriter to the Canadian Ministers of Justice and Environment, and -- from 1979 until a few years back-- as a freelance corporate and political speechwriter in British Columbia. I am a former director of the Federation of British Columbia Writers and I used to belong to Mensa Canada, but these days I'm conserving my energies to write fiction.

I'm a university drop-out from a working poor background. Before getting into newspapers, I worked in a factory that made school desks, drove a grocery delivery truck, was night janitor in a GM dealership, and did a short stint as an orderly in a private mental hospital. As a teenager, I served a year as a volunteer with the Company of Young Canadians (something like VISTA in the US). I've been married to a very patient woman since the late 1960s, and I have three grown sons.

In late 2007, I took up a secondary occupation -- that of an unpaid housesitter -- so that I can afford to keep on writing fiction yet still eat every day.

You can find me at: *http://www.matthewhughes.org*

ALSO BY
MATTHEW HUGHES

Fools Errant
Downshift (as Matt Hughes)
Fool Me Twice
Gullible's Travels (omnibus edition of Fools Errant and
        Fool Me Twice)
Black Brillion
The Gist Hunter and Other Stories
Majestrum, A Tale of Henghis Hapthorn
Wolverine: Lifeblood (as Hugh Matthews)
The Spiral Labyrinth, A Tale of Henghis Hapthorn
The Commons
Template
Hespira, A Tale of Henghis Hapthorn
The Other
To Hell and Back: The Damned Busters
Song of the Serpent (as Hugh Matthews)
To Hell and Back: Costume Not Included
Old Growth (as Matt Hughes)
To Hell and Back: Hell To Pay
9 Tales of Henghis Hapthorn
The Meaning of Luff and Other Stories
Paroxysm (as Matt Hughes)
The Compleat Guth Bandar
Devil or Angel and Other Stories

.